OF ART
AND
EROS

ALSO BY GJ BABB

Lara Bliss Loves Rose Madder Genuine
ISBN 9781838590147

Nude Not Naked
ISBN 9781838594053

OF ART
AND
EROS

GJ BABB

Matador
9 Priory Business Park,
Wistow Road, Kibworth Beauchamp,
Leicestershire. LE8 0RX
Tel: 0116 279 2299
Email: books@troubador.co.uk
Web: www.troubador.co.uk/matador
Twitter: @matadorbooks

ISBN 978 1800464 377

British Library Cataloguing in Publication Data.
A catalogue record for this book is available from the British Library.

Printed and bound in Great Britain by 4edge Limited
Typeset in 10pt Sabon MT by Troubador Publishing Ltd, Leicester, UK

Matador is an imprint of Troubador Publishing Ltd

'She was scarcely pugnacious by temperament, but belonged to that more successful class of fighters who are pugnacious by circumstance.'

– Saki

ONE

Where shall I start? With Gustave Post or with the Collarii Foundation? Well, let me start with a thumbnail sketch of Gustave; an old, old friend from way back. He was born into an Anglo-Irish family in nineteen thirty-seven. His father was in the Irish diplomatic service, holding several quite senior posts in Eastern Europe. After the war he became the resident expert on the Eastern Bloc, based in the Irish Foreign Office.

What comes to mind when I think of Gustave? Ego, bloody-minded persistence, a chaotic domestic life, restlessness, rambling properties and studios like barns, which he had a habit of filling with his paintings and then moving on. There was a property for every decade, sometimes less than that, and a new love too, never much more than twenty-five, which was the age of Waverley Smith when she entered this story… but I'm getting ahead of myself.

Gustave is dead; has been these past four years: November fifteenth, two thousand and fifteen. I went to his funeral: a crematorium out in Suffolk. I can't remember where exactly but I recall the remembrance service vividly. The art world was there in force, looking exceptionally sober and well dressed. Well, the latter was aided by the weather and the time of year: it was mid-January and raining, so there were no safari jackets and only one or two garish anoraks.

Gustave painted in a straight line. When I met him at the Royal College he was already fully formed. His paintings sat – still sit – at the point where the three markets for contemporary art overlap: the museums of modern art, the high-worth private collectors and the corporate clients. For nearly fifty years they rolled off the production line: sublimely simple, positively elemental… and nobody else could do it like he did. He turned his personal life into

1

a mythic fable, making sure-footed moves from motif to motif, subject matter to subject matter, symbol to meaningful symbol. And underpinning what the art historians call his "narrativity" there was always what the French sometimes term "*saveur*", the ability to convey in everything he did his sensuous delight in his medium.

Even as a student he was never in need, and even from his first exhibition he kept back work. He was a hoarder, and what he liked hoarding most was his own work. It was a good thing, really, because when he was in the mood he was extremely productive. I was with him once when he painted five pictures in a weekend and still had time for cocktails at six.

In nineteen seventy-two, aged thirty-five, he teamed up with Daniel Collarii. Daniel was an ambitious and wily art dealer who developed the Keyline Gallery into an international art business. He took control of Gustave's waiting list and made sure it never disappeared. Gustave bought a sprawling property in Majorca. One in Manhattan followed, and it just went on from there. He changed, of course. He took up with the glitterati, did the Adriatic on ridiculous yachts and all that sort of thing. We, in England, watched with varying emotions. I thought "fair enough", most others weren't so generous, but that's the art world for you. Did he care? No. He was too busy chatting with bankers, industrialists – latterly Silicon Valley billionaires – and taking hell from tempestuous women.

But whatever else was going on, he kept that studio of his working full tilt. Wherever he settled, however briefly, the deliveries of art materials never stopped. And that line of development I described him following never failed him. He was inventive, of course, but if that line is thought of as a taut wire strung across a yawning chasm, he never wavered or lost his balance… well, once only, for nearly six months, but more of that later.

Gustave had a genius for recognising his own abilities, his own distinctiveness, and knew how to exploit them both like no one else I've ever met. In short, I thought truly he was a genius… Yes, that exceptional, although, having suffered his foibles close to, I do surprise myself in saying so. He was a monster, of course, but anyone expecting anything less knows nothing of artists or the world in which they move.

His gusto finally gave out when he was seventy-eight, in the capable arms of Neema, then aged thirty-six. There was quite a hullabaloo in the press, I remember. I knew all three of his wives. I remained close to his first wife, Clarissa, after they divorced. Some amongst the Post brood called her "the dowager duchess". They meant it unkindly, but she had a certain regal charm that continued to work its magic on the elderly men of her circle. At the crematorium I offered her my condolences. 'He never could decide whether he was a Latin or a Norman,' was her response.

Gustave had outlived Daniel Collarii by more than a decade, but Collarii's three sons, Max, Erik and Peter, had carried on the business. In fact, for several years before Daniel retired, the management of the Keyline Gallery had passed to them and they had expanded its reach with branches in Geneva, Los Angeles and Hong Kong. In Daniel's final years he established a foundation to specialise in the management of artists' estates on behalf of their heirs. The sons' considerable expertise and depth of contacts meant they were exceedingly well placed to continue this venerable business. It also called for the skills of an undertaker: probity, diplomacy, discretion and a respect for the dead. The foundation's largest asset by worth was the management of the Gustave Post estate and, in particular, the substantial body of his work vested in the Gustave Post Trust. On Gustave's death, it had quickly become obvious that a very significant accumulation of his work, never exhibited, was stored in his various properties. Most spectacular was the body of work at *Villa Besugo* in Majorca.

Villa Besugo was one of Gustave's earliest acquisitions. He named it Besugo, after the fish, despite the entreaties of his Spanish friends; he was that kind of man. Even during his two spells in New York he had continued to use it as a second home. In his final years of decline, when he was living in Suffolk with Neema and their children, there had been long summer sojourns there until his health forbade air travel.

It was a big, rambling property on the north coast, well away from the package holiday resorts. Gustave had added to the property over the years as adjacent land had become available. Besides the main building, there were extensive outbuildings, originally intended for storing agricultural produce, and a caretaker's house. For Gustave it had been a place of retreat. After his death, its protection had been a concern and security was greatly improved as the Collarii Foundation wrested control of the estate from the family's legal squabbles. Once the complex tangle Gustave had left behind him was finally sorted out, the villa was to be redeveloped as the Gustave Post Museum and Study Centre. However, more than three years after his death, his estate was still the subject of negotiations between, on one side, the Collarii Foundation and the Post family's lawyers and, on the other, the tax authorities of three countries and various museums. In the case of the latter, endowments in lieu of estate duty were gradually moving towards agreement.

A new problem for the management of Gustave's estate emerged in May, two thousand and nineteen. On Monday the thirteenth, a package arrived at the Collarii Foundation from Christies, New York. It contained photographs of a Gustave Post painting, front, back and close-ups, together with a request from the then in-house specialist in twentieth century painting for a verification of the authenticity of the painting.

At the core of the management of an artist's estate is the *catalogue raisonné*, a comprehensive catalogue of the work produced by the artist. The creation of such a document is an expensive and time-consuming task, but once complete, it allows whoever owns it to become the custodian of the artist's oeuvre. The owner becomes the arbiter of what is, and what is not, a genuine work by the artist. In the case of Gustave Post this was the Collarii Foundation. Not without consequence, it also allowed the Collarii brothers substantial control over the market in his work. That was the theory, anyway.

The oversight of the Gustave Post *catalogue raisonné* was in the hands of Professor Corey Templeton of the Courtauld Institute of Art, specialist in twentieth century art and long-time enthusiast for Post's work. Whenever an important Post came onto the market, the auction house's contemporary and modern specialist took care to check the provenance of the painting with the Collarii Foundation. Corey Templeton was informed and the details in the *catalogue raisonné* were checked against those supplied by the auction house.

This particular May morning, Corey was teaching and he did not arrive at the Collarii Building in Grosvenor Street until after lunch. The conventional white box of the Keyline Gallery, a stark, cavernous space that had been carved out of the building's palazzo-style reception rooms, occupied the ground floor. To one side of this was the building's original entrance hall and stairwell. Here, the sumptuous architectural detailing of a ducal townhouse had been lovingly restored. On the first floor were the brothers' offices, with their grand interiors: dark walls, marble mantelpieces, parquet floors that shone like mirrors, complemented by some of the best, most valuable works from the gallery's storerooms: accommodation befitting the Collarii Foundation's august reputation. The reception was at the head of the stairs where Max Collarii's PA, Angela, ruled supreme over her various assistants, and controlled access to the offices beyond.

Max's office at the back of the building looked like nothing so much as a wealthy man's sitting room: bookcases, *objects d'art*, even a narwhal's tusk vied for attention with the paintings and photographic works hung in a collector's profusion. Peter and Erik had offices too, but not quite on the grand scale of Max's. On the floor above were the staff offices and meeting rooms, and so it went upwards to the top floor where a softly spoken accountant saw to the bookkeeping. If the entire enterprise spoke of substantial wealth, only the brothers and the accountant knew the exact details of the financial flows through the two entities; the profits and losses, the risks and returns of the Keyline Gallery and the Collarii Foundation.

Corey was ushered straight through reception and into Max's office. Max was the oldest of the Collarii brothers, now aged forty-two, a big, handsome man, well-made and well-dressed. "Debonair" was the word for Max. He had the manner of the better kind of politician, the ones that inspire confidence rather than loathing. His great advantaged was that he never proselytised for anything other than the art he loved. When the gallery's most important clients were imminent – directors of museums, heads of corporations and renowned artists with reputations for being difficult – it was Max who was on hand to greet them. He excelled in the company of financiers of the more enlightened kind; the kind that hankered after important, hard-to-get art. His was the charm of a man who does not feel the need to impress or be loud. Although he was married to Luccia, and had four children, his family remained firmly in the background. On the public stage he was always available to be attentive to the rich, often elderly heiresses who seemed, certainly in terms of the attention they required, to make up a substantial proportion of the business's clientele.

Besides being the figurehead of client relations, Max directed the affairs of the Collarii Foundation. Each artist's estate the foundation managed had its own liaison officer and manager, but being the foundation's biggest and most lucrative concern, the Gustave Post estate was considered significant enough to require his personal attention.

'Ah, Corey Templeton! Do come in,' said Max the moment he saw Corey at the open door of his office. 'We have a problem.'

Corey came over to where Max was standing at a table and gazed at the photographs he had laid out in front of him.

'It's a ten million dollar painting and it's not in our *catalogue raisonné*.'

'It must be,' murmured Corey, his attention taken up almost wholly with what was lying on the table.

There was a long, thoughtful silence while the examination proceeded.

'*Berlin Wall Lament No.1*,' said Max finally.

This woke Corey from his reverie. 'I need to see it in the flesh, Max.'

'What d'you think, though?'

'Marvellous! It's the kind of big political statement I've not seen from Gustave before! I'm shocked! Could be fifteen, twenty million. I can see from the way it's painted it's his Berlin period, so the date's right. Your father had Gustave's affairs well under control by then, so we ought to have a record of it...'

'Maybe it isn't genuine.'

'Looks genuine enough, but the subject matter... I suppose the photographs might flatter; that's why we need to see it. We can't verify it as a genuine Post as things stand. Can they tell us where it's come from?'

'I've spoken to Steinhoff-Norwood: strict client confidentiality. They're certain it's the genuine thing. They'd like our blessing, even though they think it's of unimpeachable provenance.'

'Tricky.'

'Very.'

'You thinking what I'm thinking?'

Max took a seat and invited Corey to do the same. It was obvious he was weighing up something and there was a pause before he spoke, and when he did so it was with the air of a man unburdening himself.

'The family.'

Corey gave a low murmur of understanding. The Collarii Foundation's agreement with members of the family meant that their personal holdings of Gustave Post paintings were registered with the foundation and it managed any disposals they wished to make. In return for that exclusive right, the foundation ensured their financial well-being. Their incomes, as stipulated in the clauses of the Post family trust, came from the sale of paintings that, during his lifetime, Gustave had assigned to the trust. This included stock held by the Keyline Gallery as well as those works not set aside for display at the Gustave Post Museum, still stored in his various properties.

'You know,' said Max, 'we have a fifty-year horizon on the disposal of works belonging to the family trust.'

'Quite.' There was a pot of coffee on a silver tray on the table between them. 'Is that hot?'

Max indicated that it was and reached across to pour a cup for both of them. 'Milk?'

'A little. The trust's beneficiaries are a mixed bunch.'

'Ah!' Max looked richly amused. 'Familiarity breeds contempt? All of the energy, none of the application. Plenty of flights of fancy, no vision. Several wastrels, one certifiable.'

Corey gave a pained snort of amusement. 'Yes, the wives were one thing but cataloguing the paintings belonging to the older children was…. well, sometimes… *uncomfortable*. I was often made to feel like the bailiff's man.'

'Relations are, on the whole, cordial.'

'I'm sure.' Corey had no doubt about the diplomatic skills of the three brothers. He was edging towards a view. 'If someone in the family has a Gustave Post we don't know about, we need to find out who.'

Max agreed. 'It's not good, when you're trying to control the market, to have this sort of thing happen.'

'Especially when it has the look of a significant work.'

'If one of them gets away with selling off their own bat, they'll all start. It'll spread like wild fire. Sure, we have a financial stake in their sales, but we think long-term and underpin the market. We have the family's best interests at heart and prevent any in-fighting. What they all hate is the foundation having so much control over their lives. I suppose refusing to certify the painting as genuine might restore discipline. "Our records for nineteen eight-two are complete and accurate." That sort of thing.'

Corey was not sure what to make of such a suggestion. For him, attribution rested on a science of small, unalienable truths.

Max rose to his feet and cross to the window that overlooked the parterre garden behind the Collarii Building. An exquisitely groomed Acer, cropped in the Korean style, stood in the centre of the parterre. He considered owning a tree in Mayfair as one of the greatest symbols of his success.

'I want something subtle, Corey. I'm worried about nineteen eighty-two. Why wasn't this painting recorded at the time? I'm wondering what Gustave was up to. He must certainly have still been in Berlin, but what else?'

'Maybe we should get Campbell Carter in. If anyone outside the family knows, he does.'

'Agreed.'

When the meeting was over, Corey went down to the basement where the archive rooms and art stores were. In one of the rooms there were many shelves filled with copies of Gustave

Post catalogues and monographs, and several table-top filing cabinets where the hardcopy of the Post *catalogue raisonné* was stored. The digital version of the *catalogue raisonné* was available on a computer kept permanently off-line for security reasons but Corey preferred to consult the twenty-eight volumes of the original, hardcopy version. Somehow, he found its very materiality a more vivid source for understanding the past. He pulled out volume twelve covering the period October, nineteen eighty-one to November, nineteen eighty-three. The illustration of each painting was labelled with a title and an accession number. Details of size and medium were noted under the photographs. In most cases there were additional annotations in various hands, giving the provenance of the paintings up to the present day. Notes indicated that a significant number of the paintings produced by Gustave in the early part of nineteen eighty-two had been exhibited first in Venice. Corey had a moment of sudden illumination. In the summer of nineteen eight-two, Gustave had participated in the *Venice Biennale*! He trawled through the paintings dated nineteen eighty-two, but despite the sense of comprehensiveness that the *catalogue raisonné* gave off, there was no record of one entitled *Berlin Wall Lament No.1.*

TWO

Campbell Carter had made his name as editor of *The New Cognoscenti* during its influential heyday. Having had a grievous and principled falling-out with a new, son-of-new-money backer who wanted him to lionise graffiti art, nearly a decade before, he had begun in earnest his long-held wish to write the definitive biographical study of Gustave Post. Finally, "Volume one, 1937 to 1975", had been published in twenty sixteen, some six months after Gustave's death. There had been many previous biographical studies of Post, but they lacked the research and attention to detail that characterised Campbell's telling of the story. His had been published to universal acclaim. The word "blockbuster" was used of it, as was "definitive".

Although Corey respected Campbell's achievement, he considered himself to be of a more forensic turn of mind than he. True, he also sometimes judged himself over-punctilious and without heart. Nevertheless, to colleagues of similar outlook, he had been known to express reservations. Readily admitting it was a great deal better than the run-of-the-mill exegesis that passed for meaningful analysis, he was inclined to imply he found it a little florid, sprinkled with conjecture, cod psychological insights and wordy flummery. In short, Corey was not an enthusiast for prose poetry in the service of art appreciation. He regarded it as a belittling simulation of the thing it claimed to represent. Their differences were easily explained: when it came to art, Campbell Carter was a romantic, he was not. It followed that in Campbell's eyes, the Collariis were little short of well-mannered profiteers in a world of cracked geniuses, misfits and rank outsiders. It was a suspicion he kept well-concealed.

As a person, Campbell was worldly in an upper-class, English sort of way. A handsome head, somewhat leonine – as biographers like to say of men of letters – graced by a carefully tended Van Dyck. Now in his early fifties, he looked racy amongst academics, scholarly amongst his horse-racing chums. He was skilled with the witty aside, more of a showman than any of Corey's academic colleagues and, not having recourse to the lifeline of an academic salary, more of a hack-for-hire than them. His bread-and-butter was writing introductions for monographs, catalogues and the like. For him, unlike Corey, they were something he could dash off without the agonising. What is more, a devoted clientele of elderly RAs was always clamouring for them.

It was shortly after six o'clock. The meeting to decide *what to do about the rogue Gustave Post painting* had reconvened. Campbell was sitting with studied nonchalance behind a large single malt, cutting an altogether more raffish figure than the other two. His arrival had been greeted with ceremony, as befitted the biographer whose second volume on Gustave Post was eagerly awaited. His response to enquiries about its progress were enigmatic and reserved, as befits the author of a Great Work if his mystique is to be preserved.

'Dear boy,' Campbell began wheezily, having been appraised of the situation that had brought him there, 'an artist's life *never, ever* fails to turn up mucky little secrets like this! Nineteen eighty-two, eh? I'd have to check my bumf. Gustave wasn't in the habit of keeping a proper diary; certainly not any detailed record of events outside the studio, but someone close to him – assistant, model, muse, call it what you will – generally had an appointments diary to keep him on the straight and narrow as far as his social obligations were concerned.'

Max was pacing the room, his thumb and forefinger cradling his chin. 'This won't be in any appointments diary.' He made a gesture of sudden impatience. 'Have you researched Post's Berlin period in any depth, or not?'

Campbell seemed undecided as to what he should say. 'Well, I'm quite a way along, but there's still much to be done! If you recall, volume one ended in seventy-five, towards the end of his New York period. He moved to Berlin in seventy-six. His popularity had taken a bit of a dip about then, before *The New Spirit in Painting* revived his fortunes. That was eighty-one. For some, adopting Berlin was an act of exile. To be frank, those six or so years are a wee bit sketchy. It was London and Majorca for the rest of the eighties, and that's been much easier to research...' He made an exasperated noise. 'The fact is, one must indulge in these quickie jobs – catalogue introductions and the like – they're so much more lucrative than serious stuff like Gustave Post, volume two.' He shrugged and buried his nose in his glass of single malt. His appreciative twinkle said he was well satisfied with the distillery Max dispensed. 'Two snippets about Berlin off the top of my head,' he decided, following what seemed like a considerable effort of recall. 'He was very much in the thrall of living in a city under siege. Being there – American sector – made him a hero to Berliners. Also in America; the Americans liked that from a European artist. Second, I've a feeling something important... Yes, *Venice*! Sorry, my mind's a bit of a blank. It was at the end of his time in Berlin...'

'You're right about Venice,' agreed Corey.

'Ah, something of a watershed!' said Campbell thoughtfully.

'That's strange!' said Max, struck by the coincidence. 'I've only just come back from the opening of this year's biennale! Certainly, Venice was an important moment for Gustave's career. I don't wish to intrude on your endeavours, Campbell, but I want to know why we have no record of this painting. Anything you can supply about that year – diary entries, your notes, anything – would be gratefully received.' He said this as a man who could deliver great favours if and when he chose. 'Corey, I hate to do this to you, but you need to fly to New York, talk to Christies and see the painting. I want a plan of action by the end of the week, so you have to go tomorrow. And, gentlemen, secrecy is the order of the day. The family must not suspect!'

THREE

In Max Collarii's world things happened quickly when he wanted them to. By midday Friday, Corey was again in his office, having spent two nights in New York and a third on the plane coming back.

Slightly dazed in the way of transatlantic travellers, Corey found himself gazing blankly at a Kirchner painting on its way to a museum in Australia. 'Christies are very excited about it,' he said in the musing voice of one reliving a tumultuous experience. 'Look, Max, you don't fully realise this until you see it, but *it is* a major work. I mean, the political engagement is something pretty unique. It's also big for Gustave, very big.'

'So?'

'We came up with a form of words, subject to your agreement.' Corey took a slim file from his briefcase. 'Shall I read it?'

Max, who was stretching his legs before the window, indicated he had the floor.

'"We agree that the Collarii Foundation should be given the opportunity to research the genesis of *Berlin Wall Lament No.1*, and the reasons for its absence from contemporaneous records. Only then will it be admitted to the *catalogue raisonné*."' Corey looked up at Max. 'Purely on procedural grounds, therefore, I declined to authenticate it. They were none too pleased.'

Max laughed. 'I can imagine. Disagreeable to have the authenticity of an important Gustave Post put in even the slightest doubt. Excellent work! It is the genuine article, I take it?'

'Oh yes, most certainly.'

'So, what's their position?'

'They've no immediate plans to sell it anyway; the next contemporary and modern sales aren't until the autumn. They'd prefer to sell it with our blessing, but they won't be happy if we hold them up for long. I think they might have coughed up an advance on consignment.'

'Oh dear, it all lends urgency to our enquiries.'

'Quite. Consider it under wraps for the time being, but they could change their minds if we haven't sorted things out in the next couple of months.'

Max came and sat down opposite him. 'There's the rub: how, exactly, are we going to sort them out?'

'They aren't going to budge on client confidentiality, quite rightly, so we have to find out for ourselves. As far as they're concerned it's a perfectly legitimate sale; none of their business if our records aren't up to scratch. It's visibly dated nineteen eighty-two, a decade after the association between Post and your father began, so there's no obvious reason why it wasn't registered in the gallery's records. There's also the question of why it's come on the market now.' Corey leant forward to emphasise the confidential nature of what he was about to say. 'The more I think about it the more I'm certain it's one of the family trying to go behind our backs.'

'Agreed. Corey –' Max had grown confessional and winning – 'this kind of ill-discipline could affect us in more ways than one. The fact is, the artists' estates business has grown tremendously in the past few years. All the greats of the past eight decades passing on, leaving heirs with a hell of a mess to clear up and the tax authorities creating fucking –' he said "fucking" with the care of an ascetic approaching a donut – 'chaos. It's the same right across Europe… and in the States. Look, I've talked to my brothers. Collectively we're stretched; we could do with the help! We'd like you to handle it.'

'What about Campbell? He knows the human side of this better than me.'

Max shook his head. 'Campbell Carter is not the man for the job. With volume two under way he could be wining and dining some of the principle suspects. And let's not dwell on his general flakiness; I don't trust club animals.'

Corey laughed. 'I suppose I'm the next most obvious choice, perhaps too obvious.'

'Yes, a little subterfuge will be called for. Think about it, will you? You can take the weekend. Get that jet lag behind you before you make a decision.'

As he departed, Corey left a question hanging in the air. 'Has it occurred to you that since this painting is called *Berlin Wall Lament No.1*, there might be more than one?'

FOUR

Corey Templeton was American on his mother's side, with a dash of Irish, as his first name suggested. He had a slight Boston twang from his years of study at Yale. That aside, he was thoroughly European and carried a British passport. At Charterhouse he had been regarded as an aesthete; at a lesser school he would have been thought of as a swot. Now in his late thirties he was slight of stature, unmarried – although only just – and possessed the look of a man-of-letters, rather than that of a library worm. He was what, in certain quarters, might be called *a snappy dresser*. If so, it was without being loud. He liked young women, but tried to keep his relationship with his students professional. This was hard on him since many of those he taught were beautiful and talented.

He had not become a professor before forty without possessing a certain guile. His "trade" – as he thought of it – was by no means coextensive with the academic world that purported to represent it. Art historians were, on the whole, an unworldly bunch, and it was his skills in the administrative nitty-gritty essential to the smooth running of an institution that had helped to elevate him to his present status at such an early an age. Otherwise to achieve such rank one had to be a scholarly ornament, expensive and not necessarily productive, in a pedagogic sense, and his research was never quite pyrotechnic enough to put him in that category. His tended towards the discovery of small but illuminating insights in the chaotic archives of dead artists, insights generally gleaned against the grain of the destructive custodianship of wilful descendants.

Corey had taken to the task of working on the Gustave Post *catalogue raisonné* with relish. It was, in its own way, an epic equivalent to the sprawling biography Campbell Carter had embarked upon somewhat earlier. He had given it a major proportion of his research time for nearly six years. Post's prolific output had made it a mammoth undertaking. It amounted to entries for over three thousand paintings alone. One day, Corey's labours would be turned into a publishable form, but at the moment its importance lay in ensuring the Collarii Foundation's control over every aspect of Post's output, his reputation and hence his status as a blue-chip investment. It hurt Corey's pride to discover that an important Post painting had somehow escaped his methodical, painstaking research processes. He had developed the *catalogue raisonné* to the point where the sudden, unexplained appearance of any Post painting, never mind one of the importance of *Berlin Wall Lament No.1*, was extremely rare. Minor works on paper – drawings, studies, prints and monoprints – were another matter. This was an open-ended category due to Post's prolific, not to say profligate, ways.

Seeing the painting in the flesh had convinced Corey it was of unusual importance. It belonged, he was pretty sure, to the very end of Gustave's Berlin period, just before one of his major upheavals: not only new motifs and subject matters but a change of city and personal relationships. Gustave was not noted for his political engagement, but here was a stark attack on the cruel forces that had brought the Wall into being. And Gustave's imaging of it, in Corey's view, had the potential for it to be placed in the historical canon of significant works of art portraying social and political disaster.

Corey's work on the *catalogue raisonné* did not count as academic research since it remained unpublished, yet academic research was a precondition of professorial status. It was a status that allowed him to come and go as he pleased; that allowed him, when opportunities arose, to travel to see collections he had not seen previously, to devolve the supervision of his students to other, lesser, members of staff. Happily, his work on Gustave Post's *catalogue raisonné* had been used as the definitive source material for the many retrospective exhibitions that had taken place since Gustave's death. His involvement with these exhibitions, which had graced museums on every continent, certainly *did* count as academic research since he had co-curated them on behalf of the Collarii Foundation, and, for every one, written introductory material for the accompanying catalogue in his sparse literary style.

Through the weekend Corey's mind kept returning to the question of who was selling *Berlin Wall Lament No.1*. If, as seemed likely, it was a member of Gustave's family, any enquiries in that direction would be greeted with hostile silence. No, he had to manufacture another pretext to visit his three wives and seven children. Only by doing so did he stand a chance of discovering which one of them it was. Tricky. Some two hundred paintings, studies and drawings were, he knew, recorded as being in their hands, and business related to the *catalogue raisonné* – updating photographic records, or some such – was a start, but he needed more. He needed a better story and more than one way of engaging with such a disparate and unruly group of people. It called for ingenuity, and it called for reinforcements. It was at this point that his thoughts turned to Waverley Smith.

FIVE

Corey liked blonds with high ponytails cinched close to the crown of their heads. Particularly the vivacious ones who swished them as they walked, like the tails of Arabian stallions. He willingly admitted to himself that the gender switch was part of the allure. Waverley Smith was one such. Her hair had a wonderful texture like a calligraphic river in bronze and gold. Although there's always an attractive young woman in any story worth telling, Waverley Smith is not a required *effect* of fiction; rather, her beauty *was*, to no small extent, the *cause* of the train of events that follow. In some ways she was a portrait painter's nightmare. Her features were fine, well proportioned and presented no particular challenge to depict, but they had a marvellous mobility such that the most fleeting thought could be seen crossing her face. It was more than what was normally meant by the term "expression", or "expressiveness". There was, to be particular, a kind of nakedness in this mobility that suggested both an unusual candour and an unusual mind. Its special charm was that, more often than not, the moods that those with the gift of observation could so easily read were hesitation, curiosity, puzzlement, scepticism, wry amusement. In other words, the provocations of uncertainty. Hers was not an ostentatious glamour, rather the sort that rewarded the art of looking closely. To attempt her portrait would have driven a Gainsborough or a Lawrence to distraction since their portraits, lacking this aspect of mobility, would have taken on a kind of lifeless symmetry, not unlike those computer simulations of fifteen thousand people's idea of ideal beauty.

His amorous entreaties rebuffed, a neophyte poet in his cups had remarked that, "Considered as a fruit, Waverley Smith is one that only ripens slowly and even when ripe retains a note of acidity". He also maintained that she had been something of a child mystic, seeing strange things at night, caught parlaying with Apollyon, angel of the abyss. So much for the influence of an industrious Eng Lit teacher! She had come to the Courtauld and written a remarkable thesis entitled, "Man Ray, Surrealism and the Abrogation of the Past". Corey had considered it remarkable, anyway. After reading it, he saw Man Ray differently, and few of his students had ever had such an effect on his settled views. Her examiner had agreed. The *viva voce* of the thesis had been something of an ordeal.

'Did she actually write it?' her examiner had wondered after they had finished and Corey had taken him for a cup of tea in the refectory.

Corey knew exactly why he asked. The *viva* had been conducted with an air of something approaching anguish on Waverley's part, as if she were answering questions on an essay she had bought ready-made from an on-line academic cheating service.

'Oh, certainly,' Corey had replied. 'That's just her.'

For some reason he did not understand, she always brought to mind the English pangram, "the quick brown fox jumps over a lazy dog'. The connection may have been a puzzle, but he was in no doubt about which of the two animals she was. Quick, small without being exactly *petite*, supple of mind and body... and those mobile features that fascinated; a cavalcade of expressions one could contemplate with endless pleasure.

Corey had supervised her thesis for three and a half years. As she had approached the end of her writing-up period, Corey had recommended her to the Collarii brothers for an intern's post at the Keyline Gallery. He did it without fully acknowledging how much he'd done so to keep her close. He thought no more about it until the day in early May, several weeks after her *viva voce*, when he came across her in Dover Street. She was standing next to an Uber ride. The driver – he looked like an Afghan or an Iraqi – was out of the car. It was clear they were waiting. Waverley did not see Corey as he approached. She looked cute, but when she spoke to the driver, she didn't sound it.

'Do you know what Fishman's doing in there?' She smiled at the driver as though she knew, and she knew he didn't know enough about almost everything to want to know what Fishman was doing. 'Swiss watches,' she said, no longer looking at the driver but staring down the street with a frown as if something that way held her attention. '*Swiss watches!* I want to go to Harrods. Can we leave him and go?'

'Hello, Waverley,' Corey greeted her. 'What's going on?'

'Miss, I have to wait,' said the driver, looking uncomfortable.

'Oh! Hello, Corey. Sorry about this: we're having a bit of a domestic.' She turned back to the driver. 'Ah, yes, his highness says wait! But I'd like to go. It must be possible to reach a compromise whereby we go and he walks!'

The driver's discomfort was growing. Corey saw the man was dealing with a species of feminine insistence quite foreign to his experience.

'Surely,' the driver ventured, 'that would not be a compromise?'

'Oh, I think it's a very reasonable compromise. You don't know the alternatives my compromise is between.'

The driver appeared to wilt as she fixed him with her serious blue eyes. He looked to Corey, as though for help.

'I suppose you think me impatient,' decided Waverley peevishly. 'Corey thinks that, don't you, Corey?'

'I do also,' mumbled the driver, as if talking to her was anathema.

'Well, if *you* have to wait, why not let me take the car?'

That made him look at her again, sharply. His expression said he knew she was making fun of him, but she returned his look remorselessly with those serious, enquiring eyes.

Just then a black cab came by with its light showing. Waverley grabbed at her throat. A single piercing shriek froze the air. The cab halted. Corey only understood this afterwards: from the chain around her neck dangled a little silver whistle. One blast and the whole street had come to a standstill, just for her. He was struck by how effective it was: twenty seconds and, with a wave, she was gone. He looked at the driver with an apologetic smile. The man was blank with perplexity. He turned away and climbed

21

back into his car with – so it seemed to Corey – an infinite sense of relief, to await whosoever it was doing something with Swiss watches. Corey was amused by the encounter; thought Waverley's behaviour mildly outrageous. Only vaguely did he wonder what she was mixed up in.

SIX

Monday morning. Time was running fast. Max Collarii had a twelve-thirty luncheon appointment at Wiltons with a very important client. What he wanted more than anything was to get the Gustave Post business off his hands. It was triple underlined in the "to do" list he kept in the tiny week-to-a-page diary from which he was never parted. He gazed at the Acer in the garden below and thought how exquisite it looked. It comforted him to think of something so perfectly in repose, occupying its space with such a graceful sense of balance. How very like a Gustave Post painting, he thought, without the least sense of irony.

Corey Templeton was back in the building and Max knew he was going to agree to take on the Post family. Had Corey's intention been to decline the task, Angela wouldn't have allowed him any further than her desk. Now Max hoped to wrap the thing up and let him get on with it.

'Corey, nice to see you. You look rested. Over the jet lag?'

Yes, more or less.'

'So, what are we going to do about this Post business?'

'It fills me with trepidation but, to tell you the honest truth, I suspect I want this painting properly accounted for as much as you do.'

'Quite right, Corey. But I have to have the wider interests of the foundation in mind. The family must observe its obligations to both the foundation and to the Post Family Trust. *And that means no unauthorised, back door selling!*'

Corey nodded his understanding.

Good! We have differing motives but the same aim! How are we going to go about solving this?'

'Nineteen eighty-two: the year points to one of the older

beneficiaries… Clarissa? I think she's my candidate. However bitter, she's always considered herself the custodian of Gustave's work; resented any other claim. They were still married in eighty-two.'

'Only just. Didn't he take up with Ruthie at about that time?'

Ruthie had been Gustave's second wife until she grew tired of the whole Post circus, took herself off to Devon to live with cats and divorced him.

'Ruthie's not devious, unlike Clarissa. What about the children?'

'Oh God, *children!*' groaned Max. 'Edward must be sixty, Charlie not much less!'

Edward and Charles were Clarissa's sons. At the time Gustave and their mother broke up they were in their teens.

'Yes, the dreadful duo! I don't know…'

'Too young at the time?' wondered Max. 'I suppose Clarissa could have gifted the painting to either. They're both as devious as their mother. If anybody has the aptitude for something like this –' he weighed his estimation with care – 'it's Ross Post. He's been living beyond his means for years. He's never had a career, or even a job, and he runs with a very fast crowd.'

Corey grimaced, for Ross was the most bloody-minded of Gustave's off-spring. Now in his mid-thirties, eldest son of Ruthie, Gustave's second wife, he had a reputation for thuggish, unpredictable behaviour, something like the worst aspects of his father, but without his charm or talent. There had been a strong affinity with his father, though. Following Gustave's death, it had emerged that his favouritism had been expressed as a generous allowance. Once the legal teams got their grip on Gustave's estate, it had been stopped to howls of protest from Ross. Much to his further fury, the provisional annual stipend for family members provided under the terms of probate, administered by the Collarii Foundation, was significantly less than his father's largesse.

Max laughed and shrugged, as though to say he considered the matter open to whatever proof Corey could bring him.

'I suppose my credit with the family is not too devalued since they see me as the mechanic of the *catalogue raisonné*, not a biographer,' Corey decided. 'If you don't object, I think I'll start with Clarissa, I've been invited to give a couple of talks at the Venice Biennale in September on past participants. A recreation of Gustave's show in eighty-two might interest one or two museum directors I can think of. It's a good enough reason to go and pick Clarissa's brain. I'll see what she'll tell me about Berlin, without going too much into specifics.'

Max was amused by the choice of pretext. It was the kind of ingenuity he expected of Corey.

'Another thing, Max: I need an assistant. I want Waverley Smith for the duration.'

Max looked slightly startled. 'You mean that girl in…?'

'Yes, works in the gallery. She's wasted sitting behind a desk. I've seen her sticking labels on envelopes.'

'She's hardly started, has she? Didn't you recommend her?'

'Yes, as an intern. She was one of my best research students, ever. I hear somebody's made her permanent, so somebody must think well of her.'

'Ah, that'll be Peter. Yes, yes, fine by me, but you'll need to ask –'

At that moment Peter Collarii sauntered in, as though summoned to assist in their machinations. He was one of the very few people Angela could not prevent entering unannounced.

'Ah, Peter, the Post… erm… difficulty. Corey, here, wants one of your staff to assist him.'

Peter, with the youngest brother, Erik, looked after the day-to-day affairs of the Keyline Galleries. There were five: Hong Kong, Los Angeles, New York, Geneva and London. Erik was based in Los Angeles and ran the Hong Kong, Los Angeles and New York locations. Peter, London and Geneva. He was clearly from the same mould as his older brother, but leaner, a man for the ski slopes above Zermatt and Aspen; a man with silverware at home, and won in the not too distant past, either. He wasn't hearty but he had the tang of the outdoors about him. Competition, one could sense, was something he relished. He gave Corey a quizzical nod.

'Hello, Peter.' Corey pulled an apologetic expression. 'I'm suggesting to Max that if I'm to investigate the Posts I want Waverley Smith.'

Peter bridled slightly. 'Everybody wants Waverley; Erik's got his eye on her for New York.'

'Already?' Corey appealed to Max. He was adamant. 'Look, I'll get nowhere with some of the Post family, particularly Ross and his brother. She's a terrier and I want her. She'll get in where I can't.'

Peter laughed as though he found it comical to be squabbling over a junior member of staff. 'Can I have her back when you're done with her?'

Max joined in the amusement. 'Steady on, she's not a photocopying machine!'

'Oh, yes, I know *that*!' Peter responded. 'She'll do what photocopiers can't do.'

'Meaning?'

'She likes idiots, humours those beyond helping, and the artists, God deliver us, love her.'

'That, Corey,' declared Max, 'is the closest you'll get to an endorsement from Peter, so she's yours. Bring her back in one piece, or the artists will be crying into their porridge.'

The younger Collarii levelled a finger at Corey. 'Better still, find me a new intern just like her. That school of yours must be crawling with stroppy young things.'

Max ushered Corey towards the door. 'Farewell, Corey. We can't imagine how you're going to employ her, but don't tell us, we don't want to know. Report back when you have news.'

SEVEN

Clarissa Post – she had stuck with the name Post after her divorce, despite remarrying twice – came from a long line of Austrian hoteliers. With her third husband her station in life had changed very much for the better and she had settled in Kensington in a very grand house near The Boltons. She received a courteous note from Corey Templeton, to which she replied with commendable speed. So it was that at eleven o'clock, not many days after agreeing his commission from the Collarii brothers, Corey rang her bell and was admitted by her personal assistant. The PA was spick and span, looked new to the job, but very much at home.

'You're expected, come.'

Corey followed her back through the house. It – her back – was extremely straight. She walked like the CEO of everything she surveyed. He was impressed; she looked very high-maintenance and floated just above the floor.

Clarissa was at home in a large, over-heated sitting room. She was surrounded by flowers, and looked like a somewhat faded hothouse bloom herself.

'If you recall, I came about nineteen eighty-two,' Corey reminded her once the pleasantries had been disposed of.

The PA laughed to herself as though he had laid down an impossible condition for profitable discussion.

'Silly girl!' scolded Clarissa. 'Of course I remember nineteen eighty-two. *Perfectly!* It was the year Torville and Dean did something.' She spoke in a high, clear voice with a hint of foreignness in her pronunciation.

'You were living in Berlin at the time.'

'I told Gustave it was me or Berlin. I couldn't stand Berlin. We were marooned and there's a cold wind that blows from Siberia.

It turns men's minds to *lebensraum* in warmer climes. Then, when I wasn't looking, some snake brought Little Miss Elfin-tits to the studio to surmount me.'

'Supplant,' said the PA.

Clarissa frowned as though considering whether she should object to being corrected. Instead she said, 'Crack on, crack up, crack down. These are the kind of things I still find endlessly difficult. Crack and crap are hard enough.'

'Shit and sheet,' added the PA.

'Yes, that too,' agreed Clarissa.

'In particular it was the Venice Biennale I had in mind,' said Corey, wondering what kind of double act he had encountered. 'I have to give a talk, you see, in Venice in September. I wanted to discuss Gustave's exhibition when he –'

'I had no objection to Venice, of course! We stayed at the Basilica San Marco.'

'That's a church,' said the PA, smiling sweetly.

'The San Marco Palace, then,' Clarissa corrected herself waspishly.

'You were in Berlin, though, weren't you?' said Corey, hoping against hope that he could keep the conversation on track. 'I mean, most of the work he showed in Venice had been produced over the previous year, if I remember correctly.'

'The smell of oil paint: you can't forget it when you no longer have it!'

Corey could see that this was in the nature of a stop-gap answer. As Clarissa assembled the rest of her reply, his eyes wandered to the early Post painting of nineteen fifty-nine that hung on the far wall. To one side of the abstracted interior it featured his celebrated sardonic use of the flower arrangement motif. As his eyes circled back to the dowager duchess in her bower of flowers he thought, idly, how apt Post's floral invention was to present circumstances.

'That wastrel Clyde was harbouring Little Miss Elfin-tits. He'd know. He won't speak to me because I hit him with one of those golf sticks.'

'Clubs,' said the PA.

'Well, it had a very nice club end. I cornered him. Of course, being Gustave's assistant, he couldn't fight back. I doubt you'd have more luck,' she decided.

'Do you mean trying to talk to him?' said Corey, feeling rather lost.

She gave a small sigh. 'I should have been taking it out on Gustave, but he was nowhere to be seen… as usual.'

'Miss Elfin-tits…?'

'Some dreadful bird of passage.' She put the subject beyond further enquiry with a curt gesture of dismissal.

'But this Clyde might have insights…?' wondered Corey. He had not heard the name before. To work as a studio assistant was a well-known way into the art world for ambitious art students.

'I'm writing my own story,' declared Clarissa grandly. 'It's become an historical necessity, but it means there's an embargo on sharing reminiscences. Domestic detail's my strength. I regret hitting him now; there's so much I can't remember.' She looked up gratefully at the ramrod figure of her PA and reached out to touch her hand. 'Even with Penelope's assistance.'

'Get-even time,' said Penelope rather menacingly.

'Would be, if everyone weren't dead,' said Clarissa. 'Time we did a little dictation,' she decided. 'Been lovely to see you, etcetera.'

Corey realised he was being dismissed; his plan had been shredded even before he'd started.

'So, you're helping her write her version of life with Gustave Post,' he mused as Penelope ushered him back to the front door. 'Do you have a title?'

'*Life in the Bullpen.*'

Corey looked at her, unable to tell whether she was ribbing him.

'Or, *Life with the Pitbull.* Which do you prefer?' She looked at him quizzically, an amused curve to her unkissable lips.

EIGHT

Corey had thought he had a plan of campaign. Now it was clear he needed a better one. He went eastwards towards the Aldwych, ruefully certain he'd been the butt of an elaborate joke. Did it mean all three branches of Gustave's family already knew the Collarii brothers had launched an investigation into the ownership of the unknown painting? He had been ambushed. Knowing Clarissa of old, he should have expected it. At least he had a couple of useful pieces of information. When he was in his office, high above the street, he put in a call to Campbell Carter.

'Ah, hello Corey. You call as a representative of the Brothers Grimm, I suppose?'

'Well, they won't let the Gustave Post thing go, not for the moment.'

'Ah, these art world contracts...!' Campbell made a throaty sound of disapproval.

'Let's put it this way, Campbell: I'd like to complete the *catalogue raisonné* and move on. It's a scholarly thing.'

'Yes, I understand; the completist in you, and all that. Well, as a humble biographer I suppose I must applaud. How can I assist your disinterested endeavours?'

'It's Post's Berlin period.'

'Yes, yes, I've been scouring my notes; putting my sources in order. Devil of a job. I shall deliver to Max in due course.'

'And I'm sure Max will be suitably grateful.'

'What troubles you?'

'Someone called Little Miss Elfin-tits. Could have been a mistress. Does she turn up in them?'

'No. Where did that come from?'

'Clarissa.'

'Ah! A word to the wise: take anything she says with a pinch, old boy.'

'How about a studio assistant named Clyde?'

'Clyde... Doesn't ring a bell. First name or second? Could be either. I don't recall Gustave having any studio assistants during his Berlin period. I suppose there might have been the odd German helper.'

The silence that followed told Corey he was going to get little else from Campbell. With warm words he terminated the call. He had always seen himself as being in a non-competitive relation to Campbell, but a certain tension he could not fully explain had dogged their conversation. It had been cordial but Campbell had been atypically taciturn. Corey felt restless and further dissatisfied with his performance as a sleuth. On his desk was a chapter of a thesis that he had to read: "Genre Painting in Post-War Britain." He put it in his briefcase and went down to the canteen for something to eat. While consuming his sandwich in a quiet corner, he observed the hubbub. The students came and went, bright, careless, full of restless energy; he decided it was time to co-opt Waverley Smith. Max Collarii had delegated the Gustave Post business to him; perhaps he'd have more success if he delegated it, or some part of it, to her. His mind made up, he travelled back to Mayfair.

Behind the defensive barricade of the reception counter at the Keyline Gallery, three young women were peering into computers. What did they do? It baffled him. They were always there, looking as though they were about to be sucked into their screens. When, rather than continuing into the gallery, he remained standing at the counter, a resolute blot against the light from the glazed entrance, they began to register his presence, one after the other, heads popping up like buds coming into bloom. Waverley was the good-looking one, and the last to tear her gaze away from her screen. She did so with the reluctance of a victim of narcolepsy.

'You're joining me,' he said, and nodded towards the stairs.

She dragged herself up and stretched. She had a charming halter-top with thin straps that showed off her shoulders to perfection.

They took the back stairs. Half way between floors, Corey asked, 'What do you do on those computers?'

'Sudoku, mainly,' she replied.

By the time they reached the small meeting room on the third floor she was wide-awake. She messed with her hair as she prowled the room, glancing occasionally in his direction as he unburdened his briefcase of its papers.

Corey sat down and looked at her speculatively.

'What?' she said.

'Peter talk to you?'

'Yes.'

'You happy about that, or what?'

'Yes, no, great. I mean, much better.' She came and sat down at the table, opposite him.

'You know I'm a calculating sod, don't you?' he said.

She leant her elbows on the table and looked at him frowningly, from beneath a lowered brow.

'Good. Next week you're flying down to Cannes with me. There's a Gustave Post opening at La Malmaison on Thursday. On Wednesday there's a reception for the family. We're going to be there and be gracious to the ones who turn up. I want you to make yourself known to Ross and his brother, Quentin. Ross is a brute and truly his father's son… in a bad way. He's staying in Antibes at the moment. I want you to go and be curious about his work – he thinks he's an artist – and about his father's pictures. Max thinks he might be the source of this New York painting.'

She nodded as though she knew of Ross's reputation and wasn't impressed.

'In the meantime, I want you to charm Campbell Carter. He's putting together all the info he has on Gustave's time in Berlin. I want you to extract it from him as painlessly as possible. He's a biographer and it's natural for biographers to keep their secrets. He won't be expecting you; probably he'll be expecting me. Play it like you're half siren, half minion and you should get more co-operation than I'll ever get. What do you say?' He looked at her enquiringly, half expecting her to have some scruple about what he was suggesting.

'Super. We going club class?'

He gave her a chiding look and slid a folder towards her. In it was a list drawn from the Gustave Post's *catalogue raisonné*, itemising his Berlin period paintings. There were also copies of the photographs of the unknown painting that had turned up in New York.

'Do your worst,' he said.

NINE

Campbell Carter rented a tiny flat at the top of a tall, thin house off Russell Square. He owned an equally small cottage, which he liked to call his "country retreat", in Whitstable. On a good day, Whitstable was an hour from London Bridge station. His was a somewhat solitary life, not without a certain prestige and many convivial consolations. He liked his food and considered himself a gourmet. Down in Whitstable he had been known to eat at both Wheeler's and the Sportsman on the same weekend. It was therefore somewhat in the manner of taking a purge that he had just finished a lunch of toast, cheddar and a tomato when Waverley Smith reached his landing and knocked on his crooked door.

'Dear child!' he exclaimed, when he opened the door and found her breathless at his threshold. He took a step back to admire what had landed on his doormat. 'I say, you're quite the best thing the Marx brothers have sent my way in a looooong while. Do, do, come in!'

Waverley entered and made quite a business of being flustered, throwing off her shoulder bag and various carrier bags as though she could not bear to be encumbered for another moment. 'I hope this isn't inconvenient?' she mumbled, vigorously tossing back her hair. She offered him a hand, a little limply, but looked at him intensely, suggestive of someone short-sighted.

Campbell was caught in a crosswind of reactions. Why, he asked himself in his flowery, art historical way, had the Collarii brothers sent this chaste nymph? He was charmed, but had been anticipating somebody with more heft; he had expected it would most likely be Corey Templeton who arrived to take delivery of his research.

'I'm sorry,' she said, with just the right touch of deference, 'I'm Waverley. The foundation sent me... you know?'

He gave a little laugh. 'I was expecting someone... a little more mundane,' he confided, unable to suppress a note of fruitiness in his voice.

'Would you mind...?' she pointed to a nearby armchair.

'Not at all.'

She sat down with the expression of someone experiencing discomfort. She was wearing toreador pants and a frail-looking pair of slip-ons. 'My Alexander technique teacher is so demanding,' she said as she took off one of the shoes and looked accusingly at the exposed foot, as though it had betrayed her.

Carter could only see what looked like a perfectly formed foot, *au naturel*.

She wiggled her toes with a wince. 'I try to think through my forehead in an upward diagonal, but I don't think my feet notice.'

'Ah,' decided Carter, as though all were suddenly clear, 'you're footsore.'

'Yes, I guess. Do *you* think about posture?'

He chuckled and shook his head. 'I suppose you're going to tell me I should go to yoga.'

'Well, no, but you write a lot, don't you? It's terrible for the spine.' She stood up without returning her shoe to her foot and instead kicked off the other one. 'Look, if I think upward with my forehead, my spine is properly curved inwards here.' She put the back of her hand against her lower spine. 'You feel. Come.' She held her position and indicated with some urgency that he should feel the curvature of her spine.

He came over and, with her encouragement, placed his hand against the small of her back. 'That's what I'm trying to achieve every minute of the day without thinking about it!' she said bitterly, as though disgusted with herself for not doing so.

'It sounds extremely life-enhancing,' he decided, unaccustomed to, and bemused by, such intimacy.

'Yes, something like that,' she agreed, rather losing interest in the subject. 'I've come for the papers. You know, nineteen seventy-six.'

'My dear girl, that's not right, is it?' he rejoined, amused by her mistake *and* somewhat relieved to have moved on. 'The whole Berlin period, I was told.'

Waverley was suddenly crestfallen. 'Oh? I'm sure one of the secretaries told me I've to pick up the Gustave Post diary for nineteen seventy-six! Should I check?'

'Believe you me, the Collariis want what I've got on the whole time Gustave lived in Berlin. Seventy-six is when he moved there. Would you care for some coffee?'

So it was that Campbell Carter not only gave Waverley Smith coffee and biscuits but also regaled her with a somewhat fuller account of Gustave's activities in the years nineteen seventy-six to nineteen eighty-two than he had intended to share with anyone, even if it was still a great deal less than comprehensive. Waverley, whom he considered to be a soft, delicious, somewhat unworldly young woman, bewitched him. She was a spark of life in the torpid bookishness of his normal surroundings. He enjoyed the way she stood pensively besides him while he sorted through the photocopied material he had put together. Some of the pages were handwritten, others typed, although many of the latter consisted of a succession of stand-alone paragraphs with no final chronology. He apologised that much of the handwritten material was little more than jottings.

'Well, overall,' he concluded, as though to excuse the scant nature of what he was providing, 'I don't think it was a very interesting time in Gustave's life. New York was, in the end, more necessary and decisive.'

'No, no,' said Waverley, 'it's all very interesting. I've been to Berlin but I can see it was different when Post was there.'

'Indeed, *very different!* West Berlin then was an island filled with revolutionaries, but no politics.' He laughed, delighted by the droll nonsense of his aphorism.

'I love all your art books,' she said. 'You have so much information here.'

It was so; every wall space worth the effort had been clad in shelving, an effect that was cosy in sombre months, but on a summer's day, like today, stifling.

'It's a lifetime of writing about art, you know,' he said in a voice that suggested it had all been a light-hearted romp.

'Gosh, yes, I know. I love your book on Gustave Post.'

'Have you seen the catalogue for his Venice Biennale exhibition?'

'No, I'd love to see it.'

He went to a shelf where the volumes were slim, some without spines. He pulled out one with a maroon and blue cover and took it to his worktable. He laid it down for her to examine in a way that told her it was something precious, to be handled with care. She turned the pages one by one with great deliberation. At last she came to a full-page black-and-white photograph of Gustave Post in his studio. It was the usual scene of artistic endeavour: an industrial space, tabletops cluttered with cans and pots of every kind; a jacket hanging off an easel; a tall canister stuffed with lilies; half-finished and finished canvases everywhere, some propped against, some hanging on the walls.

'Fabulous! Was this where he always painted?' she wondered.

'For the Venice show?'

She nodded.

'Yes, this was in Berlin, not long before he moved on, following complications of the usual kind for a man of his age. He had his place in Majorca, of course, the flat in London and a studio in New York, but mainly he was here.'

'Oh? How old was he?'

'You know, mid-forties. He was always very restless, in matters of the heart as much as anything else.'

Waverley cast her eyes towards the window as though he were touching on things beyond her experience. 'I see.'

'By the time he had separated from his first wife, Berlin was finished.'

'What a life!' she said as she prepared to leave, gathering her scattered belongings. 'Are you coming to Cannes?'

'No, not this time. The family will be there and I've learnt not to bore them with my eternal presence. "Biographer's blight", I call it.'

Amusement, followed by a hint of uncertainty, crossed her face, as though she thought he was teasing her.

'The Collariis expect everyone to be working on their behalf because they're a power in the land...' he said, wagging a cautionary finger.

He accompanied her to the door.

'...And don't you forget it!' he called after her as she clattered down the stairs, leaving him standing at the threshold.

TEN

Waverley was well-satisfied with her afternoon's work. She caught a bus outside the site of the old Imperial Hotel and was soon in Corey Templeton's office. He had been elsewhere in the building when she arrived and he opened the door to find her gazing out of the open window. He came over to where she was sitting on the windowsill.

'What's so fascinating?' he asked, trying to identify what in the street had been holding her attention.

'No,' she shook her head. 'I wasn't really looking. It's not so intriguing, your view. I had other things on my mind.' For a moment she looked as though the weight of the world was on her shoulders but, almost instantly, she was the golden girl again.

'I did my best with Mr Carter. A charming man.' She pointed to the papers lying on Corey's desk. 'I think you're right: he's protecting his author's insights for volume two. Did you know he writes everything longhand and then has it transcribed by a secretary?'

'No, I didn't.'

'Quite archaic. Why isn't he coming to Cannes?'

'Do you know how many Gustave Post exhibitions there have been in the last couple of years?'

She shook her head.

'Seventeen or eighteen. I've lost count. And I should know, I've been involved in nearly all of them.'

She looked impressed. 'I didn't know; so many museums! Talking of exhibitions,' she went on, her voice becoming more of a drawl, 'I thought you might be interested in this.' She went to the papers she had brought from Campbell's flat and extracted Gustave Post's nineteen eighty-two Venice Biennale catalogue.

Corey gave an appreciative grunt. 'Do you know how rare this is? I haven't seen a copy in years. Where did...?' He gave her a penetration look. 'Is this his copy?'

She nodded, looking a little guilty.

'Does he know you've got it?'

She shook her head, even more guiltily. 'I'll take it back; it got mixed up with the photocopies he gave me. I didn't realise...'

He laughed. 'Why did you want it?'

She did a sudden switch and became brightly animated. 'To show *you*: it's this, look!' She opened the catalogue to show him the black and white photograph of Gustave Post's studio. 'You see? There's a photo credit on the side of the photograph, here: Geldrich. Somewhere I've seen a similar photograph of this studio, shot from a different angle.'

Corey put his hand to his chin. 'Yes, I think I know what you mean. It's in one of the Post monographs. Could it be the Phaidon one?' He strode over to his bookcase and selected a volume from his extensive collection of books on Gustave Post.

'I was wondering if there might be a chance...'

Corey already understood what she was driving at. '...that the Berlin Wall painting is visible in one of them.'

'You never know.'

He rifled through the book and at a second attempt he alighted on an illustration captioned, "Gustave Post, Henry Moore and Daniel Collarii in Post's Berlin studio, 1982". It too was credited to Geldrich.

'What if he gave the painting to Henry Moore!'

Corey shook his head. 'No, Post gave drawings and the like to his friends. But a large painting? Most unusual. Anyway, if he had it would have been catalogued before it left the studio; Daniel Collarii was very strict about such things. There should be an entry in the gallery's records of when Daniel made this visit to Berlin. That'll date the photographs.' He put the monograph down on the desk next to the Venice Biennale catalogue. 'I can't see the Berlin Wall painting in either, can you?'

'But look–' she had become quite twitchy– 'they're not taken at the same time, are they?' She pointed at the photograph in the

Phaidon monograph. 'In this one there's no lilies on the plan chest, but the container, vase, whatever it is, is still there. You can see the same length of wall in both but the paintings are different. I don't know, Geldrich must have been allowed in more than once. This is not even the photograph I was thinking of. What if he took lots that have never been published? And he might have taken some from the other end of the studio, where he'd get a very different view. They're much more vivid than Mr Carter's recollections. If we can pin down exactly when the painting was finished...' She clenched her eyes shut and shook her head. 'We should materialise its birth, if we can.'

'Good! So, how about Geldrich? Think we can find him?'

She nodded.

'"Seminal political statement", that's how Christies want to describe Gustave's Berlin Wall painting,' Corey ruminated. 'Who took it from the studio, and when?' He was still bent over the Phaidon monograph, scrutinising the photograph. 'There's something else. Look, in the background, there's a fourth man. I think I might know who that is. Clarissa, Gustave's first wife, told me he had a studio assistant; his name was Clyde. No other name though. I asked Carter: never heard of him. We'd better see if we can find him too.'

Waverley scooped up the Venice Biennale catalogue. 'Look, inside the back cover, there's a list of acknowledgements: "This exhibition would not have been possible without the help of..."' She had her finger under the fifth name on the list. '*Clyde Diggle.* That must be him!'

Corey was impressed. 'You're right.' He stood up and gazed into the far corner of his office, where the walls met the ceiling. 'There's another thing: who was Little Miss Elfin-tits? No use asking Clarissa, she says it's embargoed, but Clyde Diggle knows.'

ELEVEN

Corey and Waverley were booked onto the 17.15 flight from Heathrow to Mandelieu, Cannes. They met in departures and went straight to the Club World lounge. The flight was delayed and they were there for over an hour before they boarded.

A soft Mediterranean warmth greeted them as they stepped off the plane at Mandelieu. There was minimal passport control and the baggage hall was nearly empty. Corey had only a cabin bag so he went straight out into the arrivals hall while Waverley picked up a second bag she had consigned to the hold.

The flight had, in a small way, brought to the surface Corey's dissatisfaction with his social abilities. Waverley had responded to his conversational gambits cheerfully enough, but in between she had seemed subdued and inattentive. It was as though he could not prise her away from her private thoughts for long.

'Do you want something to eat?' he had asked when she was so absorbed.

'No, I think I'll wait.'

'What, eat at the hotel? What's the difference?'

'It's not the quality, it's the timing, Corey. There's a superfluity of food. Haven't you noticed?'

'I suppose I have. We're food-rich. Is that what you mean?'

'Yes. Don't you worry about how the supermarkets compost all those packets of smoked salmon?'

'All? Perhaps none get wasted.'

She gave him a look that said he'd said a very naïve thing.

Her obscurity made him feel uncomfortable; it was as though he failed her as a social animal. It was a knack he didn't have... and not worth struggling with. Rather miserably, he concluded he'd never stimulate her mental faculties like she did his.

He paced the arrivals hall. The concession stalls peddled the usual businessman's homecoming essentials; he looking disconsolately into the café. Waverley, he presumed, was still waiting for the hold baggage to arrive at the carousel. He wondered at the length of time it was taking to unload the plane. He poked his nose out into the evening air and sampled the sybaritic Côte d'Azur atmosphere. The taxi rank was still busy with comings and goings. The evening's aromas of thyme, coffee and warm diesel wafted around him seductively. He turned back. He heard several sharp noises like somebody rapping a metal pipe, and thought no more about it. Still Waverley hadn't come. He walked back to the doors where the arrivals debouched from the baggage hall. As a straggler emerged, Corey craned for a sight of the carousels. He recognised the straggler from the plane. 'Excuse me, is anybody still waiting for baggage?' he asked.

'Nah, mate, they've all come through.' The straggler hefted his rucksack and lumbered off.

Corey was perplexed. Something had gone wrong. He took out his mobile and wondered whether he should call her. As with many meticulous people, he didn't want her to think he was fussing. He strode back towards the exit doors, the conviction taking hold that somehow she had got ahead of him and was waiting outside. As the doors rolled back something caught his eye on the further side of the vehicle lanes. There was some sort of agitation in the short-term car park. Hard to say why he thought it unusual, but there was something implicitly violent in the movements... of what? Well, people. But what were they doing? What was going on? There was a sense of danger in the air; a shout, maybe more than one. Then he saw a blond woman and realised it was Waverley. She was heading in his direction, between two lanes of parked cars. Obscurely, it struck him that, in the declining light of evening, every car was uniformly coated with dust. Now alarmed, he crossed the taxi lane to the pedestrian island, and then the access lane. Waverley was beyond a crash barrier directly ahead. He veered left to meet her on the walkway and when he reached it he saw, further into the ranks of parked cars, a man on the ground.

'Waverley, what the–?'

She was very close now. It struck him she looked discomposed, as if their plane had crash-landed and she had disembarked by the escape chute, somehow in possession of both her hold and cabin baggage.

'We should go, Corey. I've been waylaid. They wanted my case. Look!' She indicated a Renault Grand Scenic with her chin. The centre of the windscreen was starred with what looked suspiciously like a bullet hole.

'Waverley–'

'We need a taxi. Those men had a gun.'

'What men?'

'Later, Corey.' She tossed her head in the direction of the man on the ground. 'He saved me. Get his mobile number; I'll get a taxi.' It was clear she intended they should make as fast a getaway as possible.

Corey did as she had asked, but as he made his way towards the downed man he began to have second thoughts; to think he was putting himself unnecessarily in harm's way. After all, he had no idea what had just happened. It seemed there had been a serious altercation with parties now vanquished, but vanquished for how long? Hadn't Waverley mentioned a gun? Was there not the evidence of a shot having been fired through the windscreen of a Renault people-carrier just metres from where he was standing? Was this the sort of thing one expected when travelling club class on cultural business? *No!* Suddenly, he was disinclined to go any further. What's more, the man had picked himself up, was dusting himself off and looking around for his dark glasses. Corey turned back towards the taxi rank. Already Waverley had secured the taxi at the front of the rank. The driver was out of the car with the boot open.

Corey flung his flight case in the boot as Waverley was sliding into the rear seat. 'Quick, *allez doucement!* No, à *toute vitesse!*' he mumbled, almost colliding with the driver.

Waverley reached over to open his door for him and he tumbled in, stubbing his toe on one of her cases, which she had, for no obvious reason, stowed in his foot well. She was laughing softly; he felt ludicrous and abashed. Oblivious to their sense of urgency, their driver was in a querulous exchange with the driver of the taxi to their rear. They sat for an agonising minute before he finally moved off.

When they had cleared the barriers flanking the exit, Corey felt able to enquire as to what he had just been an unwilling party.

'What the hell, Waverley?'

She looked at him coolly. 'I know... bad! I have thirty-two Swiss watches in that case with an average value of ten thousand dollars.'

'Jesus, that's a quarter of a million!'

'Thirty-two thousand, actually,' she said primly. 'And somebody knew I was coming. Not one party, *two!*'

'What... what... *what the hell* are you doing with *Swiss watches*?'

'Somebody asked me to take them to Nice. I thought, *why not?* I didn't expect anybody to try and stiff me.'

'Stiff you? What, *exactly–*?'

'I don't know. People are unreliable. They have Afghan partners. They deal with Internet creeps. I mean, who cares about watches anymore?'

'What happened?'

'I was hustled. These two jerks were trying to frogmarch me to their car when these other jerks intervened. There was a lot of – you know – foul language...'

'What, in French?'

'No, Geordie... *I don't know!* This businessman guy going to his car tried to intervene. I mean, I was a damsel in distress and so on. Somebody produced a gun. There was more pulling me back and forth. The gun went off accidentally, or maybe it was fired.' She paused to think. 'Several times, I seem to remember. Somebody fell down. And then the man who was trying to rescue me was pushed over. I doubled back to the terminal. That's when you appeared. *Where were you?*'

'*Where was I?* I was waiting. I thought you were still at the baggage reclaim.'

'That's crazy! They nearly snatched me and the watches from right under your nose.'

'Well, if I'd known you were carrying Swiss watches I'd have behaved differently.'

'Really? I'm touched!'

'Since the Collarii Foundation paid for you to fly club class on Gustave Post business, you can't expect a gun-toting *fracas* in a short-term car park to be on my list of likely occurrences!'

'Amen.'

'Meaning?'

'I agree. I didn't get snatched anyway.'

'*Monsieur, où allons-nous?*' said the taxi driver.

Corey thought Waverley should feel contrite, but no such thing seemed to occur to her.

'*Monsieur…!*'

Corey had their itinerary in his pocket, which had been prepared by Angela, Max's PA. He extracted it hastily and showed the driver. 'So, what you're saying is that two separate teams were trying to rob you at the same time?'

'I wouldn't call them "teams",' she said, scornfully. 'Neither were competent, were they? I mean, white boys on scooters with machetes would have been far more effective. With a scooter I could have robbed myself in ten seconds flat.'

'Doesn't it occur to you they were intending to take you with them? What might have happened then?'

A troubled expression crossed her face. 'Bad stuff?'

'Yes, *bad stuff!* Those watches must be counterfeit, or stolen or something.' He kicked the case at his feet. 'Is this them?'

'Yes.'

'When we get to the hotel you get rid of them. They're not going in your room safe; they go in the hotel safe where you can't access them. Then you won't be a target.' Corey wanted to see her as an innocent victim under the sway of bad company, but the picture didn't quite gel. 'Robbing a mule; that's pretty standard stuff,' he said with a slight air of disparagement.

'*Mule!*' she said mockingly. 'Oh really? Do I look like some Mexican *peon*? That's American TV crapola. I am not a mule; I was acting as a *courier!*'

'Yeah, well, you can buy me a big fat gin Martini when we get to the hotel… *and* explain what's going on.'

She was aghast. 'Corey, I don't buy men drinks! Show a little respect! That's not right!' She gazed truculently out of the window, her lips slightly parted in what might have been a pout.

He softened. 'Okay, I'll buy, but you'd better explain so someone with normal mental faculties – *that's me!* – can understand.'

TWELVE

The Majestic on the Croisette was one of those grand, icing sugar hotels beloved of the fabulous and those who would be so. The Collariis were protective of their prestige and would not have had anyone associated with their business staying anywhere less. Corey thought it a typical Riviera playpen for the gilded ones, and its architectural style a little over-bearing, but he had to admit that it suited Waverley: she looked a million bucks in the shining, wind-blown way some starlets do before things go awry. On his tours around the world he had watched them enjoying the game of being close to the myth of Gustave Post, and he had to admit that Waverley more than looked the part.

They checked in, and went to their rooms to shower and change. Corey came down first and ordered a gin Martini seated at the bar. When Waverley joined him, they moved to a table away from the bar's back-lit glamour. She was wearing a simple Audrey Hepburn dress in black. He felt weary; the drink had induced a deepening of his lethargy.

'God, you look so alive,' he said as she collapsed graceful onto the banquette.

'I should explain,' she said gravely.

He waited, letting her take her time, although there was something of a rebuke in his silence.

'Fishman buys and sells second-hand Swiss watches. Expensive ones.'

'Who the hell is Fishman?'

'*Who is he?*' she said, as though the idea of explaining was an insufferable bore. 'Stanley Fishman, but nobody calls him Stanley, do they? You wouldn't, would you, with a name like that? I suppose, if you were really to stretch a point, you might say he's my boyfriend… although the "friend" part seems slightly disproportionate at the moment. Mainly, he buys watches at auctions and sells them in London, to collectors and jewellers looking for something special or rare. They go very well down here in the south of France. He knew I was coming and he asked me to bring some for a jeweller contact in Nice. It's all supposed to be above board. His name's Gabriel de Grandhomme and he's coming tomorrow to collect them. That's the whole arrangement, as far as I'm concerned.'

'So, have you spoken to this Fishman about what happened at the airport?'

'Yes. He claims he's coming; says he knows nothing about it… Shocked…'

'You believe him?'

'I don't know. I don't know what to think… I don't understand what happened myself.'

'Tell me again.'

She looked into the middle distance as though to recollect. 'Two men grabbed me, and then two other men tried to snatch me from them. They had a gun. Well, somebody did. Then the businessman intervened. It was kind of crazy.' She took a sip of her gin Martini. 'Did you get his number? I should try and thank him.'

'Forget it.' Corey shut the matter down with a dismissive gesture. 'I decided against it; we had to get away.'

'De Grandhomme's driving over early and then it'll be done.'

Corey grunted his understanding. 'Good. And tomorrow I don't want this Swiss watch thing coming up! You're going to beguile Ruthie's sons: Ross and Quentin. You on board for that?'

'Sounds immoral.'

'Yes,' he admitted despairingly, 'it is. Ross is difficult.'

'So you've said. You could come too.'

'No, together I'd just get a lot of hostile verbals. Ross is house-sitting in Antibes, and Quentin is supposed to be around too. Ross spends money.'

'He does?'

'Max thinks he might be selling the Berlin Wall painting to fund his lifestyle. All you have to do is talk to him about his father's paintings; see what he says. He and Quentin are idiots so they could say absolutely anything. And no Swiss watches!'

He thought Waverley was about to reprove him for harping on about the watches, but her eyes were across the room and she exclaimed, '*Max!*' in an alarmed voice.

Corey turned and saw that Max Collarii was, indeed, heading their way; what's more, he was accompanied by Clarissa Post. It was a shock to see Max was already in Cannes and at the thought of Clarissa for company he uttered a short, sharp expletive beneath his breath.

'Charming scene of debauchery,' said Clarissa when the two arrivals reached their table, before Max could offer a word of greeting. It put him on his metal as far as diplomatic niceties were concerned.

'Ah-hum! Clarissa, you know Corey, I believe. And let me introduce Waverley Smith. She's Corey's assistant. They're working on Gustave's eighty-two Biennale exhibition. It's in the air we might do a recreation.' He adjusted his stance to address Corey and Waverley. 'Clarissa and I have been having a little preview of the exhibition. It's very good. Very, very good! I can't get over how fresh it all looks.' There was a droll look on his face. 'Clarissa was almost overwhelmed.'

'Pomp and circumstance!' she said, lowering herself into a chair. 'Every recipe he ever concocted!'

'I wasn't expecting you,' said Corey. 'You weren't on our flight.'

'No,' agreed Max, 'we came via Nice from London City this afternoon. I had someone to see. So, what have you both been up to?' It amused Max to think he and Clarissa had caught them in an amorous tryst. 'You both look thoroughly guilty,' he added teasingly.

Corey noticed that Waverley had slid along the banquette, into a patch of shadow, as if to lessen his scrutiny.

'No, no,' Max decided, '*not guilty enough!* You look like you're on your honeymoon.' He turned around and caught a waiter's attention. With an unerring instinct for a good tipper, the waiter bustled over directly. Max was in an expansive mood. With much bonhomie he ordered for himself and Clarissa, and was at pains to ensure Corey and Waverley's drinks were replenished. He moved round to sit on the banquette, next to Waverley.

'I think it's going to be rather a glorious occasion,' he said, with a cheerful grin. 'The French have always been a little slow to warm to Anglophone artists, but they love Post's *élan vital*. Bergson's mistake was to spread *élan vital* around like butter. The fact is, hardly anyone can materialise it and turn it into something concrete, not like Gustave could.' He looked around the table with what appeared, to Corey's eyes, like boyish enthusiasm. It was a side of Max to which he was unaccustomed. *The Riviera*, he thought, *the infectious, carefree lightness of being!*

'All those ghastly people,' said Clarissa, without making clear of whom she spoke. 'Gustave was a bastard – *yes, of course!* – but even he had to admit I encouraged the good in him. He was surrounded by sycophants from morning to night, so no wonder! Not your father, Max; he was a pillar, an absolute pillar. I intend to blow them all *out of the water!*'

'Ah, yes! *Your book!*' exclaimed Corey, still unforgiving of how convincing her pretence of encroaching senility had been at their last meeting. Her present demeanour confirmed his every suspicion and he felt moved to pay her back. 'Max, do you know about Clarissa's book?'

Clarissa fixed Corey with a gimlet eye. 'He thinks, Max, my book is going to be kiss-and-tell nonsense. Don't you believe it! I will, however, reveal the secret of my recipe for *patatas a lo pobre*.' Her Chartreuse cocktail had appeared and she took it up with surprising relish.

Max studied her with new interest. 'You're writing a book about Gustave?'

'I've insights nobody else could have… except his mother!' She made the sound of a mewling baby.

'Seriously, it sounds very… *exciting*,' said Max cheerfully.

For Corey the *patatas a lo pobre* crack had been the last straw. 'What about Little Miss Elfin-tits?' he asked, acting a little drunker than he actually was. 'Is she in it?'

'Bah! I despatch her in two sentences, both cutting.'

Max gave Corey a puzzled look. 'Little Miss *who*?'

'I don't know, that's what Clarissa calls her. She's a Postian mystery.'

Clarissa wagged a finger at Corey. 'Ingrid Pingle-dingle-grid, or some such; good on her back with her legs in the air!' Furiously she flicked the subject away. 'She didn't get Gustave, the scheming little bitch, she got zilch!'

'Well! Well!' said Max humorously. He turned to Waverley, who had been silent for some time. 'Do you play tennis, Ms Smith? We could have a game in the morning before breakfast.'

Waverley stretched and nodded like a child who had been brought into the conversation by an indulgent grown-up.

Tough, but not armour-plated, decided Corey; more affected by the incident at the airport than she's letting on.

THIRTEEN

Corey was having breakfast on the pool terrace. He glanced up to see a young woman in whites and sunglasses making her way between the tables. For a moment he thought no more about it, so perfectly did she belong amongst the blues, creams and lemon yellows of the terrace. On second thoughts he looked again – focusing this time – and saw it was Waverley wearing a tank top and matching pleated skirt. She looked blithely happy.

'Did you bring a racquet too?' he joked, faintly surprised she had thought to pack tennis whites.

'No, there's a tennis professional; I borrowed one.'

'Did you win?'

Waverley had been gazing about her, as though to orientate herself in the unfamiliar surroundings, but now she turned to look at him over the rim of her sunglasses and gave him a smile that said she was not going to be clear on that point. 'Ah…! In the battle of wills, who says who won?'

Corey found that suitably politic. 'Too true! Have you got rid of those watches?'

'Not yet; they're at the concierge desk. It's all arranged, though. De Grandhomme's going to show his passport when he picks them up; I don't even have to see him.'

'Good. How about coffee?'

'Yes, and juice too.'

She wandered off to see what was available at the buffet. Corey took idle pleasure in watching her go. He should, he felt, have been displeased with her after yesterday's events, but her loveliness swept aside all thoughts of displeasure. Her hair was tied loosely at the nape of her neck; it flowed between her shoulder blades in a river of gold. He followed her progress and saw her meet Max, coming in the other direction. They exchanged a few words in the manner of partners in an enterprise both had enjoyed, and then Max came on. He had changed out of his tennis gear and looked, in a studied way, casually rumpled.

'Morning, Corey.'

'Morning.'

A waiter arrived as though out of nowhere.

'Coffee, scrambled eggs and fresh orange juice,' ordered Max, without hesitation. 'Oh, and toast, please.' He turned to Corey. 'How's our little project going? I couldn't ask last night because of Clarissa.'

'Where is she?'

'Preparing to make her entrance, I suppose. Any developments?'

'Mmm. Waverley dug stuff out of Campbell Carter quite successfully. Gustave had a studio assistant named Clyde Diggle that Campbell didn't know about. Heard of him?'

Max puckered his lower lip in a way that said no.

'A Clyde Diggle exhibited at the Greeson Gallery in the late eighties.'

'That gallery's gone, hasn't it?' said Max.

'Yes. Sloane Avenue, if I remember rightly. Apparently, Diggle won the John Moores painting prize in nineteen eighty-something. We found him through his website. He lives in Northumberland now. Twenty years teaching art in a girls' secondary school; recently took early retirement. I've written to him. Then there's the photographer who visited Gustave in Berlin. Name of Andrew Geldrich. Seems he was around on the scene – quite successful – in the seventies and early eighties. He's dead, but his wife lives in Hastings, and apparently she has a huge archive of his work.'

'What's the idea there?'

'Oh, he visited the studio at least twice. And Waverley thinks on one occasion he might have photographed *Berlin Wall Lament No.1* while it was being painted. If he did, we might get some insight into how it left the studio without being recorded, and where it went.'

Max nodded appreciatively. 'Bright kid!'

'I thought we might buy the negatives and prints, for the Post archive.'

'Good; you're right. Essential... gathering that sort of documentation. I wonder if there's one of Clarissa? She'd love it for her book.' He glanced at Corey. 'We need to keep her on side.'

'Ah!' said Corey. 'Talking of Clarissa, who's this woman she's got a thing about: "Little Miss Elfin-tits"?'

'Yes, where's *that* come from?'

'Clarissa said she's called Ingrid something-or-other.'

'She made an enemy in Clarissa, whoever she is. She must have been one of Gustave's flings. Nothing I know anything about. You going to find her?'

'Yes. If Gustave gave her the Berlin Wall painting, it's none of our business, and the family's in the clear. It'd be a neat closure.'

Max laughed, shaking his head knowingly. 'Too damn neat! He may have sprayed drawings about like confetti, but a major painting...?'

'No, certainly not in a Biennale year.'

'Well,' decided Max brightly, 'you seem to be making progress. Good! I'm going back to the exhibition this morning. What about you two?'

'I'm setting Waverley loose on Ross.'

Whereas Corey readily admitted to finding Ross odious, Max liked to maintain the impression he was above disliking anyone. Even so, Max looked noticeably uneasy, even a little disapproving. 'Keep an eye on her; that man's a danger to himself, never mind anybody else!'

'Are you saying she shouldn't go?'

As ever, Max was oblique. 'I'm saying he's a bloody fool.'

Corey felt a prick of guilt and a little frustrated at having to defend sending Waverley. 'I've never been able to get anywhere with him. I sense she might have more luck. He's your suspect, after all.'

Waverley reappeared: she'd found fruit and croissants. Then coffee came followed by Max's scrambled eggs and more coffee.

Eventually Waverley rose to leave. 'I'm going to get ready to visit the Post boys,' she announced for Max's benefit.

Max gave her an inscrutable look. 'Take care. He thinks he's a bigger genius than his father. And keep him away from me, we're *not* offering him an exhibition!'

Corey chuckled wearily. He knew all about Ross's self-belief and his attempts to further his career.

They both watched Waverley wend her way towards the hotel. When she was lost to sight, Max rolled his eyes heavenwards. 'Ross has heard it before… but, *my*, does he persist!'

FOURTEEN

At the last moment, Max insisted Waverley use his chauffeur-driven Mercedes to go to Antibes. She told the driver to stop at the corner of the Chemin des Nielles, and not to wait for her. She knew the lane she was looking for was a right turn somewhere ahead, but wasn't in a hurry to arrive. She slung her satchel over her shoulder and sauntered. There were no pavements, the neighbourhood not being of the kind to encourage pedestrians. Both sides of the road were edged with yard upon yard of low, white-painted boundary wall, which was topped with impenetrable fencing in green sheet metal, giving the whole the look of fortifications. The uniformity of the construction of these defences suggested the local planning authority had approved them as having the status and utility appropriate to the needs of the neighbourhood. The gates looked equally intimidating. The effect was softened by the peeping tops of oleanders and bougainvilleas, and the video cameras were suitably discreet. The villas this arsenal of security devices protected spread out horizontally, ranch-style, set back from the road in densely-planted plots. The atmospherics suggested retired executives, successful scriptwriters and perfume manufacturers.

Eventually, Waverley came to a gate set back between two backward curving lengths of white-painted wall and saw the number fifteen. She would have been impressed had the place been the fruits of Ross's own endeavours, but she knew the villa belonged to the parents of some private jet-flying chum and Ross was only house-sitting until the chum's family arrived for their usual summer stay.

She pressed the bell on the keypad. Nothing happened for a long time and then a voice drawled, 'Yeah?'

'Oh, hi, it's Waverley. You remember: I work for the foundation?'

'Push when the buzzer sounds,' said the voice.

She let herself in. Ahead was a drive cutting into a lush vista of trees and shrubs, every one a horticultural specimen. It – the drive – curved round to the front of the villa: a surprisingly modest edifice with the obligatory, old-fashioned green shutters. A man, about thirty-five, as languid-looking as he had sounded laconic on the intercom, stood at the threshold. He shaded his eyes with his hand as Waverley approached as though he couldn't quite believe what he was seeing.

'If you're new, I like their recruitment policy,' he said, his face impassive. Ross Post was handsome, but looked a little shabby and over-the-hill. He was wearing a tee shirt and what looked like karate pants. The tee shirt was smeared with dabs of oil paint in an area that was in danger of becoming a paunch.

'I'm working for Corey Templeton on your father's *catalogue raisonné*. I... I wanted to meet you,' she said with a display of hesitancy. 'The Post legacy is very important to the Collarii Foundation. The reception this evening...'

'Yes, *the reception! An opportunity!* Good to meet you, Waverley.'

She smiled.

'Come in,' he said, presuming he needed no introduction. 'I'll make coffee.'

There was a spacious entrance hall and open-plan rooms off. Scant furniture and the air of a summer let, but expensive. There was a fair bit of domestic detritus scattered about the floor; some of it looked like a woman's clothing. The original villa had been enlarged greatly to the rear. The living/kitchen area was beyond generous with vast areas of glass. The view overlooked trees and rooftops. Through the live-in kitchen there was what might originally have been intended as a children's playroom. From it, open French windows accessed a covered terrace. Ross had commandeered the playroom and the terrace as a studio. The floors of both were covered in plastic, like the preliminary of a mob killing. The evidence of his volcanic spurts of creative activity was everywhere, tacked and taped to the walls. The raw materials for this activity – a messy profusion of paint in cans, tubes and aerosols – was spread across a plastic-covered table tennis table, which stood at the junction of the two spaces.

In general terms, it might be said about Ross's paintings that from *Arte Povera* he took his indifference to conventional art materials, from his father a sense of urgency and dash, from the New York school his sense of scale. The result left most people wordless, but not Waverley. Her training meant she was practiced in the social niceties of commenting on the creative act. True, she sensed danger and was more cautious in her performance than usual. The phrases came haltingly, suggesting the conjunction of a serious mind and charming diffidence.

'Wow, you're well set up here.' She stopped in front of the largest work, a frantic melange of daubs on an assemblage of flattened cardboard boxes, the original Chinese ideograms of which were not entirely submerged by the over-painting. 'I love the dynamic shapes you find when you deconstruct the boxes. It must have taken a lot of work for you to achieve this... this spontaneity... gestural artifice... Tachist meta-piece? I don't know how you prefer to think of it.' She murmured the latter in a manner that made clear her deference to him as its creator.

Ross had remained in the kitchen, putting together the coffee percolator. He laughed to himself and shook his head despairingly. 'All those clever words! *Interesting!* But what do you think, *really*?'

Waverley hunched her shoulders and looked a little crestfallen. 'You think I'm not really saying what I think?'

'Maybe.'

'You mean I'm double-crossing *you*... or perhaps myself? Is that what you think? I must be cleverer than I think.'

'*Think?* Stop using that word; I don't want you *to think;* not in front of my work! It's about being overwhelmed by sensation and the evidence of my activity. *I'm me!*' He beat his chest and laughed again, this time fiercely as though he thought of himself as a lion roaring from atop some rocky eminence.

Yes, like the bloke in the stage version of *Lion King*, thought Waverley.

'You must have been to art school to imbibe all that shit,' he said with a flash of aggression.

'No, I studied art history. I was at the Courtauld.'

'Ah, verbiage, verbiage, *verbiage*! I lasted one term at the Royal Academy. Shit place, shit teaching. Don't study art, just do it!'

'Your father went to the Royal College. He was an art student for – I don't know – six years?'

'I learnt from him. I short-circuited all that shit.' He made a grand gesture of dismissal. 'I'm at the heart of darkness where art really comes from.' While they were talking, she had come closer to where he was making the coffee. Suddenly he reached out and grasped the little silver whistle visible in the open neck of her top.

'What's this?' he said, tugging at the chain so her face was forced closer to his.

'It's an anti-vermin alarm,' she said, curling the fingers of her right hand around his hand and digging in with her nails.

He released the whistle with a dismissive laugh. 'Ah! You, *darling*, only need protecting from yourself!' This he said as if a definitive judgement.

He continued in the same intense, intrusive vein while he finished preparing the coffee and, while he did so, openly appraised Waverley as though he found her unaccountably fascinating. In turn, she examined him, but obliquely, disguising her inspection with inconsequential questions about the house. She was disconcerted to notice that amidst the kitchen clutter on the island unit there was an open box of Viagra tablets. Erectile dysfunction, she decided, was unlikely to be his thing. From the nervy energy he put into every action, she judged premature ejaculation to be a more likely *dénouement* of his sexual dalliances.

'Have you heard of *mise-en-scène*?'

She nodded. 'Of course.'

'If you want to make art you have to be attentive to the creative *mise-en-scène*.'

He put down his cup and walked into the studio space. There was a stepladder leaning in a corner. He lifted it into the centre of the room, opening its legs to set it upright. He jerked his head towards it. 'Come on, you can do something useful. Pose for me.'

She was amused and, at the same time, alarmed. 'But,' she protested, 'you're not a figurative painter!'

'I'm everything,' he replied impatiently. 'It's all in the mix.'

That, she thought, was exactly the problem, but to keep him sweet she made her way towards the stepladder.

'You have to take your clothes off,' he said as though she were a little slow, or being obtuse. He hooked a finger under the hem of her top and lifted, exposing her midriff.

She looked him up and down. '*No way!*' she said with great firmness.

'The model's always naked,' he said as though it were a self-evidently truth.

'No crazy shit, Ross! You don't know me, and I certainly don't know you well enough to take off my clothes. That's not going to happen.'

He didn't argue any further, but turned towards the stepladder and gestured for her to climb. 'Very well,' he said blithely, 'but you *will* pose for me. This –' he gestured towards the top of the ladder – 'is the plinth that raises you above the artist. I like the symbolism of my model being naked but elevated above the field of action, which is the zone of the artist. In painting the artist – male – and his model – female – is an archetypal *mise-en-scène*. Today I accept clothes. Next time: *no!*'

There followed for Waverley an excruciating hour, perched like a flood victim atop the stepladder, while Ross occupied the zone of the artist with a frenzy of painterly activity. She spent half an hour being a ball of fluff, the next "a speeding bullet".

While he worked on his chosen canvas of flattened cardboard boxes, he kept up a rambling monologue, which was immoderate and revealing of his delusions about his artistic standing, his lack of clear thinking and, even, common sense. At one point he got on to the subject of his mother, Ruthie. 'She's mad, you know. I mean, literally insane. She lives in a nowhere dump in Devon and paints, paints, paints to absolutely no avail. She's like my dad, but going backwards. She says Clarissa tried to kill her when she took Dad away from her. Brides for life, those two!'

'How did Clarissa do that?' asked Waverley.

'Run her over; a car thing.'

At last he had exhausted himself and the possibilities of the flattened cardboard. He threw his brushes down in a tub of water and started to find lids for his tins of paint. Waverley climbed down, her eyes firmly fixed on the mess on the floor. 'You have paintings by your father, don't you? I can see the family connection.' She immediately feared she had gone too far and he would recognise what she had said for the flattery it was, but his susceptibility to praise saved her.

'Yeah, well, it's not easy being Gustave Post's son. He gave me some good paintings when – you know – I was growing up. You should come and see them and... pose for me again. Next time, properly.'

She gave him a doubtful, maybe-you-can-persuade-me look. 'Yeah? You know there's a plan afoot to recreate your dad's Venice Biennale show?'

'No. Whose idea is that, Corey Templeton's?'

'I don't know. Maybe the second volume of your dad's biography is due.'

'Ah, that bloody leech, Campbell Carter!'

'Have you any paintings from that era?'

'No, my father gave me what he was painting at the time. Mine are turn of the century, and on.'

She nodded her understanding, her gaze apparently fixed on the paintings in his studio.

'You're going to be there later, right?'

'Yes, of course, I'm looking forward to it,' she said as she returned her satchel to her shoulder. 'Is your brother coming too?'

'Yeah. He'll be around, you know. He wanted to DJ, but the museum didn't want it. Maybe we'll go on somewhere afterwards. You'll come?'

'Sure.'

They had reached the door.

'This Templeton you work for... The *catalogue raisonné* thing is a bit... anal, isn't it? How long is he going to go on about that?' He looked past her, his eyes fixed on something somewhere in the garden.

She shrugged and sighed. 'It's digital technology. We need to up-date the quality of images, where we can. I think that's the answer.'

He fetched something out of his pocket. He held it out. It was a key. This was clearly something he'd been planning.

'What's that?' wondered Waverley, looking at the key with misgivings.

'You take it, yeah? Keep it safe. When I call you, you come and use it.' He didn't give her time to respond, but turned and re-entered the house, trailing his final words over his shoulder: 'See you at the museum.'

Waverley felt the need to decompress. She knew Ross had meant to impress her with his vitality, his focus, his dynamic interaction with his raw materials, but the work he had busied himself with on the flattened-out and taped-together cardboard boxes told her that the things her training had taught her to prize – talent and technical ability – were entirely absent from his endeavours.

She let herself out through the gate.

He was of a kind she had come across before: the alpha male seen through a cracked glass. Painting was a solitary business, and here she had met the superficial party animal, craving a captive audience. *Grand gestures with no substance; crude and unlovely!*

So, she fulminated as she wandered back the way she had come, relieved to be out in the untrammelled air and sunlight. She was quite some way back towards Cannes before she mustered the impulse to call a taxi. By then her mood had turned to mirth.

FIFTEEN

Corey Templeton looked drowsy; looked as though he hadn't moved since breakfast. The same table, only the remnants of breakfast had been cleared away. Waverley stared at him askance. 'Is it just me suffering the Posts?' she demanded, sliding into a chair.

Corey was amused by the hint of outrage. 'I assure you I've been as busy as you. Quentin came here looking for you. As usual, he had things wrong. Anyway, he wanted to walk the Croisette and assure me he values what Max is doing on the family's behalf.'

'Does Quentin have Bad Personality Disorder, like Ross?'

Corey smiled. 'Cool, groovy and babbling. Edward, Clarissa's eldest, has arrived. Max has taken him somewhere for lunch with somebody or other. Made quite a fuss of him.' He waved his hand, vaguely indicating the direction they had gone. 'Clarissa's taken quite a shine to you. Max told her you'd gone to see Ross. She thinks you're going to save him.'

'From what?' she said indignantly.

'Oh, what she describes as "his mother's madness", mainly.' There was a moment of introspection before he added, 'And himself, of course… There's a lot of venom there.'

Waverley was less than forthcoming when he tried to question her further about Ross. So close to actuality, she didn't want to dwell on her morning. 'Move on,' she said, rolling her eyes. 'I feel faintly soiled.'

Corey was intrigued, his earlier guilt a little rekindled. 'Were you in moral danger?'

She leant forward. 'No, *mortal* danger! *And* I'm to be summoned, apparently.' She produced the key Ross had given her and, with a triumphant grin, held it aloft like a specimen.

'I see,' said Corey dryly. 'Any chance the Berlin Wall painting came from him?'

She gave a shudder of mock horror. 'I couldn't say. He's going to show me what he's got when he's back in London.'

'I really can't see him having it. My money's on Clarissa; she's the cunning one. I've got Max's mind churning, but he can't figure out why she would be trying to sell one of Gustave's paintings behind his back. That's why he'll keep this farce going until he finds out who it is.'

'Well, for what it's worth,' decided Waverley, inspecting her fingernails, 'Ross is a psycho and he says his paintings are much later than Berlin; his dad gave him them straight from the studio when he was growing up.'

'Yeah, but Ross has this reputation; he's had it a long time, when his father was still alive. For some reason his father favoured him, even though he was stealing stuff from his –' Corey's mobile signalled a message. He looked. 'Neema and her brood have arrived.'

At the mention of Neema, Gustave's third wife, Waverley became extra attentive. 'Remind me.'

'You've not met her, have you?'

'No.'

'Final chapter in the Gustave Post story: *Senility in Suffolk!*' He pulled a face, as though offended by his own levity.

Waverley had no such scruple. 'You should give that title to Campbell Carter for volume three of his biography.'

'Neema was Gustave's dental hygienist. She attached herself like a limpet; took command, cleared out the riff-raff, regulated what was, at the time, a pretty chaotic situation. Neema's the straightest one of the lot: she has that stately calm many Muslim women have. God knows what she saw in Gustave! Escape, I suppose. Ruthie had been absolutely impossible. She thought she was Gustave's equal – *he* was stealing *her* ideas, if you please – and had gone off to Devon to paint. Actually, under Gustave's influence, Ruthie did wonderful things for a while. She took Ross and Quentin with her; both ran away before long. Neema bore Gustave three children in quick succession... before he went into that sudden decline of his. You know, that famous picture of him in the wheelchair? Two boys and a girl. The oldest must be late teens now.'

Corey seemed to be ruminating on Gustave Post's decline, but when he spoke again it was clear his thoughts had moved on. 'I've been meaning to ask: have the watches gone?'

'Yes, I checked with the concierge. De Grandhomme signed for them.'

'Thank God they've gone without Max finding out. If he had we'd both be in his bad books and you'd be back in the gallery playing sudoku.'

She looked at him with a sudden, cryptic smile. 'You think so?'

Corey had no wish to debate the matter. 'Just keep it under your hat,' he advised her. 'We need to go to the museum soon. We have to say hello to the curator, Augustine, before the reception starts. Are you going like that?'

'Yes.' She had changed into a light grey worsted suit. The trousers were cut some way above the knee. She looked down at herself. 'Any objections?'

'No, no, you look great.'

SIXTEEN

The museum was a short walk from the hotel. It had a grand formal entrance: columns, stone coursework, flanking balconies, a huge Gustave Post banner and, down the entrance steps and out onto the pavement, a waterfall of red carpet in cerulean blue.

Waverley thought it delicious. The door was closed but when they rang the bell they were quickly admitted by an elegant young woman, French to the highest degree.

'Augustine will be here in a moment,' she said. 'I'm Heloise.'

Corey introduced Waverley. 'Are you new here?' he wondered.

'Ah yes, I came recently, from Montpelier. We are very proud of our Gustave Post exhibition. You have seen it already?'

'Actually no, though Augustine and I have discussed the hang.'

'He too is very proud.'

All this time they were drawn deeper into the building, through a lobby, once unmistakably that of a hotel.

'I think Post was a great man, no? He understood his inheritance in all its complexity. He carries a great deal on his shoulders.'

Corey was quite moved by Heloise's shining sincerity, by such educated politeness, but before he could respond, Augustine, the exhibition's curator, a small dark man brimming with animation, appeared out of a side door. He looked surprised and delighted in equal measure.

'Ah, you steal up on me, my friend!' He laughed and shook Corey's hand energetically. 'Thanks to you we have a great success on our hands, I think!'

'Waverley, this is Augustine. Augustine, Waverley is working with me. We're revisiting the Post *catalogue raisonné*.'

'Ah!' He turned his full charm on Waverley for a second. 'But, Corey, I thought your *catalogue* was perfection already!'

'Perfection until digitalisation began to take its toll,' said Corey, gesturing vaguely. 'And here we see the real thing!'

They had reached the threshold of the first gallery. Waverley had already decided that the exchange of pleasantries did not concern her and she had drifted away, her attention taken up with the paintings.

'This is early period,' announced Augustine, arms akimbo like a proud shopkeeper. 'Nineteen sixty onwards. See, the Petersham Diptych!'

Corey nodded appreciatively; the Petersham Diptych had not been seen in public since Gustave's death. He felt his ownership of the exhibition, if not the particularities of how Augustine had arranged the hang. It benefited from the inclusion of a number of rarely-seen pictures he had secured on loan from private Swiss and French collections, and the balance of this first room struck him as remarkably fresh and raw. He was drawn to a painting named *Ma Jolie,* after an early Picasso. Corey believed it to be of Clarissa, 'with her arse in the air', as, rather indelicately, he thought of it. It was from nineteen sixty-three, soon after her relationship with Gustave began. As he came to a halt in front of it, the doorbell of the museum sounded, and whoever had a finger on the bell push kept it there interminably.

'Would you, Heloise?' said Augustine, a note of irritation in his voice.

Heloise turned back while the others continued their appreciation of the early Posts. Shortly she returned with unwelcome news: 'It's the police.'

The others turned to gape. Indeed, it was as Heloise said: hard on her heels came two tough, official-looking men who loitered at the entrance to the gallery.

'A detective is here,' continued Heloise. 'There has been a shooting. They wish to speak to you, I'm afraid.' The latter was directed at Waverley.

Waverley put a hand up to her throat. '*Me?*'

The first policeman, still hovering at the entrance, said, 'That is so, *mademoiselle,*' in heavily accented English.

Waverley fainted. She did so prettily; a gentle swoon that allowed Corey to catch her before she hit the floor. She was light but nevertheless he subsided to the floor under the awkwardness of staying her fall. There was a moment of considerable consternation, and into the consternation strode Max Collarii, followed by the museum's director, Henri Leclerc, who was chatting amiably in French to Clarissa.

'What on earth…!' Max was instantly on his metal. He had a natural capacity for control and command, and he behaved with a magnificent sense of concern for Waverley. In a moment she was whisked into the director's office where she was laid out on his couch. The policemen were reduced to bystanders and under suspicion of having behaved with brutal disregard for her well-being.

Meanwhile, Waverley was coming to. Her complexion, pale at the best of times, had taken on a fetching green pallor, a colour Corey thought he'd seen somewhere before, most likely in a Matisse.

'No, no, it's all right.' murmured Waverley, the centre of a huddle of concern. 'I didn't have any lunch.'

'Damn it, Corey,' said Max taking him aside, 'I thought she was with you! Make sure she's okay, I'm going to talk with the policemen.'

He was gone before Corey could dispute Max's implication that he bore some responsibility for Waverley's swoon.

She was recovering fast. 'Sometimes I forget to eat,' she said weakly.

'Max thinks I should have fed you,' said Corey solicitously, sufficiently moved by her appearance to feel a little guilty.

'Oh! Too bad; don't take it…'

'How are you feeling?'

'Better. I think I'm in big trouble.'

'No, I expect it's Fishman they're after. Where's your mobile? You should call him.'

'At the hotel. I left it in my room.'

'If they'll let you, you should go back there.' Corey looked at his watch. 'There's plenty of time before the reception starts.'

'I'll stay here a little while, if I may. Could you get me some water?'

Heloise who had been sitting by her all this time holding her hand, rose to her feet. 'Corey, I will fetch; you stay.'

Henri Leclerc had disappeared, taking Clarissa with him. Having concluded his interview with the police, Max rejoined the others, looking a little shaken. He stood at the door of the director's office and signalled for Corey to join him out of Waverley's hearing.

'Corey, this is a bit of a mess,' he said distractedly. 'I'm not sure I understand what the hell's been going on!'

'It was best to get away, Max. The gun…'

'It seems fantastical…' Max began, obviously having difficulty believing what he had heard.

It now transpired that it was not simply a matter of an unexplained *fracas* in the airport car park the police were concerned about, but an armed robbery accompanied by grievous bodily harm. The jeweller, Gabriel de Grandhomme, having picked up Fishman's watches from the concierge at the hotel, had not travelled far along the coast before his car had been run off the road. Thereupon he had been attacked by two men and robbed. As he tried to fight them off, he had been shot, very deliberately, in the foot.

Since the incident at the airport, Corey had been decidedly apprehensive about how Max would react if he discovered that Waverley had brought a consignment of Swiss watches to Cannes. And had done so for a boyfriend who apparently attracted the attention of professional thieves. He was astonished, therefore, to find that Max was not in the least concerned about Waverley having been drawn into something unsavoury and potentially damaging to the good name of the Collarii Foundation. His sole worry was that the authorities might treat her harshly. So solicitous was he for her wellbeing, he insisted on attending her interview with the police to help overcome any difficulties translating either questions or answers.

When the policemen were satisfied with Waverley's account of the bungled theft at the airport, they agreed to allow her to leave, on the understanding they saw her again the following morning. Having chaperoned her through the interview, Max insisted she go back to the hotel in his car. He then sought out Corey who'd been left footloose in the gallery.

'Corey, come and speak to the police.'

During the interview that followed, Corey gained a fuller understanding of the events to which he had been a party. The attempted robbery at the airport had been caught tangentially on CCTV, but only the flooring of the Good Samaritan businessman. The rest had been off camera. Somewhat belatedly, when the bullet hole in the windscreen was recognised for what it was – long after Corey and Waverley had fled – the alarm had been raised. Due to a non-operational video camera covering the taxi rank, the police had been unable to identify who the intended victim had been, another reason for their irritation. They did have CCTV coverage of the baggage reclaim carousel of the flight from Heathrow and strongly suspected the person attacked was Waverley. Further enquiries revealed she's been waved through at passport control and the CCTV footage gave them no idea who she was or where she had gone. Understandably, they were peeved that the victim of an attempted robbery, involving a firearm, had quit the scene. It was only when they interviewed the hospitalised de Grandhomme that the name Waverley Smith emerged. The concierge team at the Majestic, and the hotel's CCTV, made it clear what de Grandhomme had not: that almost certainly she linked the attack on him to the airport incident. Hence, they had traced her to the museum.

When the policemen let him go, Corey was surprised to find Max still waiting for him.

'Here's the real news, do you know how much those watches were worth? Waverley's been used!'

Again, Corey was surprised by how lightly Max was taking things. Here, he thought, was a man adept at riding sudden changes of fortune, especially those chiefly affecting others.

'Not used, *abused*!' he said. 'But she won't have it.'

'Yeah, well, she's young and foolish, I guess. Let's not dwell, huh? The show looks splendid, does it not? I think Augustine's done a marvellous job.' Max had the fidgety look of a man with something else on his mind and he manoeuvered Corey into a corner of the gallery. 'Look, Corey, I'm sorry about this, but I've got an important transaction to complete; a client on a yacht out in the harbour. I'm going to have to ask you to deputise for me tonight.'

Corey was taken aback suddenly to discover that he was being gifted the care of the reception, the Post family and any other matter of concern to the Collarii Foundation that cropped up during the evening, but as always, Max was softly persuasive. His assurance that, "you know the foundation's business as well as any of the directors", didn't sit well with him since even a fool could deduce that his annual stipend for the continuing supervision of the Gustave Post *catalogue raisonné* was but a tiny fraction of the directors' remuneration. Feeling a little put-upon, he walked with Max to the door of the museum and watched as he floated down the cerulean blue carpet towards the Mercedes, which had returned to its station at the foot of the steps having delivered Waverley to the Majestic. Max gave him a brief wave of farewell as the chauffeur ushered him into the car. It was, Corey reflected, a scene as old as time: the faithful family retainer at the threshold of his employer's palace, bidding farewell to the head of the household as he departed on some gilded mission. He noticed, as he had done before, how Max commanded his loyalty through charm, but also the latent sense of his power over the world... well, at least those things he chose to turn his attention upon. He knew the reception mattered greatly to Max and reckoned he must have been heading for an important deal to forego orchestrating it. He had no idea what he might be buying, or selling, but there were a great many Rembrandts in the world and very few Vermeers, so whatever it was, he reflected, it was more likely to be a Vermeer than a Rembrandt.

SEVENTEEN

The Gustave Post reception was in full swing. By a happy coincidence, the arrangement of the exhibition over the four main galleries of the museum echoed the four distinct factions that had taken up occupation for the duration. Neatly, it also kept the warring factions of the Post family from one another's throats. Corey now understood why Max had taken Edward to lunch and been so solicitous of his well-being. In response to the words of welcome from the museum director, he, as the eldest son, gave a charming speech in fluent French that was a model of diplomacy: several humorous reminiscences of his father and a sly dig at the Collarii brothers. Once the ceremonials were concluded to everyone's satisfaction, which included the local *En Marche* politician, champagne began to flow. It flowed in such immoderate quantities that Corey began to feel uneasy about the permanence of the armistice currently being observed by all.

Fittingly, in the first gallery, devoted to early Gustave Post, Clarissa, wife number one, was holding court in her usual dowager duchess manner. The gallery was full of regal, elderly ladies and their diplomat-cum-politico husbands talking softly of important matters. She had been joined by her two sons fathered by Gustave – Edward and Charlie – and a third, younger son, fathered by her second husband, whose name no one could ever remember.

Edward Post was in his late fifties, Charlie a couple of years younger. Logically, they must have been children once, but now they were immutable personages, seemingly born elderly: stout, patrician. Edward was the more formidable looking of the two. There was something in the lineaments of his face that suggested, behind the bluff exterior, a calculating, mean-spirited man. Charlie was somewhat more rotund, waddling and florid, and had the look of a po-faced Tory nitwit. In their election of social class, both had taken after Clarissa, rather than Post. Not given to artistic flights, they had professional careers of the kind that require a smattering of law, financial acumen and wives with wealthy backgrounds.

Ruthie's offspring, Ross and younger brother Quentin, had commandeered the second gallery. No ex-wife formed the backbone of their occupation. Ruthie had spurned any contact with the other Posts or the Collarii brothers for many years, but remained on good terms with Corey who had been a youthful admirer of her early paintings long before he began work on the Post *catalogue raisonné*. She still painted doggedly, mainly pastiches of her former husband's middle period, but intermittently produced crazy, inspired originals. In the absence of their matriarch, Quentin and Ross had taken it on themselves to invite a substantial number of their moneyed set, at least one of which had travelled a great distance by private jet to be there. They were loud and animated, and out to enjoy themselves, as those privileged by birth must, at the expense of others.

The third gallery, to the side of the second, was smaller, more intimate, with a lower ceiling. It was here that the drawings and prints were displayed. It had become the refuge of the director, Henri Leclerc, and the local dignitaries on whom his employment and the financial well-being of the museum depended, not least the *En Marche* politician. They had first access to the canapés and were safely insulated from *les rosbifs*.

The final gallery, the largest, was devoted to Post in his full maturity and precipitate decline. Here, Neema was to be found, Post's third and final wife. She had travelled from Paris by train with her three children, who surrounded her like a praetorian guard. Augustine and Heloise were gratefully entertaining them since Neema had loaned several important late Posts for the exhibition, thought by some to be the crowning achievement of his career.

As Max's appointed stand-in, Corey, like any dutiful host, roamed the crowded galleries being gracious to those who required his attention. By the time he had reached the final gallery he'd said 'hello' at least fifty times and his smile was a little rigid. At his approach, Neema turned aside from the others to greet him.

'Ah, Corey, so pleased to see you here.'

Corey had always liked Neema. Some found her haughty; he thought this a cultural misunderstanding. The warmth of his greeting was sincere: she was always so level headed, spoke with such measured calm. Now, as during Gustave's life, she treated the Gustave Post phenomenon with a certain sober detachment, as though it were something inevitable, like gravity, and for that reason scarcely worth remarking upon.

'Quite a turn-out,' said Corey as, together, they scanned the vista of paintings, only partially visible above the heads of the crowd.

'They are pretty, are they not?' This was her way of acknowledging the lightness of touch that distinguished Post's late work. 'There are many mysteries about the attraction of this man, I always think.'

Corey responded with an uncertain smile. 'You mean his sense of colour… how it changed?'

'No, I mean he was so often sad, yet here you see such gaiety. I sometimes used to go in that studio and find him in despair. Do you think it was an act?'

He shook his head. 'Who can say now? I never saw him at work.'

'Of course, I forget. Declining powers, I think, declining powers. Could we take a breath of air outside?'

'I would like that.'

Together they made their way through the crowd. He noticed she walked in his shadow, to one side and a little behind, as if he were a shield to ward off the curious. Soon enough they were in the open air. The evening was glorious. They shared an unspoken thought that the exuberant palette of the western skies was a fitting tribute to Gustave's last paintings.

'My boys…'

She turned and, following the direction of her glance, he saw her three children had followed them and were standing nearby, as if sentinels watching for an ambush out of the setting sun.

'They think Gustave's other sons wish us harm. I cannot convince them otherwise. They want me to come away as soon as possible. They will not come to the dinner. They are afraid.'

Corey wanted to be reassuring. 'They shouldn't be. I cannot say the others warm my heart, but they are harmless, surely?'

'Something happened earlier. They will not speak of it.'

'Then perhaps it would be better if they went back to the hotel,' decided Corey. 'Ross is a brute, but it's all hot air.'

'Yes, Ross, and the other two.'

'What Edward and Charles?' He laughed. 'Surely, they're buffoons? I know they can be unpleasant about the trust, but they know it reflects their father's wishes, and nothing can be done about that!' Having to think about the situation exasperated him. 'God knows, they can say hurtful things! So unnecessary! Where are you staying?'

'At the Marriott. We go back to Paris tomorrow.'

'Tell me, Neema, did Gustave ever talk of lost paintings at all? I mean from earlier times, before you met him?'

'Some of what he had done when he was young hadn't survived, but he didn't seem that regretful.'

'Later, for example, when he was in Berlin. Did he ever talk to you about Berlin?'

'He did talk, yes, but it was when he was already ill. He was very fretful. There was unpleasantness of some kind, he said.'

'What? Were some paintings destroyed?'

'No, not paintings; the way he had treated people seemed to distress him, but he wasn't very lucid, you know.' She looked at him beseechingly, hoping he understood what a trial the last several years had been. 'I felt it troubled him greatly. It must have been meaningful since most other memories had faded by then. I'm sorry, I didn't handle it very well.'

'Neema, no need to reproach yourself, you did a magnificent job.'

'I must go back and keep watch; my paintings, you know,' she said, touching the back of his hand in a gesture of farewell. She turned and re-entered the museum, closely followed by her children.

For the moment Corey was reluctant to follow. He hated the spite and envy that sometimes seemed to be Gustave's greatest legacy to his family. For all that, he couldn't see any of the Post progeny posing a real threat to Neema and her children. It was, he thought, just another example of the febrile atmosphere that somehow clung to Gustave's memory. As he thought about Neema's final words he found himself wondering if one of the older sons had threatened to damage one of the paintings she had loaned. No, he dismissed the idea as fanciful.

He paced back and forth across the breadth of the cerulean blue carpet, and his thoughts turned to Waverley. He wondered where she was. He knew she had gone back to the hotel, but he felt an urge to know where she was at that precise moment. Even though, for the last hour or so, he had been fully occupied with the Post reception, what really bothered him were Waverley's troubles and in particular the incident at the airport. It was this that was responsible for the nebulous feeling that some kind of unpleasantness was about to erupt. He now understood Neema as having something of the same feeling, though for her own reasons. At least, he reflected, the Waverley affair seemed to have caused hardly a ripple as far as Max and the staff of the museum were concerned. That was a relief, although he knew he could not discount some form of aftermath. He juggled his mobile, wondering if Waverley was reunited with hers, but decided it would be too intrusive to call her.

EIGHTEEN

All things considered, Waverley looked remarkably restored. Once she had reached her room, she had lain down, but only for five minutes or so. As she rose from the bed, she laughed a little to herself. After a while, she showered and changed, ready to make her entrance to the reception.

Back outside on the Croisette the air was limpid turquoise with a touch of indigo. The lines of parked cars were magnificently polished, their interiors sombre. Every element of the scene was pampered and curated, as the fashionable would have it. Out of nowhere, Stanley Fishman appeared. Suddenly he was walking beside her as though they were out for a stroll.

'You've made it then. How was the flight?' she said, giving him barely a glance.

'We've got to run, Princess.'

'*Where?*'

'I've got to get those watches back.'

She came to a halt and looked at him helplessly. 'And *how* do you propose we –'

'Look,' he said, his patience apparently worn very thin, 'I didn't do this to myself, you know. It's not some sort of insurance wangle, if that's what you're thinking. As far as I'm concerned, only de Grandhomme knew you were carrying them for me, so he must have told somebody who thought stealing them would be a smart piece of work. So, first we go and see my pal de Grandhomme.'

Waverley looked at him pityingly. Something had been bothering her since the attack at the airport. It was so odd she had tried to push it to the back of her mind. Now, with Fishman present, she could avoid it no longer.

'The problem is, there were *two* lots of amateur criminals at the airport, not one. They ended up falling over one another trying to grab me. They were lousy at what they were doing: *slapstick*!'

'Okay, I understand what you're telling me, but let's not get too elaborate. First de Grandhomme at the hospital. Let's go.'

Fishman had a small Peugeot hire car parked not far from the entrance to the hotel. Once in the car, Fishman said, 'Right, which way?'

Waverley gave him a look that said the question was idiotic. '*I don't know!*'

'How do you mean, "I don't know"? He's in the hospital!'

'I've no idea which one. He could be in Nice for all I know.'

'Somebody knows.'

'Not me! I'm on my way to the reception. Someone there might.'

'Then let's go and enquire.' He lifted a mallet out of the rear foot well and passed it to Waverley. The mallet was of the type favoured by carpet fitters and the more technically adroit handyman and had a dense composite head which made it an extremely effective tool when force needed to be delivered gently but persuasively. 'Put that in your bag; we might need it.'

She tossed the mallet back. 'If you bothered to look you'd see I don't have a bag.'

Fishman drove the Peugeot to the museum with suppressed fury and left it where, earlier, Max's Mercedes had been parked, at the foot of the steps. As he got out, he threw the car keys to Waverley. 'You keep them,' he decided.

Several decorative couples adorned the entrance, dragging on cigarettes before diving back into the reception. On their way to the first gallery a glass of champagne magically materialised in Fishman's hand. He considered it for a moment and then handed it to Waverley.

'Cheers,' he said.

'Stop giving me things!' she said.

Fishman came to a halt at the entrance to the gallery, taking in the hubbub. 'Who do we ask?'

'We should find Heloise; she'll know.'

'Jesus! Where?' He hung back hesitantly.

'You can go in, you know!' she said, waving him over the threshold. 'It's just art!'

As Waverley entered the gallery, Clarissa, who towered above the crowd of men around her, immediately saw her and signalled her to come over. Waverley pulled a face that indicated she was helplessly caught up in something she would rather not be. Clarissa had an eye for an entertaining *contretemps*.

'Charles,' she said to her second son, 'you see that young woman over there? She's been kidnapped by a lout. Go and rescue her. She's the only interesting person in the room.'

Charlie Post craned his neck to see. 'Are you sure, Mama?'

'Yes, yes, I want to introduce her to you. He can't have her, not looking like that; he's crass!'

Charlie set out like a knight errant on a chivalrous mission, ready as always to do his mother's bidding, despite a lifetime of being sent to collect water in paper bags. '*I say there!*' he called after Waverley as she and Fishman made their way into the next gallery, the one occupied by Ruthie's sons and their crowing friends.

As Waverley made her way across the second gallery, Ross spotted her. A look of mischief lit up his face. He nudged his brother, Quentin, and began to shove his way through his chums, intent on intercepting her. It was only as he grew closer that he realised, to his annoyance, that she was accompanied. Since meeting her it hadn't crossed his mind that she was anything but a free agent, but now he smelt *boyfriend*!

'*Hi! Waves!*' he called in what he hoped was a penetrating voice, a call which, in actuality, was lost in the general hubbub.

Representatives of two factions of the Post bloodline were now closing in on Waverley, but *her* attention was focused on a vignette, framed by the arched entrance to the final gallery. It consisted of Heloise talking animatedly to a girl Waverley didn't know, aged about sixteen, and a sallow-faced woman in a headscarf. The girl looked very much like the sallow-faced woman's younger self. Heloise caught sight of Waverley. She had developed a protective, sisterly concern for her as a consequence of the fainting episode and she gestured, holding out an arm as though to draw her in.

At this moment, Charlie and Ross Post found themselves shoulder to shoulder.

'What the hell!' swore Ross recognising his half-brother. 'What are you doing, you chump?'

'I beg your pardon!' said Charlie, exuding ineffectual scorn. He came about-face. 'This might well be where your set has chosen to hang out – basically, riff-raff – but so what? Ruthie never did teach you to distinguish between hares and hounds!'

Ross had come to a halt. 'What does that even *mean*?' he jeered. 'If it's an insult, I don't get it.'

'Oh, *excuse me*!' said Charlie in his stuffed-shirt voice. 'I'm about to make a social introduction, something that doesn't go down in your world.'

'I don't understand that, either,' Ross snapped back belligerently.

At this moment Ross's younger brother, Quentin, intervened. To understand what happened next it is helpful to have in mind the general impression Quentin made. Quentin was a DJ. He travelled the length and breadth of Europe performing gigs of his very special sort of retro mix. He was thin and straggly, not well-built like his brother. Despite being middle-aged, he affected the garb of a trendy eighteen-year-old, from clumping boots, through ankle-length skinny jeans, a velveteen top from Uniqlo, to freshly-crushed DJ hat with several enamel badges pinned to its crown. In the shade beneath the hat's floppy rim was a pair of pebble glasses perched on a long nose that sat above a long chin.

Charlie had no idea who he was; hadn't been in the same room as him since their father's funeral and looked no further than his outfit, which amounted, more or less, to a disguise. Quentin, on the other hand, knew exactly to whom he was about to speak.

'Hey, be cool man!' said Quentin, giving him a gentle, brotherly push that rocked him back on his heels.

Charlie looked him up and down with a "what's-this-piece-of-shit?" look. 'Do you mind?' he said, as one feebly responds to an affront.

There were now the makings of a filial spate, and Ross wanted no part. Doing his best to ignore his half-brother, he again called after Waverley, louder.

'*Waves!*'

Her head turned in his direction and he made a violent pulling motion, as though he too wished to reel her in. As he did so – since he and Quentin were standing very nearly back-to-back – his elbow struck Quentin's elbow, which resulted in Quentin administering an unintended, though lifelike, punch to Charlie's midriff. In truth it wasn't a particularly hard punch, and Quentin's fist was not clenched particularly firmly, but Charlie Post had long suffered from "dicky tummy". No definitive diagnosis of his condition had ever been made, but suffice it to say the organ was prone to tenderness and scarcely disposed to withstanding a punch, even from someone as weedy as Quentin.

Meanwhile, Fishman had swung around, sensing, in his hyperactive, malevolent way, that Ross's call heralded an in-coming attack. In his reality nothing made an attack more likely than the intuition that one was in-coming. He saw the doubled-up figure of Charlie, which affirmed his sense of danger.

'Princess, this way,' he said out of the corner of his mouth.

Waverley was bent on reaching Heloise, and had no intention of joining the objectionable – to her eyes – Ross. Fishman turned back without her. Ross saw him coming and connected its approach with the fact he had twice called Waverley by name. He didn't see it as having been much of a provocation, but his long familiarity with the rowdier sort of nightclub predisposed him to caution where supposed slights were concerned.

Meanwhile, Waverley, given what she knew of Fishman, had come alive to the role he might play if a fracas ensued: she foresaw someone with a cracked skull. Fair to say, a similar thought had already crossed Ross's mind, not that he saw himself as the victim. Much as he relished a fight in favourable conditions, in the present circumstances he was disinclined to indulge an oik he didn't know.

'What *exactly* is it you want with Waverley... *exactly?*' demanded Fishman, now in Ross's face.

Ross was not to be rushed. He was quite happy to out-stare his adversary as he considered his response. While things were thus, Charlie, who had recovered sufficiently to rejoin the dispute, intervened.

'This is mine, leave it to me,' Charlie advised Fishman, indicating he should fall back. Whether he deemed it necessary to clear the floor in order to punch Quentin and/or Ross, or give them a piece of his mind, remains unclear. Which ever it was, when Fishman showed no inclination to "leave it to me", Edward gave him a push in the chest. The result: without a moment's hesitation, Fishman punched him in the face. Contrary to appearances, it was a blow that was reproving rather than deadly. Nevertheless, it had the desired effect of removing Charlie as a party to the dispute.

When an affray arises, many are oblivious until engulfed by the tide of action; a few are sharp-eyed enough to identify the early signs of trouble. Corey was the latter. It is not surprising, then, that he was in a position to intervene before this one spiralled any further out of control. He had registered already that the second gallery was the loudest and the most champagne-fuelled, and the one where the crowd, in its entirety, had its back to the paintings. Thus alerted, he was keeping a close watch on it, and had spotted Waverley and her companion as they threaded their way through the crowd. His response to Fishman's strike was decisive and probably would have surprised anyone who had ever come upon him at his desk, surrounded by the monographs of dead artists. Now that he had disposed of Charlie, Fishman was squaring up to Ross and Quentin. Corey approached him from behind and said, 'we're leaving.'

Waverley came up beside Corey, a decided look of amusement on her face. 'Hello, Templeton,' she said.

'Is he who I think he is?'

'Yep.'

'Well, help me get him out of here. Come on, before somebody falls into one of the paintings, for Christ's sake!'

'Just don't tell me –' she enunciated her words with pedantic clarity, but teasingly – 'how very glad you are that Max isn't here to witness this!'

They took possession of an unresisting Fishman and propelled him out of the gallery.

'Do you know where de Grandhomme is?' Waverley asked Corey.

'Centrer Hospitalier de Cannes. Sorry, I thought there was going to be a fracas!'

Waverley laughed cruelly as she hauled her half of Fishman towards the exit. 'Are you apologising to Fishman, or me?'

It struck Corey at that moment, with real force, that he was in the thrall of a beautiful woman, charming *to the highest degree* in every aspect of the informal deportment of modernity... yet markedly lacking scruple.

As they reached the foyer, Corey realised that Ross and two of his heartier acquaintances had followed them out.

'What, Ross?' said Corey, turning to face him.

'Nothing, Templeton. Just this!' And he kicked Fishman in the groin.

NINETEEN

Outside the museum a policeman was about to ticket the Peugeot but they looked like a medical emergency. Waverley charmed him; Corey asked for directions to the hospital. They set off, Fishman lying on the back seat, groaning. Waverley drove as if they were in something high-powered and sleek. Beside her, trying to buckle his safety belt, Corey was perturbed.

'Why did I get in the car?' he wondered, as they barrelled northwards.

'Because you love the kind of adventure you know we're going to have.'

'No, I don't.'

'Fucking get out then,' groaned Fishman from the back seat.

'Sweet, isn't he? You didn't need to come, just because Ross kicked him in the bollocks.'

'I do feel rather guilty,' Corey decided awkwardly. 'I should have resolved things non-violently.'

'Oh, don't be such a namby-pamby liberal,' she scolded. 'You did fine. Ross is an oaf. Tell me, Fishman, who did you tell I'd be carrying thousands of pounds worth of watches through Cannes airport?'

Fishman heaved himself up. It was apparent the question engaged his indignation, sufficient to assuage the pain. 'I didn't tell anybody, Princess. Why would I? I reckon MI5's spying on me.'

'*What?* And they arranged for Cote d'Azur crooks to lift them? *Ha, ha!*'

'Seriously, it's big money for little men like that. They think I'm money laundering.'

'Yeah, well, good point,' decided Corey. 'Where *did* you get the money to buy them? And why aren't you phobophobic about getting them back?'

Fishman was indignant. 'What d'you mean? I flew down here, didn't I?'

'He thinks you don't look very bothered, Fishman,' said Waverley with sardonic glee. 'It all went wrong at the airport, so somebody had a second go. The question is, did the watches fall into the right or wrong hands?'

Fishman sank back, overcome with exasperation. 'Would I do that to you?'

Waverley flashed him a look. 'I'm thinking about it; mind not made up!'

'So, where are the watches?' Corey wanted to know.

'Who knows... but I know Fishman!' she said cryptically, her eyes fixed on the traffic.

'Ah, leave it out, leave it out, that's devious thinking!' complained Fishman. 'You've got me all wrong.'

'Like the man said, you look bothered, that's why you're here,' Waverley decided, a note of triumph in her voice. 'You're not bothered enough to have lost those watches, just the possibility you've lost them.'

'Fuck off, the both of you.'

TWENTY

Max Collarii was on the yacht of the fifty-sixth richest man in Saudi Arabia. He was a man with limpid brown eyes, and the ability to face both ways at once, which one must if one is to sell the world the virtues of Saudi Aramco. When away from home, he liked to think of himself as "the Jedi From Jedda". He was a big *Star Wars* fan.

Hung on the wall of the bar, above the spirits bottles, was an enormous painting of *Christ the Redeemer* by Zurbarán. It was a wildly inappropriate place to hang it, and just lately it had become a political embarrassment. Not only was it coldly sensuous in a homoerotic sort of way but also, of course, rich in Christian iconography. Ibrahim bin Salman could not understand how it was that he had bought the thing. It was, he said, "an eternal mystery. I wish to be rid of *this*, delightful cultural artefact it may be... *or not!*"

TWENTY-ONE

It took them all of ten minutes to find the hospital. It seemed Fishman was fully recovered by the time they arrived because he hurried them into reception. From there, despite the frustration of several encounters with administrative staff, the chief note of which was their indifference, they finally identified de Grandhomme's location in an annex towards the back of the hospital. As soon as this was established, Fishman rushed off to interview him, accompanied by a nurse who was telling him in voluble French that such a thing was impossible. Meanwhile Corey hung back. He wanted a word with Waverley out of Fishman's hearing. She seemed to have already divined that such a thing was on his mind because she lingered and finally gave him an interrogative look herself.

'Why are we here?' said Corey with a puzzled shrug that was almost Gallic.

'Letting Fishman go through his little act,' she replied.

'So, what's going on? This feels like a complete charade. How is he going to get those watches back by interviewing de Grandhomme? They were stolen *from him*, for Christ's sake!'

'So, who here's kidding who?'

'Well, if de Grandhomme had organised the hijacking himself he wouldn't have arranged to get shot in the foot! Somebody else must be behind it. It doesn't make sense.'

Waverley laughed, shaking her head. 'Know thy Fishman,' she enjoined him. 'He's come to see de Grandhomme so de Grandhomme doesn't think he arranged to have him shot in the foot.'

Here was a complexity Corey hadn't envisaged. 'Are you saying Fishman arranged to have his own watches stolen?'

'Who tried to steal them from me at the airport? De Grandhomme? Who else knew I was coming? No one, according to Fishman. So, who sent the other two? Fishman? It was their squabbling that turned the thing into a farce. Then someone had a second go this morning, and Fishman doesn't know whether the watches are safe or not!'

'Good God!' said Corey, 'is there no end –?'

'– to the iniquity of men? Of course not!' She came closer, exuding slippery charm. 'When I promised you an adventure, it wasn't this. Let's see if Fishman can get those watches back to London.'

Corey shook his head in disbelief. '*What?*'

'Don't you think it's time Fishman was taught a lesson? He doesn't have the money to buy all those high-end watches. He's working for somebody and they're trying to defraud somebody else… anybody! Desperate stuff! What was it at the airport? A double-cross? An insurance job turned farcical? Then what: an attempt to defraud de Grandhomme? I wonder if de Grandhomme's paid Fishman.'

'That's a heap of ridiculous supposition!' said Corey wearily. '*Count me out!*'

'No, you're counted in. Too late, I'm afraid. You're in!' She smiled her most beguiling smile.

Corey shook his head as he consulted his mobile. 'The dinner kicks off at nine. We're done here.' He pointed with his chin in the direction Fishman had gone. 'What about him?'

'Oh, he'll being doing his best to look innocent and concerned for the next hour. He can find his own way back.'

'Where's he staying?'

'Not with me! He doesn't use his mobile for anything questionable because he thinks it's being monitored by MI5, but he'll start texting me sweet nothings when he's done here. I'll deal with him then.' She dismissed Fishman with a wave of her hand and took Corey's arm. It was companionable, as if she was claiming the right to be intimate with him. He took notice and was warmed by the gesture. It did something to counteract the chill of having been dragged willy-nilly into the fog-bound mire that was Stanley Fishman.

TWENTY-TWO

The Gustave Post reception had come to an end. Those invited to dine were making their way towards the Croisette in an impromptu procession that wended its way through the mellow gloaming. The dinner was to be held at a restaurant half way between the museum and the Majestic. The restaurant's entire terrace, which was garlanded with lights hanging amongst the thick foliage of the oleanders, had been set out with a table for thirty-two.

Before long the chattering that had thronged the museum had transferred itself to the terrace. The local *En Marche* politician, as transient as a teenage heartthrob, had placed himself at the entrance to greet people of influence as they arrived, usurping a role more properly belonging to the museum's director. Pleasantries and wine flowed, and the guests were slow to take their places at the table. The seating plan, devised by Max and Henri Leclerc, artfully managed the mingling of French and English speakers by the strategic placing of those with bilingual skills. Equally importantly, it ensured that the Gustave Post factions continued to be kept apart. The last guests to take their places were still standing in twos and threes when Corey and Waverley arrived from the hospital. They ran the gauntlet of the *En Marche* Macron-lite, who ushered them onto the terrace with delighted nods and bonhomie.

Corey, somewhat breathless, found he was seated, more or less, in the middle of the table with Clarissa on his left and a woman he didn't know on his right. Waverley was seated opposite him, between Edward and Charlie. The prospect of spending the next hour and more in the company of Clarissa and her sons dismayed him, but how lovely Waverley looked in the ambient light of the terrace, her cheeks slightly flushed by their race to get there!

The waiters were pouring Sancerre.

'Such a delightful evening, such a very *delightful* evening!' said Clarissa to no one in particular.

Corey introduced himself to the woman he didn't know, determined to be pleasant to her. Now that the final guests were seated, Max's absence at the head of the table was in danger of becoming a diplomatic affront. At that very moment he came down the steps from the street, elegantly dressed in evening attire, very plain, dark and beautifully tailored. He looked every inch the plutocrat.

Clarissa had seen his arrival. 'What does a capitalist have for breakfast?' she said.

Corey merely shook his head and watched as Max made his way to the bottom end of the table.

'Other people's lunches,' she said with a gurgle of delight.

Corey could not take his eyes off Max. He was working his way up the table, a word here, a word there, in that self-possessed way of his. He was, decided Corey, even better than the *En Marche* politician at the middle-of-the-road thing. Everyone he spoke to was at ease, knowing his utterances were never politics, just *politesse*. And how different from the intensity with which Waverley was holding the attention of Charlie and Edward! He could sense her across the table, not far from him, the restless energy, the endless taking in of her surroundings, interpreting, adapting, honing her chameleon skills, effortlessly weaving her magic around the two brothers, her face a passport to their hearts. She was, he knew, inexhaustibly making stories out of the social signals he couldn't be bothered to read.

Meanwhile the woman to his right, whose name he hadn't caught, was telling him in rapid French that she was an art critic and had visionary thoughts about Gustave Post. Corey lost the thread when he realised that Ross, who was seated with Quentin higher up on the other side of the table, was engaged in some energetic arm waving intended to catch Waverley's eye. Eventually he succeeded. The signalling was to the effect that after the meal Ross expected her to go with him and Quentin to whatever destination they had in mind. Waverley responded with a gesture that could as easily be read as yes as no, but definitely implied desist.

'Those boys…!' Clarissa had watched the little pantomime and was lost for words. It was as if she had so many uncomplimentary phrases at her disposal, she couldn't decide which one to use.

As Corey turned his attention back to what the woman on his right was saying, Max's progress up the length of the table reached the back of Waverley's chair. With the lightest of touches he placed his hands on her shoulders and leant over her to address Corey.

'How did it go?' he said.

Corey couldn't take his eyes off Max's hands. There was something proprietary about the way his fingertips rested on Waverley's collarbones. It made him feel distinctly uneasy and he shifted his gaze to her face. It was enigmatically in repose, her head tilted back a little in response to his presence behind her.

'It went well, only one or two forced ejections,' Corey said, a poor attempt at jocularity. He was thinking how thankful he was not to be a full-time employee of the Collarii Foundation, as Waverley was. Yet why did he so intensely wish to bask in Max's approval? Because, he decided, he was a ninny.

Max grinned, nodding with satisfaction. Edward and Charlie were craning their necks to make eye contact and, for a moment, Max embraced them with his smile. Then he switched his attention to Clarissa and exchanged views on the success of the reception.

'There was a bust-up that your man dealt with rather adroitly,' Clarissa informed him somewhat disapprovingly, as if the whole thing had been unnecessary.

It was plain to Corey that, in the midst of the reception, the Fishman altercation had caused hardly a ripple. Certainly Max was quite impervious to the idea that anything serious had occurred, his mind apparently on other things. As he moved off to claim his seat at the head of the table he seemed, so Corey thought, to give Waverley's shoulders the slightest of caressing squeezes.

'Don't you agree,' said Clarissa, once he was out of earshot, in a voice demanding Corey's attention, 'that Gustave Post has allowed the Collarii brothers to eat our lunch for tea and supper.'

Corey took up his glass of wine and held it half way between the table and his lips. He decided not to move the glass from there. Something edible, he observed, was being delivered to the table.

On each side, swift, white sleeves, armed with plates, seemed to be thrusting clean through people. 'I don't... No...' He put down his glass. 'Clarissa,' he said, turning to look her directly in the eye, 'did something happen in nineteen eighty-two; something we don't know about?'

She gave a snort, somewhat derisive. 'Ah, your Venice Biennale lecture! Haven't you finished it yet?'

He felt tempted to fiddle some more with his glass. 'No, I'm looking for completeness. If we don't get this right now, there'll be more and more talk of fakes. That doesn't do confidence in the market any good.'

'Oh! What a predicament!' she responded, her eyes vague, watery and hooded, 'Are there fakes out there?'

Of course, it was no good; just as before, when Corey tried to question her on anything to do with her time with Gustave, her whole appearance changed. It was as if she were donning senility. The imponderable was, *what didn't Clarissa want out in the open?* Her sense of propriety was such that it could be something others would consider trivial. He smiled to himself grimly. It might, he decided, be stomach bloat. That meant he could be misled into believing she was hiding something of significance when not, making a fool of him once again.

Having turned his enquiry aside, Clarissa began, in her inimitable fashion, to establish dominion over her reach of the table. She linked barely connected thoughts with "but", "and" or "so" in a way that forbade interruption. In an extra twist she now seemed intent on using the cloak of senility to give licence to her ramblings. Her main complaint, which ricocheted back and forth, between her and her sons, was that Neema had been given the place of honour at the head of the table sitting between Max and Henri Leclerc. It was as though, for the best part of forty years, Clarissa had clung to the conviction that she was the great, abiding love of Gustave Post's life, and should be treated as such. It was a stupendous denial of the fact that Ruthie and Neema had superseded her in his affections. For Clarissa, any version other than her own was simply a matter of Gustave being led astray. The bone of contention she conjured from this concerned was the share of Gustave's estate that had fallen to Neema. Since she was Gustave's wife at the time of his death, Neema had ended up with a share that Clarissa regarded as a disproportionately large. To Neema, unfairly in her opinion, came not only status but, as she chose to put it, 'the riches due to us all'.

'I do *like* Neema,' declared Clarissa to those trapped within hearing range, as if her carping during the entrée had not been personal. She turned to Corey, barely lowering her voice. 'I was never sure what she saw in Gustave. I suppose her expectation was to be brutalised by a bearded man, and that made Gustave as good as any. Heaven knows what she thought of Gustave's paintings! She certainly didn't understand their cultural value. She's an example, I suppose, of the mute subject in the cacophony of Europe. It meant she always had a certain tranquillity. Muslim's take the axiom "contain thyself" to absurd lengths, don't you think?'

'Mama, you can't say that,' tittered Charlie.

'I do object to the term "Islamophobia", don't you? A phobia is a baseless fear, is it not? A horror of organised religion of whatever colour is scarcely unreasonable, is it, particularly the Abrahamic ones?

To Corey this was an ordeal. His irritation was increased by the collusive, rhetorical questions with which she salted her misanthropic opinions. He set himself to imagining her trying to run down Ruthie in her car and found her quite capable of the deed. His determination to break into her monologue mounted, even at the risk of falling out with her.

'I rather object to "scopophilia",' he said smoothly. 'Only some dour media academic could propose a word like that to typify the male gaze.' As he said this – he just couldn't help himself – his gaze wandered, involuntarily, to Waverley.

Clarissa intercepted his look and understood its import. She smiled and uttered a drawn-out, menacing, '*A-haa!*'

Corey realised he'd fallen into a trap. He had condescended in order to beat Clarissa at her own game, and in so doing had revealed his contempt for her opinions. It came out as little more than petulance.

Clarissa gathered herself to deliver the blow. 'Quite unctuous, isn't he, our lovelorn swain?' she said tartly.

Across the table Edward and Charlie sniggered.

Clarissa pondered a moment longer and then added, like a guttersnipe, '*Scrotophilia!* Sounds like an affliction of the scrotum, does it not?'

Her sons sniggered some more. Miserably, Corey contemplated Clarissa's rebuke. Had Waverley understood the "lovelorn swain" jibe? She had thrown him a look of commiseration – or was it pity? – before Edward again commanded her attention. He felt thoroughly trounced. It was, he decided, game set and match to Clarissa, although, in fact, he had temporarily silenced her.

An air of things coming to an end was creeping over the evening. Up and down the table, dessert plates were being scraped. Already one or two of the guests had absented themselves to smoke. Others had taken to moving around the table, dropping into vacated places to exchanged words with acquaintances they had not been seated near. Eventually, Ross, followed by Quentin, swaggering down the table and stood expectantly over Waverley, a drunken parody of Max's pose of an hour before. They had the wilful, wily look of a couple of hyenas. Ross made a great show of his surprise that Waverley was seated between his two half-brothers as if it were something he had not previously noticed.

'You must have had enough of your present company,' he said to Waverley. He leant forward, close to Charlie's ear. '*Eh, Charlie?* My, did that chump hit you? Never mind, I sorted him out, didn't I Waves?'

Charlie covered his head, as if protecting himself from further attack.

Ross lowered his chin to just above the crown of Waverley's head. 'Let's fuck off, Miss Spoilt.' He said this with sudden malevolence and then chuckled to himself.

Waverley took it with marvellous forbearance, as she had Clarissa's rants all evening. From his side of the table, Corey regarded Ross with distaste. Very visible was the thug that his father could be. He was about to remonstrate with him when Edward said, 'Yes, you bugger off too, Ross.' He said it with cool deliberation. There was note of menace in his voice that made

Ross's grin slip. Now affecting to ignore Ross and Quentin, Edward leant across the table to Corey.

'A private word, sport, if you would be so kind; a word.'

Mutely, Corey consented, but to do so entailed a walk to one end of the table or the other. Around him the guests were rising to their feet as though a signal to leave had been given. Clarissa, he noticed, had already disappeared. To his consternation, he saw Waverley was drifting away between Ross and Quentin. She seemed happy to be going. Even more, she seemed readily to have forgotten him. He met Edward at the lower end of the table. From there he could see Max at the high end, talking to Henri and the *En Marche* politician. He had a glum feeling that Edward was about to indulge in a little arm-twisting. He wished Max would float the length of the table in that majestic way of his and prevent what was about to happen. Edward was not the fool that Charlie was. Indeed, there was something more than a little formidable about him.

'I understand,' Edward began, scoping their surroundings in conspiratorial fashion, 'you're interested in nineteen eighty-two. So Mama tells it.'

Corey assented. 'The Venice Biennale year.'

'Well, dear boy, it's been all round the houses, all round the houses, so leave it out, eh?'

'I see,' said Corey, playing for time.

'Mama has been trying to say this, but perhaps you haven't been listening.'

Corey started to protest, but Edward overrode him. 'The fact is, the family – I speak not only for myself – is a little tired of the constant interrogation. Campbell Carter is a sweetie… of course he is! But that's more than enough when we're all trying to get on with our lives. *You know?*'

These last two words, a question as a matter of form only, were delivered with the persuasive force that implied it would be reasonable and gentlemanly for Corey to desist. Corey knew he was obliged at least to pretend he would do so.

'I want to help where I can, and I think it would be for the best – the absolute best – if I were the one you consulted should you have anything on your mind… anything at all.'

Corey gave his assent without scruple. He was aware that were the family to discover the real reason for his interest in nineteen eighty-two he would become an outcast instantly, but along the way, as a by-product of that reason, he was doing original research into the life of an important artist. That was justification enough.

'After all,' Edward continued in his colourless drone, 'as the oldest Post, I think I have a thorough grasp of the essentials, don't you? I mean, there *is* a limit to what can be thought, said, or done in the name of our father. Don't misunderstand: I want the facts out there, we all do, but I do especially; it's the only way to pay tribute to a great man. Having a father like mine – I'm sure you know this – is a burden; marvellous man though he may have been.'

At the thought of his father, Edward's eyes glistened with warmth and benign emotion but, Corey knew, Edward was propagating his own falsehood. For all the fine words, he resented the overbearing shadow of his father's fame; resented growing to manhood in a broken family once removed from Gustave's current affections. After all, Gustave had a studio to populate and was choosy about frittering away his emotional resources on former partners and their off-spring. Corey had no reason to doubt the whispers that said Edward regarded his father as distant, precious and self-obsessed. And from his studies he was only too familiar with the wreckage artists were apt to leave in their wake. The more he thought about it, the less he felt like responding to Edward's appeal to the reasonable human in him. He didn't feel reasonable, or particularly human. He felt – how did he imagine this? – like a repository for other people's rubbish, a kind of pot standing outside the door of a communal building used promiscuously, collectively by the Posts for all their grubby little enterprises. He felt the only thing that made them worthwhile was Gustave Post, in all his dreadful egotism.

Corey fervently hoped that shortly Max would leave Henri Leclerc to his buttering up of the *En Marche* politician and accompany him hotelwards for a gin Martini, but then he had drunk a great deal of wine at dinner and he was upset at having lost Waverley to Ross's swagger.

TWENTY-THREE

Waverley was already in the lobby when Corey came down from double-checking his room. Despite the early hour, those who had stayed at the Majestic to attend the Gustave Post reception had already scattered. Max's chauffeur-driven car had left for Nice. Corey didn't know if Max had taken Clarissa with him, but he didn't care to check. He followed Waverley out to the taxi waiting to take them to the airport.

'Where did you go last night?' he said, trying not to sound like she had to answer to him.

'Oh, a nightclub. It was boring.'

'And what about Fishman? I was half expecting to see him this morning.'

She shrugged. 'I suppose he's gone to Nice.' She wasn't very communicative.

When the taxi dropped them off at Mandelieu's departures, who should be waiting for them but Ross Post. Corey's heart sank. Ross looked cheerful and had taken some care to dress to suit the time of day, and his role as mendicant to Waverley. He handed her the flight case he had with him. Although he did not say so, it struck Corey as remarkably similar to the one she had brought with her from London. She smiled rather stiffly at him, as if embarrassed to be receiving it in front of him, and left immediately to check in one of her bags as hold baggage. Corey was left standing with Ross, who nodded to him absently, his bitter, confrontational self temporarily dormant. His eyes were on Waverley's receding back.

'She's going to be a singer, you know,' he said.

Corey was disbelieving. He had never heard her mention any such ambition, although he had no trouble imagining her embroidering such a story if she thought to do so would serve some end.

'She sang last night, at the nightclub. She was rather fabulous.'

Now Corey was properly surprised. 'She really sang?'

Ross nodded. '*Fool for Love.*'

'I thought you were pretty rude to her last night,' Corey upbraided him, 'calling her "Miss Spoil". What was that about?'

'I guess I had her wrong,' he said blithely. 'Last night I saw her in action.'

Corey raised his hands in surrender. 'Yeah, well, she has many talents. Time I went through customs. Nice of you to see us off.' The farewell was brusque for, in truth, he did not care to be polite to Ross, not so early in the day, but then he had a last thought. 'What was in the flight case?'

'Remind Waverley I'll be in London from July fifth. Tell her I expect a call.' He looked at his watch. Corey caught a glimpse; it was the type of watch drug dealers wear to match their purple Louboutins. 'Time I was gone.' He gave Corey a condescending pat on the upper arm as he turned to leave. 'By the way, Templeton, I hear you've been warned off. It applies to us too, so farewell and goodbye.'

Corey made for departures. In so doing, he passed BA's baggage drop-off. Waverley had already disposed of one of her flight cases and gone on. He caught up with her at the departure gate.

'What's in the case?'

She looked at him speculatively. 'Do you want to know, *really*?'

'I think I do. But you tell me, *do I*?'

'No, probably not. It's the watches.'

He was mystified. 'How come you have them again?'

'Oh, we went to Fishman's hotel.'

'*We?*'

'With Ross and Quentin. There was a bit of a bust-up.'

'I bet.'

'As I said, it was a double-cross. I'm taking them back to where I first picked them up. It's Justice League stuff. Fishman can start again with those watches, the conniving cretin... no, *moron*!'

'I hope you know what you're doing!' he decided ruefully. 'Did he see you?'

'No. Probably. I don't know.'

'But you're going to return them?'

'You bet, otherwise I'd be in trouble, wouldn't I? Perhaps Fishman won't try messing with me again.'

'I don't think he will.' He laughed. 'I really think he won't.'

'I'm deleting him from my social diary; he's become a bad idea.'

'Well, thank God for that! Mind you, exchanging Stanley Fishman for Ross Post sounds an even worse one.'

'Yes, I know; that thought's crossed my mind too.' She took a quick intake of breath and rolled her eyes. 'You need me close to Ross and Quentin; they're my muckers.'

Corey didn't know, and didn't ask, what was implied by "muckers". He had one last question before they boarded the plane. 'Weren't you meant to be interviewed by the police this morning? About the robbery?'

'Yes,' she said, 'but they forgot.'

'*They* forgot?'

'Yes, they forgot I was going to the airport early.'

Corey stared at her, truly fascinated. 'You've run out on them, haven't you?'

'They were only going through the motions,' she said dismissively.

'Yeah, "the motions",' repeated Corey bleakly, 'and I think you ought to know Ross was wearing a very garish, expensive-looking watch.'

'Oh, *fuck*!'

TWENTY-FOUR

Northumberland may have the city of Newcastle-upon-Tyne in its bottom, right-hand corner, but in essence it is a desolation of wild, northern beauty. In the folds between its moorland reaches lie villages and pocket towns where the slow chug-chug of yesterday stifles the present. Not the kind of place for artists to follow their calling, but nevertheless some do, driven by regional ties, or economic calculations that are an affront to artistic ambition. Some, of course, are roundly contented and pursue art as a modest craft – say, limpid watercolours of autumnal skies washed onto a handmade paper scarcely distinguishable from *papier-mâché*. For some, though, the compromise forced by the accommodation with domestic necessity rankles, and as the years go by, and the horizon of artistic endeavour shrinks, it is not unknown for rancour to set in; a feeling that the world has dealt harshly with them.

Clyde Diggle was not wholly of either camp. His had been a career that had started full of high hopes, but had gradually withered in a way that was hardly discernible; just small compromises once too often, one little misstep at a time, internally a sort of ossification of the inspiration and influence that had originally driven him. He had become a kind of museum of his most influential teacher's ideas. Odd though it may seem, this was not Gustave Post, but a lecturer he met on his return to England. He lacked the sensibility to follow Gustave's way with painting, his visual inventiveness, his mastery of the expressive line; instead he became a formalist making geometrical arrangements of well-judged proportions, some quite complex, rendered in muted, earthy colours. It was a large version of this idea that had won him the John Moore's prize for painting, but since then each new version had tended to be smaller than the last so that now, eighteen months into his retirement, he had made one no larger than a Post-it. It was on the morning of completing this triumph of the miniaturisation of the modernist aesthetic that, at about half past ten, a letter from the Collarii Foundation was delivered by a red post office van. The envelope looked exotic and inviting, and Clyde was in the mood for adventure as he sat down to open it at the table in his studio.

'Dear Mr Diggle,' he read. 'I am writing on behalf of the Collarii Foundation, which acts for the Gustave Post Trust. We understand you were an assistant to Gustave Post in the early eighties, when he was living in Berlin. The foundation's research department is currently re-constructing Post's exhibition held at the Venice Biennale in 1982. As part of this endeavour, we are seeking to identify every painting Post produced in the last years of his Berlin period. We would appreciate it if you were able to help us in this regard. In particular, we have been made aware of a Post painting, dated nineteen eighty-two, of which we have no record. It would be of enormous assistance to us if you remember the painting, and know to whom it went when it left Post's studio.

'Further to this, we would deem it an important addition to our knowledge of Post's Berlin period if we were able to record an interview with you about your experiences of working for him. We would gladly pay your expenses to allow this to take place in London at your convenience. Yours sincerely, Professor Corey Templeton.'

Clyde rose slowly to his feet. He was not a man of great resource. He still had a few friends in London he had not seen for many years. The thought of an expenses-paid "jolly" appealed to him enormously.

His studio occupied one of several stone buildings straggling alongside a track that ran aslant a bleak hillside. In the valley below, a stream wound its way towards the river. He walked up the track to the house where his wife was making bread. In no time at all he had despatched a reply to Corey's email address, saying he could travel to London on the following Monday and make himself available on Tuesday morning, were that suitable, provided the offer to pay for his travel and hotel still stood. He then climbed the little, crooked staircase to the matrimonial bedroom and went to the bottom drawer of the chest that sat in a corner. In it was a small document box. He took the box to the bed and sat down. For the next half an hour he went through its contents, refreshing his memory about events that had occurred nearly four decades before, and one much more recently.

TWENTY-FIVE

Although he was back in London by early afternoon, the rest of Corey's Thursday was a washout, and Friday wasn't much better. At eleven he was at the Slade at the invitation of an academic colleague. He gave a lecture on composition to a roomful of art students, his narrative woven principally from Uccello's *The Battle of San Romano* and Seurat's *La Grande Jatte*. Afterwards he had lunch with the colleague, then walked to the Gagosian Gallery in Grosvenor Hill to see a Francis Bacon exhibition somewhat literally called *Couplings*. Still not over the trip to Cannes, he was thankful that the gallery was quiet. Rather glumly, he noticed the most recent painting in the exhibition, *Two Studies from the Human Body*, was painted at about the time Gustave Post moved to Berlin. Bacon was of a generation earlier and what a contrast in styles! He lowered himself onto a bench in front of a particularly fraught painting from nineteen fifty-three.

A middle-aged man with a superior air about him came into the gallery, trailing a younger companion. The former was wearing droopy red leggings under a pair of khaki shorts and gave the general appearance of having just stepped out of his kitchen to empty the garbage.

'Do you think the fact that gay congress was illegal in Bacon's formative years conditioned his iconography of the body?' the older man asked, as if they had the gallery to themselves.

'How do you mean?' said his companion softly.

'All these couplings, and not a sign of a penis, erect *or* flaccid! Such a shame!'

After they had gone Corey stirred himself and walked around the gallery looking for penises. The man was right, there were none. Something about the experience was melancholic but he couldn't decide what.

It was three o'clock before he reached the Collarii Building. He walked into the Keyline Gallery on the ground floor.

'Where's Waverley?' he asked of the girls sitting in front of their computers. One, Vivien, looked up from her screen almost immediately, eager to help. His status, Corey reckoned, had risen; news of the mystery painting was spreading.

'She's in Hastings,' she replied. 'I thought you knew.'

Weakly, Corey raised his hand to his brow. 'Ah, yes, I forgot.' She had gone to meet the widow of Andrew Geldrich, the man who had photographed Gustave Post's Berlin studio in nineteen eighty-two. 'She's not expected until Monday, is she? I just thought I'd drop in on the off chance.'

He wandered around the exhibition, something fairly characterless from the Far East, and then back out onto the street. It was that hour of Friday afternoon when men and women stream through the streets of Mayfair, heading for Green Park tube station or some other means of quitting central London. He was overtaken at nearly every step. A sneaking yearning to see Waverley gripped him. He would have to wait, his sensible self said, and he would be obedient, all weekend long, not only to his sensible self, but to what he considered his better self.

TWENTY-SIX

At two o'clock on Monday afternoon a meeting was convened at the Collarii Building, in the basement room that held the Gustave Post archive. Attending were Max Collarii, Corey Templeton and Waverley Smith. Max's attendance was, in a way, purely procedural. He was there to give his blessing to what happened next, now the trip to Cannes was behind them. On the worktable that occupied the centre of the room, Waverley had spread out the results of her visits to Campbell Carter and the widow of Andrew Geldrich.

At the near end of the table she had laid out the photocopies of Campbell's assorted notes on Post's years in Berlin, together with a complete photocopy of the Venice Biennale catalogue. The original she had sent back to Carter accompanied by a small mauve card on which she had written, "Oh gosh, so sorry..." etcetera. The card had butterfly marginalia and a pink ribbon.

The photographs she had acquired from Andrew Geldrich's widow as a result of her trip to Hastings were laid out on the rest of the table, occupying much more room; they were quite a haul.

'How come she let you take all these away with you?' enthused Corey.

'Oh,' said Waverley, looking away modestly, 'she said she was glad to be rid of them. She's donated his portraits to the local museum. They weren't interested in these.'

Max, too, was impressed at the amount of photographic material spread out before them. 'She didn't want anything for them?' he said.

'A contribution to her local donkey refuge.'

Max and Corey laughed. They began to examine the photographs. There were so many that at first glance it was bewildering, and Max was quick to say so.

'I can see we have lots of photographs of Gustave's Berlin studio, and some taken elsewhere, in bars and restaurants.' The latter hadn't been enlarged and he peered at a contact sheet showing several men and a woman sat at a table covered in glasses, ashtrays and used plates. 'Is that Gustave?' He shook his head dubiously, bending to study one particular image. He turned to Waverley. 'Have you had a chance to go through these?'

'I've started,' she replied. 'Dating the photos shouldn't be a problem, the dates they were taken on are written on the negative bags, so it's only a matter of matching the negatives to the prints. As far as I can see, Geldrich made three visits in all. The first in January, the last in June.'

Max nodded. 'Okay.'

'We have contact sheets for every film, but we have enlargements of maybe a third of the negatives. The ones Geldrich chose to enlarge are marked up on the contact sheets. Everything was stored in that.' She pointed to a battered archive box sitting atop the array of filing cabinets behind Corey. Geldrich had printed "Post. Berlin '82" with a felt tip pen on the side of the box.

'I haven't had time to sort them into groups by date and location. In the main this is the focus.' Waverley drew their attention to the line after line of photographs of Gustave Post's studio. The studio's layout was immediately evident: it was a large, open-plan workspace occupying the top floor of a light industrial building. Skylights illuminated it from above. At one end of the long axis there was a view through open double doors into a second space. It had tall, metal-framed windows and there was a glimpse of a table and chairs, suggesting the room was more domestic in character.

'I've drawn a plan,' she said, showing them a sheet of cartridge paper on which she had sketched two rectangles joined by a gap in their common short side. Within the larger rectangle there were three overlapping triangles. 'I'm beginning to work out where the different groups of photographs were taken from.' She indicated the three triangles, which represented the three cones of vision. 'These three views, give or take a bit, seem to be his favourites. The long side of the triangle is the width of the view the lens of the camera gave.'

Max was voluble in his appreciation. 'As I said, *a veritable coup*, Waverley. *Very good! Excellent!*'

'There are some other things you need to look at.' She glanced hesitantly at the two men, hoping for their agreement.

Max demurred, his eyes on his mobile. 'I'm going to leave you and Corey to get on with it. Let me know if you find the Berlin Wall painting in any of the photographs. I'll have Angela see to the donkey refuge thing.'

After he had gone, Corey stretched luxuriously, as though released from some form of restraint. It was as if only now did he feel free to express his feelings. 'You did well, to get these. We couldn't have hoped for more.' He gave her a fleeting smile. 'What did Max mean…?' A half-formed question was bothering him, but he lost it in thinking about how they were going to proceed. 'Have you already looked for the Berlin Wall painting?'

'I have, but I haven't seen it yet, not in any of the enlargements.'

He hesitated. 'And how about Fishman?'

'I spoke to him. He's been avoiding the police. I told him where the keys for the Peugeot were.'

'I guess he was pleased about that. Is he back?'

'I don't know. I haven't seen him. I didn't ask. How about these, though?' She brought his attention back to the spread of photographs.

'What do you want me to look at first?'

'Let's start with who's in the studio photographs. I don't know who they all are, but some are quite interesting. I've put all the photographs with someone in them at this end of the table.'

Corey picked up the photograph closest to him. 'This looks like the one in the Venice Biennale catalogue.'

'Yes, and Henry Moore's in this one as well.'

'So he is! Who else have you found? Clarissa, I suppose, although she says she didn't like Berlin. What about Ruthie? He must have met Ruthie in eighty-two.'

'What about him?' Waverley pointing to a view of the studio that included a young man who was present but not, somehow, part of what the photographer had in mind. He was, as it were, part of the furniture. In the next frame, which she pointed out to him, he had his back to the camera.

'That must be Clyde Diggle,' decided Corey, glancing at his watch. 'He's on his way from Northumberland right now.'

Waverley placed before him a photograph quite distinct from the rest. It showed two young women posing in front of a painting, one of whom was wearing a costume, fanciful in a Chelsea Arts Ball kind of way. Over a leotard, she was dressed in a painted cardboard corset or breastplate splashed with black and white paint. Ruched fabric veils fell from her bare shoulders. A geometrical cardboard hat reminiscent of the Brussels Atomium topped the costume. There was something about the exaggerated pose of the woman wearing the costume, and the gleeful smile of the other, that suggested they were staging a prank.

'Well, well!' declared Corey. 'And who are these beauties?'

Waverley waited while Corey digested what he was looking at. When he spoke he didn't disappoint her.

'Could one of them be Little Miss Elfin-tits, aka Ingrid? Ingrid Humblecrumble-Something I seem to remember Clarissa called her.'

Waverley agreed. She let her excitement show. 'These weren't casual visitors. Geldrich took quite a few photographs of them. There's something significant about them, don't you agree?'

He picked up a second photograph of the women. 'Here's one taken of them with Daniel Collarii. He was there when Henry Moore visited. When was that?

'New Year.'

'One of them must be Ingrid. Which one... and who is the other?'

Waverley shrugged. 'We don't know. We need some help, and we've only got Clyde Diggle! What now?' She said this in a business-like way, as though she wanted to stop speculating and start doing something concrete. It struck Corey as a laudable attitude. True, part of him would have preferred to detain her in some idle chatter, just for the pleasure of the moment, but he could see that she was not in the mood and it was not to be.

'Okay,' he decided, 'let's not discriminate. Let's get a new enlargement made from every negative here, irrespective of whether we already have one. How about that? Have them here, ready for Diggle, first thing tomorrow. If you go and organise that I'll go through the photos we already have.'

She gave him a magnifying scope so he could examine the contact sheets and collected up the negative bags. As she gathered her things to leave, with that indefatigable sense of purpose she had, he experienced a reoccurrence of his desire to detain her. He recognised in it a kind of vampirism, for he did not wish for anything other than to be near her and drink in her vitality as she went about whatever task she had in hand.

Much later in the afternoon, Corey ran her to ground sitting on the backstairs between the second and third floors. She looked subdued. Her sense of purpose was eclipsed and he guessed immediately what had happened.

'Fishman's back, isn't he?'

'No, not yet,' she said wearily.

'Have you taken the watches back?'

'No, but, what do you know, there's an Omega missing. *Eight thousand pounds!*'

He pulled a face. 'Ross; as I suspected.'

'Yeah, I'm for the high-jump.'

'Leave it to me, I'll get it back, or give Fishman the money,' he decided.

She looked up at him sharply. He couldn't return her look. His rashness had utterly surprised him. It seemed like the only thing he could say and now he had said it he thought it madness. Just like that! A switch thrown! Heroic interventions were not his thing!

'When are you seeing Fishman?'

'Hopefully, I'm not.'

'Avoid him, if you can. I'll sort it out. How come you're with someone like Fishman anyway?'

'Oh! We go back,' she said. 'He was sixth form when I was doing my GCSEs.' She looked defeated, as if having lost control of her affairs. 'What can I say?' she added miserably.

'Don't say anything.' He made it sound like a warning. 'But for God's sake, take the rest of those watches back to wherever you got them from, and tell them they're Fishman's.' Corey flicked his right hand in a gesture releasing her from any further obligation.

Waverley was grateful, but vexed to have required his help. Corey, though, had other things on his mind. 'Are you sure

Campbell Carter gave you everything he had on Gustave's Berlin period?'

'Why do you ask?' she said, somewhat cheered that he wasn't going to linger on her plight.

'I've been through everything he gave you. Considering Berlin must be quite a lump of volume two, I'm surprised there's not more. Usually he's a stickler for the minor comings and goings. He doesn't seem to have dug down to that level at all.'

She thought for a moment. 'My impression was that I wheedled more out of him than he wanted to share. Perhaps I'm deluded.' She was momentarily pained by doubt. 'Do you think he's got more?'

Now it was Corey's turn to be uncertain. 'No, not necessarily, but to write about Gustave's time in Berlin like he wrote about the sixties and early seventies, he'll need more research than he's given us! For instance, he doesn't even mention Henry Moore. His detailed grasp of the New York period was masterly and Gustave was only there three years!' He offered her his hand. She put hers into his and he hauled her to her feet. As he did so, he caught from her body the subtle hint of a fragrance. Was it *Obsession*? On he went, resolutely in factual mode. 'Maybe, as Campbell says, it's that he's been too busy with other commissions... Or perhaps he has stuff he doesn't want to share. After all, original insights are a biographer's gold. It means we're going to have to do more. I don't want to compete with Campbell, but we need more detailed information about Gustave's time in Berlin.'

Just before Sotheby's closed, Corey walked over to their galleries in New Bond Street. They were crowded with the season's Modern and Contemporary sale. There were three Gustave Posts to be sold in the evening auction on Wednesday. Although the catalogue entry for all three said "property of a private collector", Corey knew who their current owners were, and when and from where they had acquired them, and at what cost. One belonged to a privately funded museum in Switzerland, originally launched on the back of the endowment from a pharmaceuticals heiress. He wondered why the museum was selling. It struck him as odd. He looked at the estimates of all three lots and thought them conservative.

TWENTY-SEVEN

When, first thing Tuesday morning, Corey descended the stairs to the archive room he saw, through the open door, a scene that seemed to speak of intimacy, perhaps conspiracy. A man – he presumed Clyde Diggle – was sitting at the table with his back to him. To his left, balanced on the table and leaning in to him as though sharing some secret, was Waverley. Deep in his uncontrollable, yearning self he experienced a pang of unappeasable want as it struck him afresh how adorable he found her. She was, he thought, already bewitching Clyde Diggle. How would he react? How completely would he succumb?

'Well, Mr Diggle!' said Corey as he entered the door, briskness itself, his words spoken as if they were a call to arms. 'Welcome to London.'

The man before him was small, perhaps a little shrunken. There was a faint stamp of vigour about him, as though when young he had been energetic but now was just stolid, his flesh having turned somehow morbid in the way of freckled men in old age. In the photographs his face was a characterless blob, but now, in life, it was freighted with detail. There were studs in his ears, Specsaver glasses with green plastic frames, a ginger goatee beard, and deeply-etched lines to his forehead that suggested any amount of Northumberland weathering.

'May I call you Clyde?'

'You may, Professor Templeton.'

They shook hands.

'And may I call you Corey?

'Certainly,' said Corey. 'Did you find the hotel satisfactory?'

'Yes, fine.' Clyde had asked for, and been granted, two nights in a large tourist hotel near Marble Arch.

'He enjoyed the breakfast,' said Waverley with a mischievous smile.

'Good. Coffee? I wouldn't mind one myself.' He looked to Waverley and she slid off the table and went to make some in the kitchen.

While they waited for her to return, Corey took the opportunity of going through some of the preamble he'd been rehearsing as he travelled on the tube. Waverley brought in the coffee as he finished, right on cue.

'Any questions?' Corey said to Clyde.

'No, no, I think that's quite clear. I am impressed by this.' He swept his hand over the ranks of prints. Overnight Waverley had had fresh ten-by-eight enlargements made of every photograph Andrew Geldrich had taken during his three visits to Gustave Post's Berlin studio. They covered the entire table.

'You appear in some of them,' said Corey.

Clyde glanced from Waverley to Corey, as if wondering what they revealed, almost as if he feared an indiscretion might be brought to light. 'Gustave was quite careful about allowing photographers access, but this chap.... What was his name?'

'Andrew Geldrich.'

'Yes, I remember...'

'You know we're going to record our conversation, don't you, Clyde?'

'I sure do.'

'Good! I think, perhaps, we should kick off. We'll come back to the photographs later.'

They all settle down with great solemnity as though something meaningful, even portentous, were about to occur.

'Let's start at the beginning,' said Corey, feeling like a stock cop in a stock detective drama. 'How come you were working for Gustave?'

'I'd just finished my BA. I was helping in a print workshop. Transartifact, it was called. Gustave did an edition there and I printed it with him. He liked the way I worked, so when we finished the prints he asked me to go and work for him. I couldn't at first, but I'd always wanted to go to Berlin, so I said I would when I could. I deferred entry to my postgrad course for a year; Reading University.'

'So, you went to join him?'

'Yep, he had a push on.'

'This was autumn of nineteen eighty-one?'

'Yes, September. In those days he didn't buy ready-stretched canvases; we stretched and primed them in the studio. I did lots for a month or so. He was working at a furious pace because of the Venice exhibition. Berlin in those days was like an island. He loved that; "head to head with the Commies", he called it.'

'Where were you living?' said Waverley, chewing on her thumb.

'Oh, there was an empty studio on the floor below. The artist had gone to the States on a travel scholarship, or something. It was okay with me. It was full of paintings, but it had a shower.'

'And Gustave?'

'He had a sort of living area off the studio, and he sometimes stayed overnight. He had a flat nearby.' He broke off to ask a question. 'Do you know about Clarissa, his wife?'

Corey nodded.

He gave a kind of grimace as though she were an unpleasant thought. 'He stayed at the flat when Clarissa was in Berlin.'

'She wasn't there all the time?'

'No, she came and went; she had the boys... They were in school in London and she wanted to be with them.'

Corey nodded his understanding. He knew Clarissa had insisted on Edward and Charlie going to a private school in Wimbledon. He wanted to move on. 'Was there a routine in the studio?'

'Oh yes. He started late morning, after a lot of minor things had been dealt with. I mean, stuff had to be got in; there was a fair bit of coming and going. Then he'd work until maybe six or seven. Usually I went out for a while to buy food and whatever. When he'd had enough, he packed up and ate somewhere local. I went with him a bit. He met other artists, Germans mostly. Gustave could speak some German, and they all spoke some English. Then he'd go back to the studio and quite often went on painting. I could hear him through the ceiling banging about. In the morning I'd see he'd started something new, or changed something, even repainted a whole picture. First thing, before he started, I cleaned the studio; washed brushes; that sort of thing. It was a routine.'

'It sounds quite humdrum.'

'Yeah, after a while. I mean, I had opted out for a year, so I wasn't in a hurry or anything like that.'

'You stayed until the following summer.'

'I did. I came back to London after the Venice exhibition opened, middle of June. Most of the recent work went to Venice in May. After the opening, Gustave didn't need me; he wasn't going to work there during the summer, so he said. Frankly, I'd had enough anyway.'

'I don't think Gustave ever really worked there again.'

'No, there was a feeling of things coming to an end.

'Was a visit by someone like Henry Moore usual?'

'Yes, in the morning people would drop in. I don't know who most were, but Gustave thought them important. I remember Moore. I think the first time the photographer came was with him. That was just after Christmas. Moore had a commission in Bonn; he had friends in the German government.'

'What about these two?' Corey drew his attention to the photograph of the two young women with Daniel Collarii. 'Was one of them called Ingrid?'

His manner changed. He turned the photograph to face him and for several seconds was lost in contemplation. 'Yes, that's Ingrid.' He reached into his shoulder bag for a folder and from it produced a small paper bag, yellowed, with German lettering. He tipped it up and several passport-sized photographs fell onto the table. All were of Ingrid.

'She gave me these,' he said. It was clear from his manner that the photograph had set off a rush of conflicting memories. 'Yes, I remember her: Ingrid Steinmann; she was around a lot.' Then he saw the photograph of the same two women posing in front of a painting, Ingrid in costume. 'Yeah, I remember that!' He chuckled. 'They loved to put on a show.'

'What about the other woman?'

'Alice Shawcross. She was a dancer; they were a bit of an item.'

'Clarissa told me she attacked you with a golf club when she found out about Ingrid. There was some rivalry, and you found yourself in the firing line.'

Mention of this clearly aggravated him. 'Oh yeah, I don't know what she thought she knew, but Ingrid had been staying with me, in the studio below, so, yeah… Gustave was really into her, so I suppose I know what I took the blame for. The fact is, Clarissa wasn't around much during that winter and spring, and then, suddenly, she turned up in this *fury*.'

'Clarissa told me she contacted you to tap your memory to help her with her book. You refused, so she said.'

He laughed rather bitterly. 'That's right. I never liked her; she was a haughty bitch and treated me like shit, even before the golf club thing. Then, forty-odd years on, she has someone contact me, offering me money for my memories of my time in Berlin. Four thousand pounds I was offered. I thought about it, but then it turned out what she really wanted was for me to sign a non-disclosure agreement.'

Corey was startled. '*Non-disclosure agreement?* That's weird! Why did she want that?'

'To protect her exclusive rights to her story, or some such.'

'Ah, of course… her book!' decided Corey.

'The giddy limit it seemed to me. I wasn't having it! So, I said no.'

'Maybe her publisher had asked for it,' offered Waverley.

Corey was not convinced. 'I didn't even know she had a publisher! Frankly, I was thinking it was a vanity thing. It would have to be a potential blockbuster to warrant a gagging order! Was this recently?'

'No, it was some time ago. Several years ago.'

'*Several years!* Have you ever been approached by a journalist about Gustave Post?'

'No, not once.'

'Well, Clarissa's book must be quite something! When was it she turned up in Berlin with a golf club?'

'Spring: March or maybe April.'

Waverley had her nose in the file of Campbell Carter's notes. 'Could it have been the first week in April? Gustave was away most of that week; in Venice on a scouting trip. That would explain why you got it in the neck.'

'I couldn't say; it was certainly temperament.'

'What was this Ingrid like?' said Corey.

'Oh…' he seemed to have some difficulty gathering his thoughts. 'She'd escaped from the East. She was into politics: Red Army Faction.'

For the second time that morning, Corey was taken by surprise. '*Red Army Faction?* Isn't that what some people called the Baader-Meinhof Gang?'

'This was later than that; Gustave was a supporter.'

'*Really?* Weren't they militant anarchists?'

'Oh yeah, but she was full of life. Gustave hated the idea there were fat-cat Berliners pretending Hitler hadn't ever happened.'

Corey looked bemused. 'I'd no idea about this, but then I've very little idea of what was going on in Berlin… this island… surrounded. It's difficult to imagine, in the centre of Europe, and only a short lifetime ago!'

'There's nothing about Ingrid, or about political affiliations or activities in Campbell Carter's info,' said Waverley with a nonplussed look on her face.

Clyde stirred himself and took a final photograph out of his folder. This one was much larger than those of Ingrid. 'None of the photographs you have here show you this,' he said. 'I took this photo from a window in the room at the far end of the studio.' He turned the photograph round so it faced them. It was of a stretch of wasteland taken from a high vantage point, and through it, snaking into the grey murk, was the Wall, its western face covered with graffiti. Beyond, just visible, were expanses of the death strip. 'That's Kreuzberg for you. His studio was next to the Wall. Bleak, isn't it?'

Corey could only agree. 'I didn't realise…' he said. 'Can we take a scan?'

Clyde assented and Waverley took it off to do just that.

While they were waiting for her to return, Clyde seemed to relax and grew more animated; the whole adventure of coming to London had obviously stirred long dormant memories. 'I met a couple of blokes last night, friends of mine, both artists. We were students together.' He mimed putting a glass to his mouth. 'We had a few. Living in Northumberland, I don't often have the chance...' He chatted on in this vein for some time.

'Berlin was a long time ago,' said Corey ruminatively. 'Very.'

Waverley returned. It was time to move on to the principle reason Clyde had been brought south. Corey took from their envelope the photographs of *Berlin Wall Lament No.1*. He spread them out in front of Clyde.

'This painting has just appeared in New York. It's probably the most important thing you can help us with.'

'Just appeared?' Clyde took in the painting and quickly came to a judgment. 'Well, yeah, that's the Wall,' he said mildly. 'Rather off-beam for Gustave though, isn't it? A bit angst-ridden for him!' Apparently satisfied by his cursory examination, he turned to the photographs of the back of the painting. He was particularly interested in the one showing the detail of the stretcher bar where the title was inscribed. 'I stretched this canvas, I'm sure of that. I never saw the painting though.'

Corey and Waverley looked at one another. Corey drummed the table. 'How do you know you stretched it?'

'That's my corner fold. Gustave liked to use copper tacks and secured the canvas on the edges of the stretcher bars, not on their reverse side. Even in those days most artists used a staple gun to stretch canvas. Gustave didn't think canvases stretched in that way would last. He was a bit old-fashioned like that. Towards the end of my time there he found a supplier and started buying ready-stretched canvases. This isn't one of theirs.' He looked at Corey and Waverley, satisfied he had given them a comprehensive response; his lack of interest in the actual painting was striking.

'So, that's it?'

'Yeah, that's it. Never saw it.'

'But what about the date? It seems it was painted while you were in Berlin.'

'I don't know.' He was perplexed. 'I prepared a lot of canvases for him. Maybe he painted it later. I don't remember him working on anything like that when I was in Berlin.'

Corey was disappointed. He had been hoping Clyde would illuminate the painting's genesis. He had fondly imagined the experience of witnessing the working procedures of a really important artist would be memorable, even transformative. There was little enough evidence that any such thing had happened with Clyde. Corey reckoned he knew why: he'd seen Clyde's little abstracts on his website. The words "twenty years teaching art in a girls' secondary school" came to mind. Clyde could undoubtedly be helpful about the daily comings and goings during his time in Post's studio: all the stuff Campbell Carter was interested in. Biographical minutiae were all very well, but Clyde's response to the Berlin Wall painting suggested he had had limited interest in, and perhaps access to, what Gustave was working on. He recalled Edward Post's admonishment to let the family's past be. It brought with it doubts about whether what they were doing was worthwhile. He came to a sudden decision. What he needed was to clear his head and work out where their investigation was going, whether, even, it was viable. Perhaps it could never reveal who was trying to sell *Berlin Wall Lament No.1*. He had been in the basement of the Collarii Building the best part of a day and a half. The atmosphere was stale and claustrophobic; he had had enough.

'Clyde, I can't stay here much longer. I've a seminar at two. Waverley is hoping to caption these photographs with your help. We'd appreciate any background insights you have. It's been most helpful already; we appreciate you coming. Shall we see you tomorrow?'

'My train's at eleven.'

Corey nodded. 'Okay, not possible, then. Well, as I say, thanks. If we need anything further when you're back home in Northumberland we'll contact you.' He held out his hand and shook the other's.

Clyde was grateful. 'It's been nice to come and relive Berlin. I didn't much enjoy it at the time. It was dark that winter. Bleak. But it seems kind of important, looking back.' He gave a wry grunt. 'These big personalities suck you dry, I suppose.'

'Yes, it must have been memorable.' Corey smiled and began

to gather his things. As he reached the door he turned. 'Did you *like* Gustave?'

'I can't say I did,' said Clyde, without pause for thought. 'I thought he was a bit… *unreasonable*.'

Corey smiled in a way that said he understood. He caught Waverley's eye. 'Could I have a word?'

She gave Clyde an apologetic smile and followed Corey out of the room. When they reach the foot of the stairs he stopped.

'Try and jog his memory. He didn't like what he was mixed up in, did he? Quite understandable; he was a bit jaundiced by the end. What's happened about Fishman?'

'He arrives from Paris by Eurostar this afternoon.'

'Have you taken the watches back?'

She nodded. 'Yesterday.'

'Really?'

Yeeeeessssss!'

'Who to?'

'Miss Moneypenny.'

'Meaning?'

'Oh, she was extra hoity-toity.'

He knew now when she was blocking him. 'Well, all right; hopefully, that's final. Let me know if Fishman comes after you. Remember what I said, I'll sort out the watch business with Ross.'

'Sure.'

'Can't stand that airless room! When you've finished with Clyde, pack everything up and bring it to the Courtauld.'

As Corey travelled east on the bus, he tried to decide whether *Berlin Wall Lament No.1* had been painted in Berlin in nineteen eighty-two. If it had, why hadn't Clyde Diggle seen it? The open character of the studio as it appeared in the photographs made it unlikely that Clyde, however inattentive, could have missed it if Gustave had been working on it while he was there. Yet, given the subject matter, it seemed unlikely that Gustave had painted it *after* he left Berlin. What made it even more baffling was Clyde's conviction that he had prepared the canvas for painting. All in all, it didn't make sense. If Clyde had somehow missed it being painted, then there was still the mystery of why it was not recorded in the gallery's records. Geldrich's photographs made it clear that Daniel Collarii definitely paid Gustave a visit during the time Clyde was there, and would have expected to see everything Gustave was working on, even if Clyde somehow hadn't. All in all, it suggested *Berlin Wall Lament No.1* had been painted elsewhere, at some other time, and bringing Clyde Diggle down from Northumberland had largely been a wasted effort, but for two names: Ingrid Steinmann and Alice Shawcross.

TWENTY-EIGHT

Waverley arrived at the Courtauld soon after five. Corey was still sitting in the empty seminar room where he had been discussing research protocols with some of his students. There were several tables on which they could spread out the Geldrich photographs, so they decided to stay where they were.

Corey came straight out with what he had been thinking since his class had finished. 'I don't think this is helping. We can't reconstruct nineteen eighty-two with enough detail to find out what happened to that painting. It's too elusive.'

'We haven't tried very hard,' Waverley pointed out.

'How do we research an absence? It's not possible.' He looked at her and saw an enthusiasm for the chase that he was lacking. Was she right? Perhaps, he thought, his sense of discouragement was temporary and he should buck up. 'Well, tell me what we've learnt that gets us nearer who owns *Berlin Wall Lament No.1*.'

It was a challenge for which Waverley was prepared. He should have known that she was more spirited than to fall in with his mood; he should have seen that she looked very pleased with herself. 'These photos,' she began, 'haven't given up all their secrets yet, and, yes, they may tell us a lot we don't need to know about Gustave in Berlin, but there's good information there if we look, and it will lead us to other sources.'

Corey was not convinced. 'It was a long time ago. I was one year old!'

'Gustave Post painted *Berlin Wall Lament* in secret for somebody in particular. That's the only explanation. Look, when I was alone with Clyde he was... he was a bit more forthcoming. He had a thing for Ingrid, didn't he?'

'I suppose, yes. The snaps he brought with him...'

Waverley went on eagerly. 'Exactly! But Gustave trumped him, so to speak. And he's pretty bitter that when Clarissa found out she treated him as though he'd pimped Ingrid. I think Gustave painted *Berlin Wall Lament* for Ingrid. He couldn't have Clarissa knowing what he was doing, could he? Ingrid was from East Germany and a political radical. What if she encouraged Gustave to make a big political statement about the iniquity of the wall, the deaths on it, the division of families and loved ones? It was inhumanity piled on inhumanity and proved that the East German authorities had learnt nothing.'

'Good grief, have you been rehearsing that?'

She smiled modestly and looked at the floor. 'Did it sound fake?'

'Yes.'

But, he thought, rather wonderful. She had drawn out Clyde. Perhaps she had come to a much fuller understanding of what was going on in Gustave's life than he had reason to expect.

'I know we can't follow Gustave's every move. But somewhere along the way he painted the Berlin Wall painting somewhere else. We can find out when and why, I'm sure! Especially if it was given to Ingrid.'

Corey laughed. 'Yes, I like that final bit!' He was lost in thought for a while. 'You know, if Ingrid's been living somewhere in Germany, or wherever, and kept possession of the painting until now, it's case closed: she's a legitimate right to sell, whenever.'

Waverley nodded her agreement. 'You leave it to me; I'll find out.' She handed him a printout. 'Here's how: we couldn't find Ingrid but we did find Alice Shawcross!'

It was a Wikipedia entry that read. "This is a stub, unverified. The biography of a living person needs additional citations for verification. Please help by adding reliable sources. Alice Shawcross, born 1951. Dancer and choreographer with modern dance companies. Worked for ABC in New York. Choreography. 1990s worked on Broadway musicals *Gavotte* and *Versification*. Created short dance programme for gala performance, Sadler's Wells, based on the music of Queen, 1997. Associate Director of Dance, Festival of Northern Dance, 1999-2005..."

Again, he was impressed. 'It's something…! Did you find anything else?'

'She has a website. She runs a private dance school in North London. We can go and see her… *now*!'

TWENTY-NINE

The house, their destination, was off the Caledonian Road. The district had been going up for so long, some of the houses were now going down. They tended to be the twilight homes of bereaved old ladies who had given up on window cleaning, repainting the porch and trimming the privet. In this particular street the percentage of houses in such decline was probably similar to the proportion of the elderly and infirm in the population as a whole. As they approached the gate, Corey feared their destination was one such. He had calculated that if Alice Shawcross was about thirty in nineteen eighty-two, she was now in her late sixties. Old enough, but not yet twilight zone. Nevertheless, the imposing, double-fronted house had a closed-up, forlorn look. There was a small sign in the garden: The Minerva Academy for Young Dancers.

Waverley rang the bell.

The woman that opened the door was small and surprisingly bright; she showed no sign of decrepitude, nor was there a dusty aspidistra in the hall. She was clearly much taken by Waverley. 'Dear me,' she said, 'with a young man, I see!'

'Yes,' said Waverley, 'this is my boss.'

While Alice Shawcross shook Corey's hand, she looked him over as though assessing whether or not he was good enough for Waverley. Clearly, with her, first impressions counted.

'Follow your noses,' said Alice, gesturing towards the back of the house. 'The front is for the little ones.'

Two rooms, one to either side of the hall, were visible through open doors. They were empty and like the house, somewhat neglected, but equipped as dance studios: full-length mirrors, bar, keyboards, audio. They made their way past the foot of the stairs.

In her forceful way, Alice was asking Waverley whether she had ever taken dancing lessons, 'in a serious way, you know?'

'No,' said Waverley over her shoulder, for she was leading the way, 'but I'm taking lessons in the Alexander technique.'

'Of course you are! But you missed an opportunity by not studying dance. You have good long legs, nicely muscled, good posture, a compact torso and excellent shoulders. I think you could have been something if you'd studied.'

Because Alice's attention was focused on Waverley, Corey was at liberty to study *her*. Although almost four decades had passed since Geldrich had photographed her, she was still recognisably the same person. What the photographs did not fully convey, and was now readily evident, was the sense of vitality she radiated. Unlike the house, she had not gone to seed. Rather, in defiance of age, her carriage and her grace of movement still suggested something of the vibrancy of dance.

'This girl,' said Alice, turning to address Corey, 'reminds me of my younger self!' Apparently, the idea delighted her. 'She has excellent bone structure, don't you see?'

Corey, compelled into an admission of admiration, murmured his agreement. In a flash of insight, he saw his manner of tuning down his feelings to the level of small talk identified him as something of a cold fish.

They had entered a bright, cluttered room overlooking the rear garden. It spoke of a life of many episodes. There were two sofas, a grand piano in the bay window, chairs of every description, both easy and upright, and a green baize bridge table readied for play. The walls were crowded with paintings and prints. Behind the piano there was a full-sized bronze copy of Donatello's *David*. The upper surfaces of piano and mantelpiece were dense with framed photographs of dancers and portraits. There was a Lenare of Dame Margot Fonteyn and a Dorothy Wilding of an aristocratic-looking couple on their wedding day.

'As you're her boss, I expect you to tell me why you want to know about Ingrid,' said Alice. She had become rather severe now they had come to the reason for their visit.

'Shall we sit?' said Corey.

'Yes, please, *do* find a chair. Or would you care for a little Amontillado? It's that time of day.'

There was further flurry of niceties before they were finally settled.

'We have photographs of you and her taken in Berlin,' said Corey, fiddling inexpertly with his mobile. He passed the mobile to Alice, indicating that she should flick through the folder he had opened.

Alice laughed. 'What fun we had! Yes, this is Ingrid all right. Gustave made her that costume for New Year. They went to a party as Pyramus and Thisbe, you know. We all went; it was called the Banquet of Love. She was a gifted terrorist; not in the least interested in dance. I suppose that made us strange bedfellows.' She laughed again.

'They were lovers?' said Waverley.

'*Of course!* Gustave made her very happy. The erotic charge... it was *tremendous*!'

'We've been told you and her spent a lot of time together.'

'We did. Well, first she was living in my flat. She turned up at rehearsals one day. Modern dance was all the rage! In Berlin the clarion call was "free expression to the barricades!" She saw a lot of Gustave. When he wasn't working, we went to all the hotspots, talked to people about the revolution. "The revolution is coming," Ingrid kept telling us, but when it came it wasn't the one she expected!' Again she laughed. 'Idealistic, you know, and a little mad, I suppose. But what happened to her?'

Corey saw that she thought he knew Ingrid's whereabouts and he gestured his disavowal. 'I was hoping *you* could tell *us*!'

'I see.' Disappointment crossed her face. 'I came back to London and she... What happened? Gustave had another studio...' She hesitated, her recall uncertain.

Waverley prompted her. 'Clyde Diggle, Gustave's studio —'

'*That's right!* What a colourless little chap he was! She wanted to be nearer Gustave, so moving in with him was perfect. Perhaps too close! I came back after the summer; she'd gone. Gustave was off somewhere. There was nothing.'

'You'd known Gustave and Clarissa for some time.'

'I had. Great friends, we were. But Clarissa blamed me for Ingrid, you see. And then she and Gustave broke up, and I lost touch.'

'But what about Ingrid? Wasn't anybody worried about her?'

'Oh yes, her brother. They'd come across together. He was living in Dusseldorf. After Clarissa had put her foot down, Ingrid told me she was going to join him there, but she never did. He looked for her. Even went to the police. She was supposed to be in touch with other members of the Red Army Faction, and somebody said she was involved with the Palestinians; a man, you know.'

'And you never saw her again, *ever*?'

'Maybe I could have found her – at least tried – but I didn't have the time.'

'You didn't find it strange? You weren't worried about what had happened to her?'

'The scene in Berlin in those days was…' She searched for a word '…*fluid*. You have to understand: some of her friends were fanatical locust eaters. It was considered perfectly normal when people went off; it was always west and most never came back. It was only natural: the atmosphere sometimes made you sick. You know how it is? Never even heard from her. It was all in the past so very quickly.'

Corey and Waverley exchanged glances; neither could tell what the other was thinking. Finally, Waverley spoke.

'And Gustave…? I mean, if they were…?' There was something indignant in her voice. 'Didn't *he* want to know where she was?'

'I did try to find out if he knew. It was a touchy subject at the time, but later, when I did ask… Well, if he knew he didn't say. Maybe it went off the boil. I'd seen that before with Gustave.'

'We were wondering,' said Corey carefully, 'whether he might have given her a painting.'

'Oh, I know he did.' She said it with such conviction her answer was beyond disputing.

'Why do you say that?'

'Why? You know, Gustave had doubts. He thought showing in Venice was the death of his radicality. Once it was decided which works were going, he was desperate to do something new. Usually he didn't allow anyone to watch him paint but Ingrid spent a lot of time with him in the studio. He fed off her zest, her energy, or something. At the time I thought it was a pity it didn't go anywhere; she was definitely a mistress, not a wife.'

'Clarissa put a stop to it,' Corey pointed out.

'Oh yes, she laid into everyone. She told Gustave what to do, and that worked… for a while. By then I suppose the Biennale was about to start. It was a pity really. I mean, Clarissa had become the ogre and you couldn't see it lasting.'

'But did you see the painting… that Gustave gave Ingrid?'

'Gustave had taken to hiding what he was doing. He wanted to keep things from Clarissa. I suppose it was his way of excluding her. Ingrid was back living with me. Gustave started painting there. He brought over everything he needed and worked there even though it was just an ordinary bedroom. Clarissa didn't know about it, and Gustave was very careful. You'd call it "clandestine", I suppose. I was going to teach summer school at Dartington and I left the flat in Ingrid's care.'

'When was that?' said Corey.

'Late May, I suppose. Gustave was still there working. There were two paintings, large ones, I remember, like night and day. When I came back in August the paintings had gone and so had Gustave. There was a kind of evaporation. *Poof! He was gone!* And there was no sign of Ingrid either… And the next thing I heard it was Ruthie. It *was* odd!'

They all sat with blank faces until Corey stirred himself.

'Very,' he agreed. '*Two paintings, not one!* And you think he gave them both to Ingrid?'

'Yes, I know he did. I heard him say they weren't ever to go back to his studio.'

'Did you see them?'

'Oh, yes, they were about the cruelty of the Wall.'

Corey found her the photograph of *Berlin Wall Lament No.1* in his mobile. He was moved to see it brought tears to her eyes. There was little more to be said; it seemed fitting they should leave. They made their way back to the front door, passing the empty rooms.

'I teach children and play tennis now,' confessed Alice, a little melancholic now the pleasure of talking about the past was over. 'Age, you know.' She turned to Corey. 'All these questions you've asked me, you're not the first.'

Corey frowned, wondering whether he was hearing something of importance. 'Oh? When?'

'I thought he was from Gustave's gallery, but apparently I was mistaken.'

'Do you remember a name?'

No, I don't. From time to time people ask me about Gustave, of course, but not about Ingrid. Anyway, it was a few years ago now.'

Waverley and Corey took their leave. They walked back to the Caledonian Road in silence. When they reached the corner they stopped, each knowing the other had been mulling over their talk with Alice. They watched the traffic for a while, the mood surprisingly serene as the aimless comings and goings rumbled past.

Corey felt a little ashamed of his earlier defeatism. 'You were right about Gustave painting them for Ingrid,' he said finally, by way of a *mea culpa*. Waverley was, he thought, reaching for an art historical analogy, Huntress Diana incarnate. He explained to her that tomorrow he had teaching obligations. He asked her to put in order all the notes from Clyde Diggle's visit and to write up the captions for the Geldrich photographs. He knew there was a good day's work there and he could leave her to get on with it. Buoyed by her enthusiasm, he assured her they would continue their pursuit of the detail of Gustave's activities during nineteen eighty-two, conceding that such minutiae were not just a matter for Campbell Carter.

At the underground station he warned her to avoid Fishman before he had the Omega back from Ross.

'It's not just up to me,' she had said cryptically.

It was then that Corey realised the extent to which his mood had improved, and the effect continued long after Waverley had gone her own way to some appointment to which he was not privy.

THIRTY

Corey spent the following day preoccupied by the affairs of the Courtauld. It was evening before he could get away. He called in on a private view of one of those new, mostly transitory, galleries with premises on a first floor in Maddox Street. It was full to bursting point with young people who looked the spitting image of Ross and Quentin's friends: young, ebullient and shining new. He left after a short while, feeling faintly discontented, a feeling that had nothing to do with the art he had seen, which had hardly registered. He sauntered west, crossing Mayfair towards the area he liked best, the streets above Shepherd Market. Ahead of him there was a brilliant display of clouds fretting the sky in thin, golden ribbons. In the other direction, to his back, indigo clouds were piling up and a menacing gloaming was growing in the streets. He reached Carlos Place. While he was standing on the pavement, waiting to cross, a large Audi came past him on the other side of the street. It was glossy and serene and travelling slowly in traffic. Corey caught a glimpse of a face in the rear of the car; he could have sworn it was Waverley. He watched the car as it proceeded towards Grosvenor Square.

As the Audi reached the drop-off to the Connaught, it came to a halt, held up by the traffic. He walked after it, his pace quickening as the driver waited for the queue to clear. As he came alongside, the traffic began to move. The car had anti-paparazzi blinds. They had been raised and the rear windows were completely obscured. He stood and watched as the car drifted off towards the square. Had it been Waverley? He felt fretful; it was as though the car represented powerful forces that were at Waverley's heels and might, somehow, be about to devour her. Was this the reason for his discontent: an indefinable fear of losing her, baseless and obsessive though that thought might seem?

Suddenly, the downpour that had been threatening since he had left Maddox Street emptied the street with its violence. It was one of those sudden summer squalls that announced itself with a terrific crack of thunder. He took shelter beneath an awning where he was marooned with two men who were discussing the cricket. He waited for the relentless violence of the rain to exhaust itself. The surrounding buildings had given up their detail and turned a grey watercolour wash. At the extreme of the reach of his sight, on his side of the street, he saw a lone figure, blurred by rain, but gradually coming into focus as its lopping gait brought it closer to where he waited. At first, he couldn't believe it when the silhouette resolved itself into the soaked figure of Waverley. She was wearing leggings and a tight top zipped up to her throat, both black. The Nikes on her feet looked ridiculously large. She didn't recognise him until she had almost reached the shelter of the awning. When she did, she threw up her hands in a gesture of exasperation, as though the weather had played a dirty trick on her.

'I'm wet through!' she complained, pulling earpieces from her ears. Her hair was plastered to her forehead.

'I didn't... So, *you jog*!'

'Bloody hell, yes! Every night, if I can; before I leave work. Sometimes I run home, but not always. It's great around here... for jogging, I mean. It blows away the cobwebs, you know?'

'Yes, I can see.'

She leant against the plate glass of the shop window and threw back her sodden hair. 'The Alexander technique is *not* compatible with jogging!' she said despairingly. 'It's still important, anyway. Where are you going? You should join me. We could get the others to jog too. We should start a jogging club.'

'We should, but not in weather like this.'

'No,' she agreed, 'not in weather like this.' She came close to him, seductive in her sporting *dishabille*. 'I found *Berlin Wall Lament No.1* in one of Geldrich's photos!' She announced it like a mischievous imp.

Corey was startled, and yes, now he could see that she was definitely very pleased with herself. '*No!* So how...?'

'Come back to the gallery and I'll show you.'

She wouldn't say more. Rather, she questioned him teasingly about where he had been going, as though the idea of him wandering aimlessly around Mayfair amused her. When the storm abated – as swiftly as it had begun – they made their way back to the Collarii Building. He was impatient to see what she had discovered. They went down to the archive room. Waverley had fetched a towel from the locker where she kept her personal things and was rubbing her hair. In the middle of the table was one of Geldrich's photographs of Gustave's studio. She relished the drama as she drew his attention to an obscure detail on the far side of the studio.

'Take a look with the scope.'

Corey picked up the scope and placed it where she was pointing. Magnified, he could see quite clearly several canvases leaning against the wall, their backs visible. The widest, to the rear, protruded sufficiently for the letters "BERLI" to be visible on the top stretcher bar. When he looked up, she was holding the New York photograph of the back of *Berlin Wall Lament No.1*. Its title was written on the top stretch bar in large black letters. Without doubt the few letters visible in the Geldrich photograph were identical.

'Geldrich took this photograph on June the fifteenth, after Clyde had returned to London.'

'*Good heavens!*'

She looked at him with wide-open eyes, willing him to reach the conclusion she had.

'By June the fifteenth Ingrid had already disappeared. So, she left without her paintings, and somehow they ended up back in Gustave's studio?' He was bewildered.

'*They weren't ever to go back to his studio,*' said Waverley, quoting Alice Shawcross.

'Why were they brought back?'

She shrugged expressively. 'Maybe she abandoned them. Who knows?'

To Corey, it was as though *Berlin Wall Lament No.1* had taken on a fresh sense of tangibility. Here it was, close to its moment of inception. He was thrilled. 'It means we've not looked hard enough! Both paintings must have come back to London when Gustave gave up his studio in Berlin! They're much too large to have been hand luggage. Tomorrow we go through the daybooks. They must be there, *somewhere*!'

THIRTY-ONE

The next morning, Corey arrived at the Collarii Building at nine-fifteen. The gallery didn't open until eleven, so the ground floor was deserted. He went down to the archive room determined to do some serious follow-up work on what had happened to Ingrid Steinmann's paintings.

The Gustave Post *catalogue raisonné* had been compiled from many sources. One it was greatly indebted to was the Keyline Gallery's daybooks. Before the digitalisation of the gallery's records, daybooks were where details of the gallery's stock, the movement of individual works of art and all other matters of any significance concerning the gallery's artists were recorded. They contained no visual material. Instead, stock numbers identified individual works of art. It meant a painting generically entitled, say, *Composition*, or *Still life*, could readily be identified from its stock number stencilled somewhere on the back of the work. Gustave Post's early work pre-dating the creation of his *catalogue raisonné* bore both a stock number, as entered in the relevant daybook, and a separate accession number relating to its entry in the *catalogue raisonné*.

In terms of their bulk, the daybooks were even more substantial than the Gustave Post *catalogue raisonné* by virtue of recording the movement of every work of art by every gallery artist as it came into and went out of the gallery, not only those sold, but those loaned for exhibition elsewhere, and those moving one way or the other between an artist's studio and the gallery.

Corey went to the stacks in the next room where the daybooks were kept. He found the three volumes for nineteen eighty-two. It was here – if anywhere – that he hoped he might trace the details of what happened to Ingrid's paintings in the summer of that year.

Almost immediately, he found the sort of specifics for which he was looking. It was only a titbit, but fairly typical of the information the daybooks recorded. It was an entry in the .second volume, listing the paintings sent from Gustave's Berlin studio to Venice in May. He knew these works tallied with those illustrated in the Gustave Post Venice Biennale catalogue. He moved on to the third and final daybook for the year, October to New Year. Here he found an entry relating to the close of the Venice exhibition, when those same paintings – bar three, sold to collectors – were shipped to London. On the next page it was recorded that in late October a consignment of twenty-two paintings came to the gallery from Gustave's studio in Berlin – all the works remaining there after those selected for the biennale had gone to Venice. Again, these twenty-two were listed and Corey knew they tallied with the *catalogue raisonné*. Almost immediately after that, the gallery, on behalf of Gustave, made a final settlement for the rent on the Berlin studio. On the following page, after several entries relating to other artists, there was a note, dated November fourth, of another consignment of items shipped back from Berlin: painting materials, a few pieces of studio furniture and unused canvases. All these, according to an entry later in the month, were forwarded to Gustave's studio in Majorca. Corey could find no further entries concerning Gustave before the daybook finished at New Year.

Frustratingly, none of this detail brought him any closer to solving the mystery of how *Berlin Wall Lament No.1* ended up back in Gustave's studio or how it, and its companion, left there. What seemed incontrovertible was that, by the time the studio was abandoned in October, the paintings had gone. Taken at face value, the entries in the daybooks seemed to confirm Gustave's avowal, as reported by Alice Shawcross, that the paintings "weren't ever to go back to his studio". Yet there, on the table, was the photograph displaying the tiny scrap of evidence that proved they had.

Corey checked the time. To his surprise it was now gone ten-thirty. He had been expecting Waverley at ten and in a moment his vague premonition that some awful enmity was ghosting her rekindled sufficiently for him to call her. Her mobile was switched off. An hour later – still no Waverley – he received a text from an unknown mobile saying, "Delayed. Sorry. W". He called the number and a man answered.

'Yes?'

'Hello... er... is Waverley there?'

'No,' said the voice. The line went dead.

Corey pondered what had just happened. He had a distinct impression he'd spoken to Fishman. He thought about calling back, but caution got the better of him. He added the number to his contacts and labelled it "Fishman(?)". He tried Waverley's number with the same result as before.

The volume of the daybook he had consulted earlier lay on the table, still open at the November entry that listed the painting materials, pieces of furniture and unused canvases that were to be despatched to Villa Besugo in Majorca. Now he noticed a line at the end of the entry that read: "Studies to be framed: 22?"

'What does that *mean*?' he said out loud.

What prompted his irritation was that "studies" could mean anything from doodles on hotel notepaper to full-scale cartoons for paintings. Gustave had drawn prodigiously, filling sketchbook after sketchbook. He was also in the habit of dashing off drawings and giving them to friends in bars, as birthday presents, to curators and critics, enclosed with letters of thanks, in settlement of restaurant bills. Corey readily acknowledged that although he might have a command of the sum total of Gustave's paintings, when it came to studies, sketches and drawings, the *catalogue raisonné* was incomplete, the absolute number of Gustave's works describable as "studies" was unknown and might always be so. What of these twenty-two? He was possessed by a powerful desire to know what they were. Without accession numbers he couldn't even begin to identify them. Were they already documented somewhere in the *catalogue raisonné*? If not, where were the actual things?

He looked again at the entry. The equipment and materials sent to Majorca were not even individually listed, and it was impossible to know whether the words "Studies to be framed: 22?" indicated that the studies were meant to be sent there too, or were a separate instruction about framing. Did the question mark mean there was a doubt about the number of the studies, or about whether they were to be framed? It was typical of some of the information recorded in the daybooks: brevity had become imponderable enigma. The entry so struck him he made a note: when he had the time, he would investigate it further. He was still gazing at the entry when Waverley finally called.

'What the hell?' he exclaimed.

There was mumbling, or possibly fumbling, from the other end of the line and then Waverley came on, very loud. 'Goddamn it, Corey, I'm stuck with Fishman. He won't let me out of his sight. It's his principals; they've turned on him. He's become possessive in a new and hideous way. You need to rescue me.'

'I've been trying to call you. How come he's finally let you use your mobile?'

'He's gone to the loo, but he'll be back in a minute. Meet us in the bar at the Westbury Mayfair. Got it?'

'God help us! When?'

'Later. Six. I don't know. *Six*.'

THIRTY-TWO

Max Collarii had on his mind a Russian oligarch, a palace in Dubai and an interior decorator who saw himself as an advisor to collectors of contemporary art. His thoughts were not entirely happy, and for that reason he was welcoming when they were interrupted by the arrival of Corey.

'Ah, Corey! Good man! What brings you here?' He stretched out his arm to consult his wristwatch. 'Still two hours to cocktails!'

'I'm troubled,' said Corey, when he was seated and provided with tea by Angela. 'This Gustave Post business is getting out of hand.' He was rueful rather than despondent.

'Oh? How so?'

'Something happened in Berlin I don't like the smell of.'

'Tell me more.'

Was it, Corey wondered, something he could describe to Max without his suspicions looking like foolish conspiracy theories? 'To put it in a nutshell, it appears that Gustave was having an affair with a young woman called Ingrid Steinmann. He painted *Berlin Wall Lament No.1* expressly for her, behind Clarissa's back.'

'Really?'

'Clarissa found out. She broke up the affair and the painting – actually, there were two – ended up back in Gustave's studio. We have a Geldrich photograph of *Berlin Wall Lament No.1* in the studio in June.'

'That's marvellous! *Two?* And a photograph of one?'

'Yes, the one in New York, leaning, face to the wall. Waverley spotted it. Even so, for some reason it didn't get recorded as inventory. That suggests it came in and went out of the studio quickly, possibly while Gustave was in Venice. What's odd is that Ingrid also vanished.'

'What, *for good*?'

'It appears so. I don't know… Enquiries were made; her brother mainly, it seems. The problem was she was a member of the Red Army Faction.'

'Good God, Corey! Did Gustave know that?'

'Apparently, yes. And when she disappeared there was a story going around that she'd gone off with a Palestinian.'

'Christ, Corey, you've done a lot of digging!' Max got to his feet and paced about a bit.

Corey watched him for a while before he again spoke. 'Did you know Gustave thought being in the Venice Biennale was the end of his artistic credibility?'

Max looked at him with a frown of concern. 'No… but artists often have that feeling when things are going well. This is about Clarissa, isn't it?'

'Somewhat. She tried to run Ruthie over with her car *and* assaulted Clyde Diggle with a golf club.'

He gave a little snort of amusement. 'Wives do that sort of thing if they've got any spirit, and Clarissa certainly had. My guess is, she drove this Ingrid off.'

'Was there more to it than that, I wonder?'

'What: threats, violence…? Intimidation?' Max looked incredulous. 'You think Clarissa demanded Gustave's paintings back and got rid of her? And what: she's now decided it's safe to sell one because it's too long ago for anybody to make any detailed enquiries into Ingrid's whereabouts?'

'Could be. And she's relying on Christies' client confidentiality guarantee to get away with it.'

Max sat back down. 'This is an incredible story, and incredible work, Corey!' He laughed, somewhat ruefully. 'I have to congratulate you, but…' He gave a perplexed shrug.

Corey didn't exactly backtrack, but he felt the need to indicate his views were by no means settled. 'You know Clarissa says she's writing the story of her life with Gustave? Well, according to Clyde Diggle, she tried to buy his reminiscences, or rather, get him to sign a non-disclosure agreement.'

'Good Lord! She's really going for it, isn't she?'

'I don't know. Diggle doesn't seem to know much scandal about Gustave, but maybe Clarissa thinks there's going to be a feeding frenzy when her book comes out. Frankly, I'm mystified. If there's a sordid secret at the heart of their time together in Berlin would she be writing about it? I mean, they were there nearly seven years; it's a significant part of her marriage to Gustave.'

'Well, Clarissa as Lady Macbeth's a bit over-wrought, isn't it? I mean, what if this Ingrid went off with her Palestinian, eschewing worldly goods and all that idealistic nonsense? She could be leading the good life in Ramallah right now.'

'Somehow Ingrid's paintings left the studio without being recorded. That's unusual; your father saw to that. But if Gustave believed they were in Ingrid's possession he wouldn't have wanted them entered in the gallery's records. Have you looked at the daybooks for ninety eighty-two recently?'

Max shook his head.

'I have. It's just baffling what happened to those paintings. The daybooks are very clear about the identity of the paintings that came from Berlin, either directly, or via Venice. I even checked the dimensions to make sure, None were the size of the Berlin Wall painting. We know at some point, after the opening of the Biennale, Gustave went back to Berlin, but apparently only for a short visit. Otherwise he was in Majorca or here in London.'

'It seems there's a riddle still to solve, Corey. I'm sure you'll succeed in doing so. It means we have another Berlin Wall painting to find!'

'I've checked Campbell Carter's notes, and there's nothing there.'

'Does *he* know about this Ingrid business?'

'Apparently not.'

'Well, let's keep it like that, eh? We can't stop him finding out, but what he doesn't know about her is best kept that way.'

'He does know Gustave met Ruthie in Majorca in the summer. That's in his notes. She was modelling for Stefan Muller. In the autumn Gustave was back in London with her, but at the moment we don't have any details. What we do know is that pretty soon they were having a serious affair, and Ingrid was completely forgotten! What the hell was Gustave thinking?'

'Nothing joined up,' murmured Max. 'Is that when Clarissa tried to run Ruthie over?'

'What do you think? Clarissa had had enough, hadn't she? First Ingrid, then Ruthie. Gustave's behaviour would have been considered appalling if it were you or I.'

Max stiffened. 'Best steer clear of moralising,' he muttered, somewhat affronted. Corey had touched a raw nerve.

'If you don't object, I think I'll go to Devon to see Ruthie this weekend,' decided Corey.

'Ah, Ruthie! You don't suspect her, do you?'

'No, I don't…' He hesitated. 'I don't think so.'

Max gave him a look that said, as things stood, it was worth bearing in mind.

Corey was not strong on the idea. 'She gave up on the whole Post thing a long time ago.'

Max conceded he had a point. 'You've always liked her wayward soul, even if Ross and Quentin *are* thugs! I wish you luck; Devon's a long way.'

'She might shed some light on what happened that summer, you never know.'

'Well, yes, by all means go. Tell her we're still here, thinking kindly of her. I never understood why we had to be estranged. For what it's worth, I still take the view it's Ross, not Clarissa or Ruthie. He's a cunning piece of work. Ask her about it; see what she says.'

On the point of leaving the room, Corey had one more question. 'Max, there's a big, black Audi with a chauffeur waiting outside. Is it yours?'

Max grinned boyishly. 'Ah, that's Phillip, ex-Guards. It's rather swish, isn't it? No, not ours, but we've taken to hiring him when the big auction weeks are on. It's to take our clients from their hotels to the salerooms; they appreciate that sort of thing. Do you want to borrow it?'

'Top of the range with all the gizmos, like anti-paparazzi shields?'

He laughed. 'If Audi fits it, it's got it! Why d'you ask?'

'Oh, nothing. I though I saw it… Oh, nothing, just… curious, I suppose.'

Max had a last thought of his own. 'By the way, did you see the prices the three Posts made at Sotheby's last night?'

'Yes, disappointing.'

Max had grown sombre. 'Economic slowdown, trade wars, Brexit! It all equals disappointing prices.'

'At least they got away.'

Max laughed sourly and nodded. 'Indeed they did! Were you aware one of the sellers was the Astrolanza Museum in Lausanne?'

'I was. Why were they selling?'

'Fishy, I know. I've heard there's a cartel out there: museums buying and selling for profit. They think it's time to unload some of their Posts. It's contrary to their philanthropic aims but they do it anyway. It's our job to discourage them, if we can.' Max didn't look very happy at the prospect.

Corey pulled a face; a mixture of sympathy for Max and distaste for the actions of the museums. He didn't know what to say.

THIRTY-THREE

For the rest of the afternoon, Corey suffered an agony of anticipation. The Westbury on Conduit Street was one of those discreet, plush hotels that dot Mayfair. Corey thought it an unlikely place to hold someone captive. The bar was low-ceilinged and intimate. There was a civilized backdrop of conversation, not too loud and of the sort that foretells of splendid dinners to come. Fishman and Waverley were there, sitting in a corner, not quite like a pair of old gloves on a hall table, but to all appearances happy to be in one another's company. Corey could see no evidence that Waverley was being held against her will. Seemingly, nothing prevented her getting to her feet and leaving that very moment. If anything, she looked bored. Turning his attention to Fishman, Corey was relieved to see that he emanated the high-octane good humour that seemed to be his default mood. Neither did he appear resentful at the part Corey had played in his misadventures in Cannes. Rather, he seemed somewhat gleeful at the predicament in which everyone found themselves.

'So... what have we here?' said Corey facetiously.

Waverley gave a shrug of exasperated helplessness. She reached for her glass of wine, but didn't lift it from the table. The bar service was obviously verging on the needy because her gesture was observed and taken to indicate a request for service. In a moment a glass of pinot was placed before Corey with a companion bowl of nibbles. While he did not question the arrival of the wine, he pushed away the nibbles as though they were an affront to the serious nature of the business they were there to transact. Fishman ignored Corey's gesture of refusal, but took the arrival of his wine as a sign that a group identity had been established. He held up his hands to indicate there were certain things he intended to say before anyone else spoke.

'Chief, as I was saying to mademoiselle,' he began in his jerky, staccato delivery, 'carelessness over stock gives my principals a bad name... *so I can't have your Post bully-boys coming to my hotel thieving stock!*'

'Wait a minute, wait a minute!' objected Corey. 'Maybe I've got this all wrong, but first you arranged to have your own watches stolen from Waverley, and then, when that didn't work, you set up your jeweller friend... *And he got shot in the foot!* I presume these were both attempts to defraud your principals, whom you're claiming to be so concerned about!'

'No, no, that's not right!' protested Fishman with a great show of righteous indignation. 'You're all back to front! I ended up with the watches in Cannes because de Grandhomme asked me to steal them from *him!*'

Corey and Waverley greeted this with cynical hilarity.

'Okay, you have to understand, *mes amis,*' Fishman resumed, striking his cuffs like a man who meant business, 'that the vintage time-piece lark in the south of France is policed, patrolled, controlled. You've no doubt heard of *appellation contrôlée.* Well, the demand for expensive timepieces here in London is good, but on the Côte d'Azur it's fabulous, and the trade's organised to regulate it, like *appellation contrôlée.* So, the *Chambre Syndicale de l'Horlogerie Vintage* is exactly that. It is, if you catch my drift, the OPEC for watches. It controls supply against demand, which is seasonal and depends on economic niceties. You can't import into their designated *terroir,* so to speak, without their say so.'

'OPEC's a cartel and nothing like *appellation contrôlée!*' scoffed Waverley.

Fishman was not to be waylaid by petty objections. 'Importing *without* was exactly what de Grandhomme was doing. Why? Because, financially speaking, he was teetering on the brink. The *Chambre Syndicale* found out. Who was at fault? *Me!* I was in breach of their quota rules by supplying him. They informed me that as soon as de Grandhomme took delivery they intended to confiscate my consignment without recompense. This was on the afternoon you two were flying down to Cannes. Too late to stop you, so – hyper quick – I arranged with a couple of my roadie mates, basking in the sun down there, to stage a heist – no violence, mind! – before you left the airport.

'Unbeknownst to me, de Grandhomme had been tipped off about the *Chambre Syndicale*'s intention and had exactly the same happy thought! Two of his brothers were despatched to the airport to stage a theft that would have also left everyone concerned looking innocent! Result: stand-off! When de Grandhomme heard, he thought my roadie mates – they were the ones with the gun – were lads from the *Chambre Syndicale* trying to exact their punishment confiscation. He took fright and that night he called me, asking me if I'd stage a robbery as he was taking the watches back to Nice; a last-ditch attempt – as it were – to foil the confiscation and lay his hands on the stock. Well, I couldn't let him think it was my lads that had thwarted his snatch at the airport, could I? *No!* So, I said, "Nah, mate, I've no assets down there!" In lieu of that, he decides he's going to divert the watches to his brothers' place instead of his premises in Nice. By good fortune – you might say – I was in full possession of his plans. Being, by now, pissed with his conduct in general, I was for getting my watches back and the *Chambre Syndicale* not knowing I'd retrieved them.'

Fishman paused for dramatic effect, noting with satisfaction that his audience was thoroughly absorbed.

'Theretofore, I spoke *very* persuasively to my roadie mates who were setting up for an open-air orchestral concert. They said they might find an hour beforehand for a little freelance.' Fishman's narrative now took on a confessional turn. 'Foolish, I admit, but I told my roadie mates, "make it look a wee bit punitive" and they, being Ulstermen both, took that to mean – as you are aware – administering a punishment shooting, as per paramilitary convention.' He sighed ruefully at the thought that unfortunate outcomes often trod on the heels of misunderstandings. 'However, the *Chambre Syndicale* is forgiving by nature. The errant child having been brought back onto the straight and narrow, they awarded de Grandhomme five percent of his loss from the theft.'

'Five percent? That's more than ten thousand pounds!' said Corey, somewhat scandalised.

'True.'

'But he hadn't paid you, so he didn't have a loss.'

Fishman glanced round and lowered his voice. 'Correct also. Let's say a large sum of money had been moved several times to make it look like he'd already paid. In any case, does not a damaged foot entitle one to a small package *de* compensation? I mean, the *Chambre Syndicale* considers him a fully paid-up member of good standing!'

Corey was still baffled. 'But they were going to confiscate the watches from him,' he objected.

'Ah, but it was intended it would be my loss, not de Grandhomme's. *Typical bloody Frogs!*'

'So, this *Chambre Syndicale* considers you at fault,' noted Waverley sardonically, 'and might be aggrieved if it discovered the watches haven't been stolen from you by some Riviera crook but returned to your principals without loss.'

'All bar one... an Omega!' Fishman reminded her. 'Which neatly brings us to where we are now!'

'I've already said I'll get it back for you,' said Corey, 'but you have to let Waverley go.'

'No, no, *no!*' Fishman went rigid. For the first time his manner suggesting that freeing Waverley might not be quite as simply as it had first seemed. 'Anyway, she likes it.'

They both looked at Waverley, who looked supremely unimpressed.

'You let her go, Fishman. That's the deal. She has to go home and do stuff.'

'That's right, Fishman, "go home and do stuff"!' agreed Waverley.

Fishman was impervious. 'My principals won't have it. They need their surety and they're very particular, down to the last penny.' He looked apologetically at Waverley.

'Yes, well, I'm telling you, I'm the surety,' insisted Corey. 'But in any case, we know Ross has your bloody Omega and I'm going to retrieve it.'

Fishman wavered. Perhaps he was making an estimation of how long it would take before detaining Waverley gave him serious problems. Maybe he didn't like the odds. Whatever the reason, he suddenly capitulated. 'It's not right,' he decided, 'but I'll take you at your word... for a while. It's irregular, and you're not doing me any favours. The *status quo ante bellum* until after the weekend. Were my principals to find out, I can't promise they won't rebuke me and insist Waverley be returned to her present condition for the duration.' He paused. 'However, they know how to find you both, so I'm willing to take a gamble.'

The whole thing struck Corey as barbarous. 'Where do these people get their ideas? I mean, it's not on, detaining someone against a piffling loss that I've promised to cover.'

'Well, I'm not holding *you*, that's for certain,' said Fishman, as though this made everything all right. He gave Waverley a soupy smile, which she returned by arching her eyebrows in disgust.

Corey was relieved to have come to a resolution, although he could see Fishman's body language was not what it had been. The stark realisation came to him that Waverley's actions all day had been guided by the knowledge that she was in the hands of someone with unstable, possibly psychotic, tendencies. For his part, Fishman seemed to be making a new calculation that, unless Waverley was obligated to him, he was at risk of losing her, a prospect he was at his wits' end to prevent.

They got up to leave. As they crossed the hotel's foyer, Corey sensed that Waverley was having her own doubts. There was something beseeching in the look she gave him as Fishman went ahead. Corey caught hold of Fishman's sleeve. 'Look, Stanley –' the name came out weirdly – 'can I have a word with Waverley? We'll meet you outside.'

He nodded mutely, his face a picture of misery.

'What the hell, Waverley?' Corey demanded, once they were alone. 'Was he really going to stop you going home whenever you liked?'

She put her hand on his forearm as though she was about to explain the obvious to a simpleton. 'It's his principals, Corey. They'd hurt him if they didn't think it was all tied up. They're like that. Fishman can't step out of line or they come down on him, *really*! You don't know these people! They're animals, and they're never going to let him go; you should think yourself lucky!'

'Is he in serious trouble?' Corey wondered.

Waverley gave a little snort of derision. 'He shouldn't be. If the *Chambre Syndicale* had got their hands on the watches they'd have confiscated them without a penny's compensation. But his principals are not logical people, as far as I can see. They're vindictive and nasty.'

Moodily, Corey stared off into the distance. He could see that in the face of abandoning Fishman to his fate she had had a change of heart. She had wanted him – Corey – to save her, but somehow he had given her the will to continue in her role as hostage.

'He's a bloody fool.'

'Yes, but the watch Ross took was the best of the Omegas.'

'Typical! Entirely to be expected! He's back tomorrow.'

Waverley gave a mock flinch and laughed. 'And I have the key.'

All in all, decided Corey, not without a certain mordent amusement, Ross's imminent arrival meant Waverley was stuck between superlative idiots. 'You're not using it,' he insisted. 'There's no way you are posing for him! It's not safe!'

'Well, you'd better be my knight in shining armour, then,' she said mockingly. 'We have to get that Omega back to save Fishman's skin.'

'Leave it to me.'

Her face lit up with a sudden grin. 'Okay, then. Over to you.'

He looked at her sternly, but saw her change of heart was not to be reversed. Despite his misgivings, he nodded his agreement, thinking it rather admirable of her to continue as surety for the return of the Omega. Out in Conduit Street there were a few awkward moments while Corey bid them goodbye. And then – to Fishman's utter surprise – she was gone, walking with Fishman in the direction of New Bond Street.

THIRTY-FOUR

Eight fifteen the following morning, and Corey was having breakfast. He sipped his coffee, gazing without focus across the landscape of rooftops that spread northwards towards Shoreditch. His mobile began to jiggle against the sugar bowl and he picked it up. It was Waverley.

'Morning. How's it going?'

There was a hesitation from her end of the line. 'I know you're going to be cross about this....'

Corey groaned. He was beginning to see a pattern whereby events in Waverley's life had a habit of encroaching on his peace of mind.

'What is it?' he said, rather frostily.

'I think you'd better come. Fishman's laying a trap for Ross.'

Corey was exasperated. 'How long do you expect this to go on?'

She lowered her voice. 'It's his principals. Call it revenge, although he seems *very* light-hearted. It's weird: I've had nearly twenty-four hours of it, and I still can't tell you what's going on in his head.'

'Okay, but this time, if I come, there's no going back to him after half an hour. Where are you?'

'At Ross's place.'

'*What!*'

'Yes, we used the key he gave me.'

'Christ, Waverley, that's not good! What's Fishman doing?'

'Oh, he's turning the light fittings into Molotov cocktails.'

Corey spluttered incredulously.

'He says when Ross turns up, he's going to lay him out cold... or some such.'

Corey reached for his jacket. '*This has to stop!* I'm coming. Keep Fishman there and hope to God Ross doesn't get there before me!'

Corey went out into the street with the intention of hailing a taxi, but thought better of it. Aldgate East tube station was only round the corner and he could go directly to East Putney on the District Line. He checked his mobile and saw that the early morning BA flight from Nice was well on its way to Heathrow.

When Corey arrived at Ross's address, the first thing he noticed was the large, black Audi parked in the street, and as he got closer he saw that Phillip, the ex-Guards driver, was sitting behind the wheel, reading a newspaper. It was so unexpected, he couldn't help but stare. As he drew level, he slowed almost to a halt with such a look of surprise on his face that Phillip lowered his window enquiringly.

'Can I help you?'

'Is Max Collarii *here*?' said Corey, feeling rather ridiculous.

'He's inside. You have… business with him?'

'Yes. I'll go ahead and ring the bell.' He did so, not at all sure he wanted to know what was going on inside. An unnerving complication had arisen, yet a sense of obligation impelled him onwards.

Ross lived in an ex-Presbyterian primary school building, which had been divided into live/work studios a decade before. The building was late Victorian, almost Arts & Crafts, rather vertical, getting progressively more interesting as it approached the roof, with some fine stone detailing breaking up the brickwork. Ross had a large, ground-floor apartment with a studio extension built out into what had once been the playground.

Corey rang the bell in some trepidation. Nothing happened for a while but then, quite suddenly, the commanding presence of Max was at the door. He did not look in the mood for pleasantries. He turned, silently gesturing for Corey to follow. It struck Corey his demeanour was that of a potentate forced to deal with a minor insurrection in some distant province.

Max spoke over his shoulder as they made their way through the apartment. 'I'm glad you've come, Corey. Waverley told me you might. It'll be most helpful if together we can sort things out, once and for all. To be honest, I can't understand why they've been allowed to fester for so long!'

There it was again! Another example, thought Corey, of Max's habit, when things were not running smoothly, of inducing in others the feeling that their conduct had in some vague, but troubling way, disappointed him.

By now they were threading their way through the living area of the apartment. Fifteen kinds of refuse were scattered about, some decidedly unsavoury. As in Antibes, Ross's kind of rubbish was not the commonplace variety; it was Terminal Five rubbish, the Prada, Versace, Champagne & Caviar type. Without doubt, the place was a dump, but the effect had been expensively acquired. Ahead was a small flight of steps that took them down to the level of the studio. As they descended, Waverley and Fishman came into view. Fishman was lounging in a large, throne-like rattan chair beneath one of Ross's collage concoctions that rested precariously on an easel. Waverley was further away, standing under the skylight. It cast down on her a sharp, vertical light, almost a spotlight. She looked incredibly pale, near spectral.

Max came to a halt. Corey circled to one side and flashed Waverley a hello smile. She wasn't in the mood to respond. It was Fishman who broke the ice, greeting him with apparent good cheer.

'Here we are again, old chap!'

'Yes, here we are indeed!' interjected Max dryly. 'And, as I was saying, *I* want to get matters straight, once and for all.' It was clear from his tone that he was going to conduct proceedings as if in a business meeting where mature, responsible people signed up to contracts they honoured to the letter. 'That means, Fishman, *you're out!*'

Fishman looked surprised and indignant, seemingly not expecting anything so forceful.

'Do you understand, Fishman?'

'Pardon you!' said Fishman with an attempt at jocularity. 'I'm a party to the parties!'

'No, you're not. She's told you, *it's over*. You're using this feeble business to entrap her. Now, *I'm telling you*, it's over!'

Fishman turned to Waverley. 'Princess, tell the gentleman the truth of the matter.'

'*Truth, Fishman!*' she said in a rage. 'We're finished. Get it into your thick skull!'

Fishman leapt to his feet, in a sudden fit of agitation. 'This is your doing, isn't it?' he snarled at Max, '*Droit de Seigneur* is it, old chap? We were bobbing along nicely until she started working for *you*!'

Max regarded these comments with contempt. 'Your "principals", as you call them, waive any requirement that you hold Waverley against this watch business.' Max said this in a low growl, effectively menacing. It was obvious that his use of the term "principals" – implying familiarity with Fishman's business affairs – took Fishman by surprise. His front of wounded outrage sagged. 'Also, in future, they expect you to devote yourself to that business, one hundred per cent. Do I make myself clear? This dalliance is over!'

At that, the only Waverley Corey knew, the resourceful, redoubtable Waverley, burst into tears. It was a sight that completely unnerved him. He simply didn't know what to make of it. He looked to Max for guidance and saw in his expression, in his tender, protective concern, in his righteous domination of Fishman, that he was smitten. It was a perceptual jolt. But... but Max, reason told him, was patrician, sage and married with a family! Could it be true? He recognised then, in that moment, the signs had been there to read for as far back as he and Waverley had been working together. He – Corey – had, almost single-handedly, lifted Waverley out of the obscurity of her internship in the Keyline Gallery to a position of prominence, and now something intense, clandestine, touching the senior Collarii brother, had occurred. He was appalled and rendered mute!

'You're stealing the light from my life!' protested Fishman.

Max was unmoved.

Fishman crossed the studio to the window. On the windowsill stood a line of ceramic vases of various sizes. He picked up the largest and, raising it above his head, he hurled it to the floor. It made the most extraordinary noise as it broke and a great splash of five pence coins, mixed with ceramic fragments, spread across the floor.

It was a pathetic act of bravado that offended Corey sensitivities. However incongruous it might seem, he couldn't resist condemning it. '*That's a Bernard Leach!*'

'Get out!' Max ordered Fishman. 'Back to the only thing you're good for: *Swiss watches*!'

'Then where's my Omega?' shouted Fishman.

'You'll have your Omega by Monday, now leave!'

Fishman looked for a moment as though he was thinking of arguing further, but he changed his mind, deciding, perhaps, he was a beaten man. The contortions of his face suggested he had a Parthian shot in mind, but yet again he refrained and headed for the front door, banging through the apartment, his jaw clamped shut.

Max held out an arm and Waverley came across to him. 'I'll take you to the car,' he said, 'but give him time to clear off first.'

'I suppose,' ventured Corey, feeling very much a spare part, 'I should go.'

Max looked at him kindly. 'Yes, I thought you were going to Devon?'

'Well, you're right, but tomorrow.'

'I could come with you,' said Waverley tearfully.

Corey shook his head, depreciating the idea.

Max led them towards the front door. When nearly there, he turned to Corey. 'Listen, Corey, would you wait here? There's something I'd like to talk to you about. Just let me put Waverley in the car.'

While Corey waited, he examined Ross's living area. With the mess being almost archaeological in its complexity, it was difficult to fix on any detail, but one thing stuck out: a notice in felt tip on a sheet of A4 held on the fridge door with magnets: "EDDIE SAYS YOU'VE RUN OUT OF EQUITY – Q." Another sign of a chaotic life, he thought.

Where, he wondered, were the paintings his father had given him? He decided to take a look at the rest of the apartment but before he could make a move, Max returned; he was in a hurry. He studied Corey with an even gaze.

'This is my responsibility.' He held out an envelope. 'I want no more said about this, Corey. Is that understood?'

Corey was mystified but, even so, nodded his assent. 'What's this?' he said. He attempted a lightness of tone, but failing miserably.

'I'd like you to stay and give it to Ross when he arrives. It's two thousand euros. It's for the return of the watch. A little reward, let's say.'

Corey was quietly dismayed at the thought of attempting a financial settlement with Ross – appealing to his better nature had been the extent of his plan – but since he had offered to intercede, having realised Waverley had a problem, he saw Max's request as his just deserts. 'A reward... and compensation for the Bernard Leach, I suppose,' said Corey wryly.

Max laughed and clapped him on the shoulder. 'Exactly! And, Corey, he mustn't know it's come from me. That's an absolute.'

Here was the catch! Corey was beginning to feel he'd fallen into a trap. 'Where shall I say –'

'Tell him it's from you. Tell him you're in love with Waverley and you promised to retrieve the damned Omega. You are, aren't you? We all are, come to that!' He smiled broadly, the merest glint of triumph in his eyes.

Corey began to object, but Max raised an admonishing finger. 'Believe me, I know Ross. There's only one thing that talks where he's concerned. Dangle the money; he's always short.' He sized up the apartment. '*Squalor!* This looks like a drugs den to me. I wouldn't be surprised if he deals, in an amateur sort of way... in the manner of everything he does.'

And then he was gone, leaving Corey in a sudden limbo. *What the hell?* Corey thought. He looked at the envelope, aware the money was going to lead to trouble. Why had he agreed to take it? To be so obliging was a curse. No, it was a curse *to have to be* so obliging. Damn it, why did he carry on with the Post archive and *catalogue raisonné*? Prestige, he supposed. There wasn't enough prestige to go round, not by any means.

After several minutes of bemoaning his lot, he pulled himself together and began to think he should devise a strategy to deal with the imminent arrival of Ross. Ross was vile, malicious and unpredictable, and it wouldn't help that his apartment had been invaded and an *objet d'art* he used as a moneybox smashed. Corey groaned. Should he clear it up? No, better leave things as they were.

He went from room to room looking to see if he could find any Gustave Posts. Somehow, he wasn't surprised to draw a blank. Not the place to keep valuable art, he decided. After all, Fishman and Waverley had gained entry using a single key and he didn't see any signs of an alarm system. What Ross's father had given him over the years was, he was sure, stored elsewhere. He made a mental note to check the *catalogue raisonné* to remind him of exactly what works Ross owned. Finally, he opened a cupboard in the main bedroom and leaning on its side against the back of the cupboard was a small Gustave Post, an exquisite still life with fruit and magazines. It was familiar but he couldn't quite place it, although he could recall other paintings in the same manner using similar objects. If the precise date eluded him, he was still sure it was middle-period Post. That meant it was suspiciously early to be one of the paintings given to Ross by his father. He photographed the painting with his mobile and returned it to the cupboard.

As he made his way back to the living area he noticed a table lamp with a lightbulb lying by it. He remembered what Waverley had said about Molotov cocktails. Discussing Fishman on the flight back from Cannes she had told him: 'Fishman knows how to blow a hole in the top of an old-fashioned tungsten filament lightbulb with a blowtorch. You half-fill it with petrol and when you turn it on it goes boom.' Sure enough the lightbulbs had been switched. He switched them back, emptied the petrol in the sink and dropped the bulb in the waste.

He had an overwhelming desire to leave and his stomach was reminding him that Waverley's summons had interrupted his breakfast. It occurred to him that it might be less fraught if he met Ross in a coffee shop rather than to be found waiting for him at home. He decided to walk down to the local shops. On the way, he took his mobile from his pocket, checked the time and decided Ross might already have left Heathrow. He braced himself to call.

Ross, it turned out, was even closer than he thought.

'Templeton, what *the hell* are you doing in my coffee shop?'

The first thing Corey noticed was that Ross was unshaven and looked as though he'd gone straight from bed to plane. He'd travelled from the south of France like a hobo, carrying everything in what was little more than a shoulder bag, but the bag was supple, tan leather and sported a LV logo.

'How come you keep turning up like a bad penny?' he added in exasperation. 'I thought you'd been told to bog off.' He slumped into a chair opposite Corey. Superficially his posture was relaxed, but the effect was strained and his foot jiggled relentlessly.

'Yes, Edward did say,' agreed Corey, 'but how come you know he did? I thought you weren't on speaking terms.'

'Oh, we all talk, for God's sake,' he replied impatiently. 'I mean, nobody wants anybody working for the Collariis sticking their noses into our business. It's the same for everyone.'

'Oh, really? I'm surprised! Okay, let me tell you what's up and I'll get out of your face.' He laid the envelope on the table. 'First thing, I want the watch.'

Ross seemed disinclined to hear him, but he had noticed the envelope. 'What's that?' he said.

'It's the reward for finding the watch.'

'What sort of reward?'

'Two thousand euros. And to cover the cost of a broken pot. Fishman broke it.'

'Did he? *I like it!*' He chuckled as if he relished the reappearance of Fishman. If he understood Corey and Fishman had been in his apartment, he seemed unmoved by it. He slid the envelope over to his side of the table and checked its contents. 'Where's this come from?'

'Don't ask. Just take it.'

'Okay, but if Fishy broke something, *Fishy* can pay for it.' Recollection of his encounter with Fishman in Cannes occasioned more amusement. 'How's Fishy getting on with his *principals*? When Quentin and I parted him from his watches, he went on and on about his principals. According to him they'd rip out our tongues. Oh, yes, and gouge out our eyes with teaspoons.' Ross gurned, his tongue protruding, his eyes starting out of his head. 'They haven't, have they?'

'They might have, if Waverley hadn't returned them.'

'Took them back? Who to?'

'Miss Moneypenny.'

They looked at one another blankly. Ross didn't understand what Corey meant; Corey realised he had no idea why Waverley had used the name.

'In Dover Street,' Corey added weakly.

Ross seized on that. 'Ah, Dover Street! That's interesting! Fishy doesn't know it, but he and I are going to rip them off.' He wagged the envelope. 'This just covers the watch.' He lifted up his left arm to rest his elbow on the table, displaying the Omega. 'Shall I try and undo it?' he lisped. He held out his wrist in a parody of helplessness. 'Or will you?'

'You,' replied Corey.

'Why the fuck I bother, I do not know,' Ross said, switching to disdain as he released the watch. 'Only for Waves, because she's my pocket Venus of the moment.' He didn't for a moment question the legitimacy of being paid for something he didn't own, because he disdained the idea of a monetary exchange.

Thankfully, Corey took the Omega. 'Listen… check there aren't any booby traps in your apartment: the light fittings. Fishman's principals might not have gouged your eyes out but they told him to blow you up, according to Waverley'

'Blow me up, eh? That's perfect! And Waves was here too, was she?'

'She had the key.'

'Of course she did! Where's she now?'

'They've all gone.'

'All?' Ross scrutinised his face, suddenly suspicious. 'Was Max here?'

'No.' He recoiled from the lie.

'The key?'

'She still has it.'

Ross hadn't entirely let go of the suspicion that Max was somehow involved in the transaction they had just completed. 'It's good she's still got the key; she's promised to pose for me. I'm going to do a Waverley series. I've got it all planned... if you and Max let her off her leash, *that is*!' He gave a gross, sardonic laugh. He tossed the envelope in front of Corey. 'Write down her mobile number for me. I don't want to call her through that gallery.' He laughed again and got up, ready to leave.

'I'm going to Devon to see your mother. Any messages?' said Corey coldly. 'Maybe you should try talking to her.'

Ross eyes narrowed, and for the first time seemed close to losing his temper. '*Oh!*' He drummed his fingers on the edge of the table. 'You're a chum of hers, aren't you?' He raised his eyebrows in mock, or was it real, exasperation. 'If you're looking for her paintings by my dad, you ought to know they're mostly kept in the Collarii Foundation's store.'

'I know hers are; where are yours?'

'That's none of your business, matey.' He snatched up the euros.

'You weren't even born in nineteen eighty-two,' said Corey as he put his pen away, 'so why are you so concerned about us researching it?'

'You know why; it's like we're under investigation –' he leant in closer to Corey's face '– *all the time! You're the bloody art police!*' He straightened and his face took on a kind of musing expression. 'Tell Waves I'll call... Tell her I'm expecting her, otherwise I'll have to come to that gallery to get her. And sign it with a kiss.' He bunched his lips in a parody of kissing and was gone.

THIRTY-FIVE

Corey had various things to attend to at the Courtauld, but by late afternoon he had made his way to the Collarii Building, curious to check Ross's holding of his father's paintings. He found the accession numbers listed in the Post family records. There were twenty-five, and from the prefix letters he could tell eight were paintings, fifteen were drawings and a couple were early prints from the *King's Road* series. Apart from the prints, nothing was earlier than nineteen ninety. It was just as Ross had told Waverley when they were in the south of France: all the paintings Gustave had gifted him were painted in Ross's teenage years, or later.

Now Corey had the accession numbers he could find images of the paintings in the *catalogue raisonné*. So far, so good, but that, he decided, could wait. What was at the forefront of his mind was the small painting he had discovered in the cupboard in Ross's bedroom. He called up the photograph he had taken of it. Now he had time to examine it, he knew he was right to have been suspicious. He was certain that if he searched for Ross's paintings in the *catalogue raisonné* he wouldn't find this one; the date was wrong! Corey could generally date Gustave's paintings to the span of a year or two and the more he looked at the image the more certain he was that Gustave had painted it in the seventies, probably during his early years in Berlin. He began to search through the appropriate volumes of the *catalogue raisonné*. Eventually he found what he was looking for: *Composition with Movie Magazines IV, 1976*. The entry said it belonged to the Gustave Post Trust. It shouldn't have been in Ross's bedroom; it didn't belong to him. It should have been at Villa Besugo in Majorca. There was only one possibility: Ross had stolen it.

As he digested this, he began to feel slightly nauseous. It wasn't that he had uncovered another blatant piece of nastiness so much as the drive of his investigation had suddenly wilted before a reoccurrence of the thought that Waverley could be nearby, but had somehow become a stranger to him. The effect made it difficult for him to concentrate. It was as if something had been stolen from him and he was left choking on knowing who the thief was.

THIRTY-SIX

Paddington Station on a Saturday morning carried the promise of western skies, Atlantic breezes and the carefree holidays of Corey's youth. He was glad to be going. Not just because of his visit to Ruthie, although he expected the twenty-four hours he planned to be in her company to be bracing. Nor was it because south Devon was the favourite holiday destination of his childhood: private estates with barred gates, crooked lanes buried under tunnels of foliage and almost impossible to reach secret beaches beneath fawning cliffs. No, the truth was that the last thing he wanted was to be in London, "languishing", as he saw it, in the backwash of his intimations that Waverley had become the subject of Max's attentions. It was a relief to be leaving London when he could only imagine Waverley giving zest to Max's morning, on a sofa with her chin resting on one knee, quizzical, that mobile face so alive in the shadows beneath a curtain of golden hair.

After what seemed like an age, he was beyond Exeter, with the local train stopping at Ivybridge on its way to Plymouth. The station was as he remembered from his youth: two stone-edged platforms, unchanged since the line was built. But the huge car park was an unwelcome surprise. It was empty, but he could imagine it on a weekday, full of the SUVs of the West of England's finest: middle managers gone to work by train to invent the petty swindles and garish straplines that were their stock in trade. Thoughts of the gruesome cavalcade caused him a grim smile.

Ruthie was waiting. Her ancient Yaris creaked in a gust of wind as he approached. She was intent on something on her lap and didn't see him until he tapped on the window. With a hoot of delight, she tossed the *Telegraph* onto the back seat and wound down the window.

'Corey, at last some enlightened conversation!' she cried with a broad, delighted grin. 'Better than talking to cows, I'll be bound!'

'Let's hope so, Ruthie,' said Corey wryly, thinking cows were little enough competition.

Ruthie drove him south into what she loved to call "bandit country", though more likely the last home of clandestine foxhunters, every fold in the land camouflaged, every feature passed on one side destined to reappear on the other, five bends later. An invading army could be encamped in one field, the home guard in the next, without the two knowing they were close enough to parley. Ruthie's house, a sturdy but ramshackled stone building, was half-way up a hillside, half-buried under a bank that gave onto a combe that opened out into a pasture, fifty per cent thistles, half a mile to the sea. Whenever Corey visited, he always found himself wondering why artists were drawn to such places. One night as a guest was enough for him. The staves on the gate at the top of the bank were painted alternately pink and baby blue. As they drew up in the yard there were cats everywhere. Ruthie climbed out and gave a loud yip. The cats came running.

'*My babies!*' she cried.

Ruthie had been nineteen when she first met Gustave. A real beauty by all accounts. At fifty-six she had become matronly in appearance, but her gaiety of spirit remained. She still had a marvellous open-faced sense of optimism about things. It was true that she didn't take much care with her appearance but a vigorous regime of country living and a clear complexion gave her the look of a horsewoman about to muck-out the stables. Her blond hair had turned a steely grey yet it still flounced about her temples in the way that Gustave Post had found entrancing when first he saw her on the beach below Stefan Muller's villa. Corey knew she would try and seduce him later. He would resist weakly, as he had done before, and she would dismiss her failure with a mad laugh.

'I saw Ross yesterday. He's back from the south of France.' It was something he had to say, even knowing she and Ross didn't get on.

She gave him her frozen-face look. 'How is he?'

'Seems well enough. Where does he keep Gustave's paintings he owns? I was in his studio and I could only see one.'

She laughed. 'Nothing is ever what it seems with Ross. Are you sure he still has some?'

'Well, he's only supposed to sell them through the Collarii Foundation and it certainly hasn't handled any sales for him.'

'Ah, yes, those Collarii boys! They've everything sewn up, haven't they?'

'You could say that, although I understand the lawyers are still wrangling over the details. The Collariis *are* paying you, aren't they?'

'Oh, yes, they're scrupulous enough, in their way. Do they pay you, Corey? That's more the question!'

Corey smiled ruefully. 'They know I'm full-time at the Courtauld, so they tend towards the view that pocket money and generous expenses should suffice.'

'Well, that's something, I suppose. I've got a new studio. My neighbours, the Farleys, have loaned me a barn. It's wonderful. We'll go and see it after lunch.'

They drove down lanes at dizzying, dangerous speeds to arrive at the Dolphin in Kingston. Corey had but one thing on his mind – nineteen eighty-two – but he knew better than to hurry things.

'I love this pub,' said Ruthie. They ate sandwiches and talked of her life in the sticks. As they left, she booked them in for their evening meal.

She drove him to her new studio to see her latest paintings. She also insisted on showing him earlier ones going back over the years. A gallery in Totnes sold her canvases and drawings from time to time, but not enough to prevent her storage needs becoming ever greater. The studio was an old workshop, not a barn. The massive bench still sat in a corner. At least it had windows, but Corey knew it would be damp and cold once autumn set in. He suspected many of the paintings were likely to suffer damaged, should they remain there all winter. Did she care? He couldn't tell. He genuinely admired some of what he saw, and besides that he flattered her, as a supplicant must.

'We first met when you were a student, didn't we?' she said, as she always did. Fortunately, she loved to reminisce. 'I was the wrong Post!' She laughed.

As usual, he was abashed that he had admired her paintings before he knew anything very much about Gustave. 'Well, it was genuine admiration. I spent the inheritance from my grandmother on that drawing of yours. I still have it!'

Later, in the gloaming, on a road luminescent with moonlight, they walked from the parked Yaris to the pub, scarcely-seen things flitting through the air above their heads.

'How well did you know Gustave?' wondered Ruthie.

'He was pretty far-gone when I first met him. Two thousand and twelve, I think.'

'He was a vampire, really!' She grew restive. 'In the end I was glad to get away. They thought I was mad: *the crazy woman with cats*. There's a lot of us; I'm in good company. The male thing in Gustave could make you pretty apprehensive. You know how we first met?'

They had reached the pub.

'You were in Majorca, weren't you?' said Corey.

'Yes, like a young fool I was posing for Stefan Muller. We were on the beach, having drinks; several people dropped by. Gustave got me by myself. You know what the first thing he said to me was? He said, "You should try me in the bath"!'

Once their hilarity had subsided, she continued. 'Gustave did have a nerve! He came into Stefan's studio to look me over.' She laughed again. 'Was I embarrassed! Mind you, I could be pretty abandoned in those days. I'm not saying I was abused like the poor creatures we hear so much about these days; nobody had heard of power relationships then. Of course, it got serious, as things do. Then Clarissa found out and there was a rumpus. He was in a bind, really. He got me pregnant with Ross within a month. I didn't care; we fooled around like crazy. After all, he was the great artist.'

Their food arrived.

'Everybody was obliging where Gustave was concerned. He lived in a kind of bubble. It was a charmed life at first, when you were with Gustave, but then you had to deal with his expectations. My God, *his expectations*!' She laughed again, ferociously. 'Cats expect little or nothing from humans.'

'Did Clarissa try to run you over?'

Ruthie's knocked her spoon to the floor. 'Who told you that?'

Corey had to think. 'You know, I can't remember.'

'Ah! So, that's the gossip, is it? Gustave tried to keep it quiet. I was one thing too many for Clarissa. I had a war on my hands! There was an incident, in London. I was nearly crushed. Gustave actually saved me. She wasn't prepared to run him over, not then anyway. The thing is, after Berlin, Gustave decided landscape was the great neglected modern subject matter, but it was me who showed him how to release it from its *École de Paris* impediments. He thought it was a matter of less raw umber!' She giggled.

'There's something I can't fathom, Ruthie. It's a bit personal, though.'

The desserts came. Corey handed Ruthie's spoon to the young girl serving them and asked for a fresh one.

'Go on, it's all history now.'

'There was a woman in Berlin called Ingrid. She and Gustave were having an affair and he painted a couple of paintings for her. Ingrid and the paintings then disappeared. Do you know anything about it? Forgive me for saying this, but when he took up with you, he could have only just… I don't know… ended his affair with her. It seems weird, the way she suddenly wasn't around.

She scoffed cynically. 'Gustave was permanently on the rebound; he was that kind of man, *and* given every encouragement to be so by his blokey friends! Was she something special?'

'You never heard anything?'

'No, not really… but Gustave was having a bad time that autumn. Black days in the studio; nothing worked. I always thought it was Clarissa. Maybe… I don't know, in those first months I wasn't with him all the time. Gustave didn't want to go back to Berlin, I know that. He told me he had a reoccurring dream. He was Macbeth. He lived in a black castle. There was a dark tunnel leading to a black forest… Everything in this dream was pitifully gloomy!' She laughed mercilessly. 'He murdered Clarissa and dragged her down the tunnel to the forest where her body was consumed by savage beasts.'

'Oh.' Corey remembered that Max had mentioned something about Clarissa and Lady Macbeth. He couldn't recall what, but something superstitious stirred in the back of his mind.

'*Yes!*' she giggled. 'I thought, after murdering her and ridding himself of her body, he had decided I was the one... *Oh, vanity!*' For a moment her peel of laughter filled the bar, challenging all conversation.

'But you and he...'

'Ah! I was safe enough until I was thirty. You couldn't help love him all right; he was golden in many ways. But I had my own career to consider and he was the vampire of vampires.'

'So, you never saw a painting called *Berlin Wall Lament No.1*?'

'No. Show me.'

Corey fetched out his mobile and found the image.

'That's interesting,' decided Ruthie. 'This is one of the paintings that disappeared, is it?'

Corey nodded.

'I haven't seen it before, but the thing I was telling you about him wanting to paint landscapes is a kind of version of this painting, without the cruelty. Could it have been he felt some sort of revulsion? Come to think of it, I think Clarissa had become a horrible presence in his life, and he wanted to change; to get out of the angry, depressive stuff. Maybe this painting is something to do with his landscape period. Maybe he was at a point of transition.'

Corey knew the landscape paintings she was talking about and could see the sense in what she was saying. They were of a kind of uplands arcadia he had focused on for several years in the mid-eighties, work quite contrary to the *sturm und drang* of his German *New Spirit* counterparts.

'Well, this was painted in the spring, before he came to Majorca. It's a bit of a one-off, isn't it? That makes it all the more valuable.'

'I suppose so. Who owns it?'

'We've no idea. It's suddenly appeared out of the blue.'

She looked at him sternly. 'Ah, I know what this is about! You're thinking Ross might have got hold of it somehow, aren't you?'

Corey denied it, but he could see she didn't entirely believe him. 'Well, you could have ended up with it, after Gustave left Clarissa. And you could have given it to Ross later.' He said it teasingly to see her reaction, but he really didn't believe it. She was vehement and her view about where the painting had come from didn't surprise him.

'It all points to Clarissa.'

'Maybe. The thing is, Clarissa, of all the Posts, is the one least in need of money. I can't see why she would try to sell it this way. Mind you, it's got us raking over all this eighties stuff, and she really doesn't like it.'

Ruthie stretched her legs; their table in a corner of the bar was cramped. 'Clarissa was devious and competitive,' she said fatalistically. 'I was a babe in arms. Let's have another drink and then walk down to the estuary. It's very beautiful at this time of year.'

Corey got to his feet and pulled out his wallet. 'Same again?'

'Yes.'

As he reached the bar, he experienced a sudden perceptual jolt. 'Oh, fuck!' he groaned. In a flood of emotion, the realisation had come to him that he was in love with Waverley; in love with someone who still led the vagabond life of a student. How could that possibly work?

THIRTY-SEVEN

On the evening train back to London, Corey tried to grapple with his Gustave Post perplexities. He did so despite Waverley haunting his thoughts, like a nagging migraine. When not beset by images of her in the arms of wraiths and satyrs, he was developing a picture of how nineteen eighty-two had marked a turning point in Gustave's personal life and career. As far as his personal life was concerned, he had an increasingly vivid picture of a series of chaotic entanglements. Gustave's estrangement from Clarissa seemed to have become open warfare by the spring, but the relationship had staggered on a little longer while he was taking solace, first with Ingrid, and then, once he had quit Berlin and Ingrid had disappeared, with Ruthie, a nineteen-year-old girl he had absurdly propositioned on a beach in Majorca. The way he had thrown himself so precipitously into his affair with Ruthie suggested a desire to be done with both Clarissa *and* Ingrid. All in all, Corey supposed, it didn't show Gustave in a very good light, although in a general sense there was nothing about his behaviour with which he wasn't already familiar. By the autumn, and after Venice, Ruthie had described a man unusually distracted, having difficulties with his work, preoccupied by other matters. It was as if whatever happened in Berlin had left him battered and eager to forget, however hard that might prove to be. Of course, as Max had suggested, it could be down to a sudden loss of confidence in the direction of his work as a consequence of his success in Venice. But now, more certainly than ever, Corey saw, in the disturbance of Gustave's working pattern, a disturbance of his mind caused by events beyond the studio, and it made him fear for Ingrid. Everything he had learnt from Ruthie had intensified his suspicion that she had been treated badly; discarded peremptorily and deprived of the canvases Gustave had painted for her under the spell of her political activism. Corey could imagine all this being biographical gold for Campbell Carter, but still, for him, the reoccurring frustration! Despite getting ever closer to the detail of Gustave's life, none of it did anything to bring him closer to knowing what had happened to *Berlin Wall Lament No.1*, or its pair. At least his visit to Devon had dispelled the faint possibility that both had somehow come into Ruthie's possession and she was trying to dispose of one of them in secret.

Now and then, thoughts of Waverley would seize up this narrative, causing him anguish as the train roared eastwards. What it came down to, he decided, was his inability to gauge the pitch of his expressions of affection. Either he was too business-like, or he was buying her with an impetuous act of extravagance. Too used to playing solitaire, he was incapable of attempting anything without producing an unattractive, flatfooted, cold-hearted caricature of himself. Max, he concluded, had trumped him in much the same way as Gustave had trumped Clyde Diggle.

THIRTY-EIGHT

Monday morning: a new day, a new week. Corey could not shake off the feeling that things were precariously poised. "Things" was a misnomer; too plastic and material, too much like physical "stuff". It was more as if some part of his mental machinery was wary that an imminent disaster was about to sweep away the coordinates of his settled existence. It registered as a kind of jangling interference lying beneath his usual thought processes. Swirling the dregs of his coffee occupied him for several minutes. Finally, he put introspection aside and brought his mobile to life. He'd avoided looking at his mail all weekend and there were dozens of new messages. Amongst the mass of institutional notifications and subsequent amendments was a press release announcing that Dermot O'Flynn would be reading his poems at Waterstone's, Piccadilly, that evening. The event was being held in conjunction with the publication of *Barriers to Barricades,* a new collection of his poems.

Corey didn't have much time for poetry and he nearly binned it. What stopped him was the premonition that some significance was attached to the announcement. He couldn't think what. He checked the sender's identity and, to his surprise, saw it was Campbell Carter. That convinced him he'd come across the poet's name before, and recently... Then it clicked: wasn't it a Dermot O'Flynn who had written the introduction to Gustave Post's nineteen eighty-two Venice Biennale catalogue? He had a photocopy of the catalogue in his briefcase. He fished it out to see if he was right. He was. O'Flynn's text was brief: it had large margins and, even so, barely filled a two-page spread. He knew backwards the kind of things such texts said. Inevitably, they were anodyne and laudatory, and, as a consequence, he had never more than glanced at this example. Now he read it with a sharpened sense of attention.

He had to admit that O'Flynn laid on the effusive admiration with a certain sly charm. It was a more than competent piece of hagiography of the sort successful, middle-aged men write who are long-time admirers of one another. The biographical background to the piece was that they had met when Gustave was a student at the Royal College of Art. The occasion had been one of O'Flynn's poetry readings at a bookshop called The Lighthouse. O'Flynn gave the slight but persistent impression that he had "brought Gustave on". He was somewhat older than Gustave and the essay suggested that as a consequence of his influence, Gustave had come to share his anti-establishment, if not revolutionary, political and artistic agenda, although what its principles were was left unsaid.

Corey's curiosity about O'Flynn was aroused. He turned his attention back to the press release. Scrolling down through it, his surprise redoubled on reading that Campbell Carter had written the introduction to *Barriers to Barricades*: "A remarkable testament to Ireland's greatest living poet, his life and work, by Campbell Carter."

Corey now understood why Campbell was distributing the press release, although the extent of his involvement puzzled him. Why had Gustave Post's biographer felt moved to become the interpreter of "Ireland's greatest living poet"? It seemed a curious side-step. The only way to find out why he had accepted the commission, he decided, was to acquire a copy of *Barriers to Barricades*.

He didn't feel inclined to speak to Waverley, so he sent her a text: 'Find out all you can about Dermot O'Flynn. He's part of Gustave's Berlin scene. I'll be there soon so get on to it.'

He left his office and took the number nine bus west. He received a call from Waverley, which he ignored. In one of the windows of the Waterstone's in Piccadilly there was a large display board advertising O'Flynn's reading from *Barriers to Barricades*. He examined the photograph at the centre of the display. From it shone the likeness of a weathered man with a spark of something uncompromising, even wild, about him; a man in the fullness of his years, yet still in command of his life and destiny. Not the sort of man to hanker after fashionable dinner parties or lodgings in grand hotels; an old-fashioned socialist, patriot and nationalist.

Corey went into the store and on one of the tables near the door he found a pyramidal display of the books. It was a substantial hardback, beautifully presented, produced by the same publisher as Campbell Carter's biography of Gustave Post. Had some editor there, he wondered, put Carter and O'Flynn together? He took a copy to the nearest till and paid. There was a café on the fifth floor where he knew he could read without being disturbed. He took the lift and ordered a coffee. On opening the book, he saw the dedication and again his attention sharpened. It read:

These poems I dedicate
to the memory of Gustave Post,
the great friend, ally and fellow patriot of my youth.

The next page was blank but for the following epigraph: "'The truth of my life lies always in my work.' – Gustave Post." Corey's initial reaction was to think, *small world* with a slight sense of disdain. He gazed at the cover, which bore the same portrait photograph that filled the window announcement. Taken together, the dedication and the epigraph were a gracious nod to a kindred spirit and compatriot. The cynic in Corey took the gracious nod to be somewhat strategic: Post was much more famous than O'Flynn, so there was no doubt who the association benefited. He leafed through the introductory matter until he came to Campbell's appreciation. Its length surprised him. It had the look of a detailed piece of work, not some thousand-word, jobbing panegyric. An introduction to a collection of poetry, however substantial, was unlikely to put bread on Campbell's table. Well, it might put bread, Corey decided, but not much else. Why would Campbell choose to spend his time on O'Flynn when he could be getting on with the second volume of his Gustave Post biography? He thought it odd. If the publisher had not been pulling strings behind the scenes, could it be, he wondered, that Campbell Carter had Irish blood. The latter was certainly a motive, but he was almost certain that

Campbell hadn't. He could only think that O'Flynn intrigued him as a contributor to a larger artistic and historical canvas.

When Corey had read sufficient to get a sense of Campbell's drift, his concentration began to falter. Several paragraphs made much of O'Flynn's early association with Gustave, but, as he'd suspected, critical writing about poetry was not the man's metier; his effusive style was too akin to his subject and Corey didn't feel particularly engaged. He put down the open book on the table. The pages slowly flipped back until they came to a halt at Gustave's epigram: "The truth of my life lies always in my work." *Where did that come from?* Corey wondered, somewhat irritably. And what the hell did it mean? He tried to see its profundity. Various truths about Gustave Post's life came to mind. There were the paintings on public display around the world, complete with explanatory captions written by curators of interpretation. Together they might be considered an approach to the truth of Gustave's life. But then there was the unseen surplus, the Collarii Foundation's stock of Posts, strategically held back from the market. When they were all finally in circulation they might subtly alter the truth Gustave's paintings told. Another truth was the sum of Post's dependents and heirs. Their rancorous disputes were his legacy. Were they not a truth: a truth of celebrity and careless living? And finally, there was Campbell Carter's still incomplete biography. Was Campbell not laying out the recoverable facts about Gustave's life to capture the truth? No, Corey reflected, a little cynically, there was biographer's gold, but there was also biographer's baloney.

All three were attempts at truth, but mundane ones. It was more likely, Corey decided, that what Gustave meant by his smart little epigram was that some kind of transcendent truth was to be found in his synthesis of the grand progress of Western art and his personal life into a mythic, painted fable. It was in understanding that synthesis, Gustave seemed to be hoping, that a higher, nobler truth was to be found. Corey regarded the proposition as suitably egotistical. He gave a caustic grunt, something like a laugh. Where, then, was the small matter of the truth of what happened to Ingrid Steinmann, and the reason Gustave had so readily forgotten her? Certainly, *Berlin Wall Lament No.1* could not speak to that: Gustave had created it at the height of his passion for her. What happened next? A year later, he was painting landscapes that Ruthie had described as "a kind of version" of *Berlin Wall Lament No.1*, but "without the cruelty". In between lay a period about which he was still unclear. Ruthie had said that Gustave had struggled with work. What story did the work he had produced in that period tell? Perhaps it said something about what had happened in Berlin that resulted in Ingrid's disappearance. That span of time was where he needed to look. He rose from his seat as though propelled. He went down in the lift and made his way along Piccadilly towards the Collarii Building.

THIRTY-NINE

Corey entered the Keyline Gallery shortly before noon. It was between exhibitions and full of technicians. The work of the Chinese artist had disappeared and preparations for the gallery's summer exhibition were in full swing. A large González had already been removed from its packing case and five Brancusi sculptures, still in theirs, had just come out of a van. Most of the technicians were ex-art school students and Corey knew them well enough to have to speak to each in turn. Today he cut it to a minimum.

The archive room in the basement was a haven. He sat for a while, unsure what he should do first. There was a text from Waverley that he ignored. On one of the shelves, at the end of a long line of Gustave Post monographs, there were several new copies of volume one of Campbell Carter's biography. He took one down, opened it, taking care not to crack the spine, and searched the index for Dermot O'Flynn. His search did nothing to lessen his sense of puzzlement. What he wanted, he decided, was a pretext to quiz Campbell about O'Flynn's relationship with Gustave. He took up his mobile, resolved to congratulate him on his introduction.

'Ah, thank you for such kind words, sooooo kind,' rumbled Campbell as he lapped up Corey's praise. There was a faint hubbub in the background. It sounded as if he was already in one of the Bloomsbury pubs he favoured for lunch. 'A kindred spirit is Dermot: succinct, language full of visual imagery, as blustery as a County Sligo morn.'

'I was looking through your biography of Gustave, and I noticed you mention O'Flynn only once... in passing. I suppose in writing about O'Flynn you've come to revise your view... you know... of their relationship? Your essay seems to suggest so.'

There was an awkward silence from the other end of the line, followed by a sigh.

'You could say that.'

However stilted it might sound, Corey was determined to press the point. 'Well, I hadn't previously grasped its importance… as you describe it. Of course, Gustave's biography only goes up to nineteen seventy-five. Should we assume you'll be dealing with their relationship much more extensively in volume two?'

'Dear boy, Gustave was important to Dermot, the other way round not so much. You know how it is with fame?'

'Were there any hidden depths I should know about?'

There was laughter from the other end of the line. It went on for some time; it seemed Campbell was much amused. 'You're fishing! I'm sure O'Flynn'll take his place in the great scheme of things in volume two, especially since you've pointed to the inadequate attention I've paid to their relationship up to nineteen seventy-five.'

'Who suggested the Gustave Post epigram, you, O'Flynn or the publisher?'

Campbell's voice had taken on an edge, between mocking and teasing. 'Ah, that's pure O'Flynn, but you'll have to wait for volume two to find out where and when Gustave said it. But how goes it with you? What rabbit holes have you been down of late?'

'I teach, Campbell: the Great Calling.'

'Indeed, yes, I had heard you have one of your exes in tow. Ex-student, I mean. Is it true she's made a great splash with the Collarii brothers? My spies tell me she's been seen in the most unlikely company.'

This allusion to Waverley flustered Corey. 'I don't know what you mean, Campbell. It sounds like rank gossip. You've been listening to those RA cronies of yours again. Anything to keep them out of their studios, I suppose.'

'Oh, cutting today, Corey! The art world is a village, dear boy, and I like to dally by the village pump.'

After a few more such forays, Campbell terminated the call.

Corey was annoyed with himself. He'd handled the call badly: he'd meant it to be collegiate but he had ended up striking a sour note. Campbell's attitude hadn't helped. Corey didn't consider himself in competition with him but, not for the first time, he had treated him as though he were. Did that suggest Campbell knew something about O'Flynn's relationship with Gustave he was determined to keep to himself? Corey was intrigued. He resolved not to miss O'Flynn's reading at Waterstone's.

He was about to put his mobile down on the table when it rang. His first thought was that Campbell was calling back to mend bridges but it was Angela, Max's PA. Max wanted to see him upstairs in his office.

'You know David at the Morandi Gallery?' Max said abruptly as he entered.

It wasn't like Max to dispense with the affable preliminaries.

'David Ashworthy?'

'Yes, exactly. He's been approached about a private treaty purchase of one of Gustave's paintings. He gave me the contact: one of those hedge-fund guys from Curzon Street. The name's Marc Bastion. Know anything about it?'

'No, should I?'

'I've sent you the image. It should be on your mobile. He's saying he's got several more, all for sale.'

'*Who* says?'

'The hedge-fund guy! Come on, Corey, keep up!'

That jolted him. He didn't like the sound of Max's impatience. Something was poisoning the atmosphere. 'I'm sorry, I don't under —'

'It's called *Falling Woman XI* and it's from nineteen ninety-nine. It's come from Ross Post. I think they all have.'

'Really?' Corey was thinking out loud. He knew the falling women series. 'Well… I only saw one painting at Ross's studio. Did you *notice*? There weren't any hung anywhere.'

The question touched on Max having been there, and with Waverley. Corey saw he wasn't going to acknowledge any such thing. As far as Max was concerned it hadn't happened, whatever the circumstances.

'This Bastion,' Max began with great deliberation, 'is saying these paintings are collateral in an equity release scheme and, given the prices the Gustave Posts fetched at Sotheby's last week, they've fallen below the threshold for forfeiture. In other words, the paintings no longer belong to their owner. If, as I suspect, it's Ross, the stupid man's signed up to some scheme to fund his lifestyle and now there's no equity left. It was probably a trap, and the lenders have a perfect right to recover their loan by selling the paintings.' In measured fury he slapped down on his desk the folder he was holding. 'And who, according to David Ashworthy, facilitated this scheme? Edward bloody Post! It's a cobbled-together piece of financial engineering intended to get round the family's agreement with us under the terms of the Post family trust... And it's gone wrong for entirely short-term reasons because Ross has borrowed against the paintings up to the hilt!'

As he was finishing, Peter Collarii entered the room.

'Have you heard?' demanded Max.

'Yes.' Peter seemed amused, inclined to regard the whole incident as an instructive study in human folly. 'So, how long has Ross been borrowing money against his paintings? He's about as savvy as *Ginger and Pickles* when it comes to money, if he's run through everything he owns. He's had millions!'

The mention of *Ginger and Pickles* halted the conversation as though two picaresque strangers had entered the room. Max struggled to get his thoughts back on track.

'So now the paintings belong to an off-shore trust,' he continued irritably, 'and this guy Marc Bastion is touting them round Mayfair! What he and his mates want, is to force us to step in and buy the paintings at gold-plated prices to protect the value of our stock.'

Peter was still ruefully amused, like one observing someone caught in a clever trap. 'I wonder what the default level was. Knowing Ross, there will be plenty of headroom for them to make a profit.'

Max nodded. 'Yeah, he's fallen for a racket and now we're the patsy!'

This was all startling news to Corey. He felt like a child in a room of adults discussing the sort of thing adults only talk about behind closed doors. Vaguely he wondered about collateral damage: was this the first tremor in the collapse of the house of Collarii? 'Surely, he said, 'Edward couldn't have persuaded Ross!'

'Edward's always been the family money man. Money talks if you don't have any,' observed Max bitterly.

'Don't touch the paintings, Max,' urged his brother. 'Let them sell them off at distressed prices. The market will rebound before long.'

Max wasn't having it. 'That's contrary to everything father taught us. We're here to ensure an orderly market!'

That troubled Peter and he didn't conceal it. 'Yes, and that's why we bought one of the Posts auctioned at Sotheby's last week. But what if this downturn is serious? We haven't the resources to keep on buying Posts.'

Here was a possibility that hadn't occurred to Corey. He was further astonished. '*You bought* one of Gustave's paintings from last week's auction? Which one?'

'The one about to fail to meet its reserve,' said Peter dryly. 'We felt we had to step in. After all, *we are here to ensure an orderly market!*'

Max put his hand to his head as though struck by a sudden pain. 'All right, maybe we don't buy them. We'll see what Erik says. What do we do about Ross?'

'Kick his arse,' said Peter with sardonic relish.

Max closed his eyes, deep in thought. 'One of us has to go and talk to him. We need to hear his side of the story. What d'you say, Peter?'

'I'll go,' said Corey.

The two brothers looked at him in surprise.

'It isn't really something for you,' said Peter.

Max agreed. 'No, we can't expect you to deal with this.'

'I think it's just up my street.' It was a rash offer, but Corey relished the thought that while the loss of the paintings was fresh, Ross might be vulnerable and let slip something of interest about paintings that had escaped his *catalogue raisonné*. 'What if you're right, Max, about him trying to sell *Berlin Wall Lament No.1*? What if the situation he's got himself into explains its sudden appearance now? He might have known for some time that he's had all the money out of this equity release thing. No, I think I should go and see him. I saw him Friday; I should see him now. It'll give me a certain pleasure to have the boot somewhat on the other foot.'

Max looked at his brother. 'Well, Corey, we were hoping you might go and see this Bastion character; get a look at the paintings he's trying to sell; confirm they're Ross's. It would be good if we had an intermediary for that... but Peter or I ought to deal with Ross.'

'We'd treat Bastion as a new consultancy,' offered Peter.

'I'll do both. They're connected, so why not both?'

Max looked at his brother again, who remained expressionless. 'Okay, if you're happy to...'

In this way it was settled. The brothers shared a politician's preference for dealing with things at arm's length and saw little downside in sending Corey as an emissary in the first instance. For his part, Corey had intended to tell them that it was likely Ross had taken *Composition with Movie Magazines IV, 1976* from Gustave's studio in Majorca. He now drew back from the idea. If he was going to see Ross, he wanted to confront him with everything he knew before sharing his suspicions with anyone.

FORTY

Ross was prowling the pavement like a caged animal; one of those animals that think they can fight anything. In truth, the effect was more pugilistic reef fish trying to catch prawns with a barracuda in the offing than a big carnivore prowling the savannah. He was perspiring and in a rage. He was thinking he needed to make some kind of physical impression on the people who, for whatever the reason, held sway over his existence. As he prowled, the Uber ride he had called drew up. He climbed in, but as it was about to move off a black cab came alongside, blocking the way. As if by magic, Corey Templeton appeared at the front passenger's window.

'Are you coming or going?' he enquired.

'Going!' roared Ross, flicking him into oblivion.

'Not without me.' Corey yanked open the door and climbed in beside the bemused driver. He gave the driver an instruction that sounded like 'drive around as long as I say', and then spoke to Ross as though in private. 'How are things going, Ross?' It was fake solicitousness.

Ross pulled the euros Corey had given him from his breast pocket and wagged the envelope at him. 'Who put up the money for the Omega? God knows, it wasn't my kind of thing. It was for some midwit ponce from Surbiton with two brats and a Range Rover, for Christ's sake! Her lousy boyfriend broke my bowl!'

Corey looked at him placidly. 'He did. So what? You've been paid for that. It's in the two thousand. Remember?'

Ross looked at him as though he was purposely missing his point. 'Recompense, damages, a token of respect and an apology! How about that for starters? Mind you, that Fishy knows how to make a mean booby trap out of a table lamp. He and I are going into business together, you watch if we don't.'

"He was upset. Give him a break. He was being warned off.'

'If you must know, Waves is *my* little blondie.'

'*Jesus, not you too!* That watch was worth nine thousand pounds, you know.' He hoped he was rubbing salt in a fresh wound. 'Anyway, I thought you made money dealing drugs for your druggie, rich-kid friends.'

'That's entertainment value only.' Ross dismissed the idea with another flick of his fingers. 'The big time is for homicidal black teenagers only.' He raised his chin as though he was about to say something further, but thought better of it.

Corey had a feeling he'd better explain why he was there, before things turned violent. 'I suppose you'll have to retrench. I hear you no longer have a single work by your father, not a single one. Somebody called Marc Bastion is flogging them round Mayfair.'

'What in the name of shite are you talking about?' Ross roared, aiming the blast right in Corey's face. He gave a hideous groan and clapped his hands over his ears. *'Don't even mention this!* That bastard Eddie's screwed me. I'm going to get his fingers in a vice and turn and turn until they're mush! I've been fucking ripped off!'

Corey shot a look at the driver and saw he was shrinkingly not present, fearful of what kind of passengers he had picked up.

'The Collariis know they're yours. They're concerned.'

'*Oh, yes?*' Ross said it with fierce scepticism.

Corey's intuition told him the moment was ripe to see if Ross knew anything about *Berlin Wall Lament No.1*. 'Did your father ever do a painting about the Berlin Wall?'

'No,' sneered Ross. 'What does that even *mean?*'

'You know what it means. *Do you own it?*' He held up his mobile and showed him the painting.

Ross was staring out of the window, his chin resting on the back of his hand and a sulky look on his face. 'All right, yes, that's the Berlin Wall, isn't it? No, of course, I don't own it. If you want it you need to get on to fucking Edward. Go tell the Collarii brothers!'

'Meaning?'

'Yeah, well, Edward gets what he deserves since he's screwed me.' He grimaced and shut his eyes tight as an aid to his recall.

'What the fuck can I say? When Ruthie pissed off to Devon, Quentin and me didn't want to go. We went anyway, but we wanted to be in London. *I was sixteen, for Christ's sake!* So, we ran away. Quentin and me, we came back to London, stayed with father. Because Ruthie had pissed off, Clarissa and he sort of got back together for a while. He was trying to get a painting back from her. Called it "the Berlin Wall painting", said it was one of a pair and they were important to him. I overheard them arguing about it more than once. She said there was nothing she could do; she didn't have it any longer.'

Corey couldn't credit what he was hearing. 'So, your father had one? This one?' He waved his mobile in front of Ross's face.

'I don't know. I never saw it, did I?'

'Any idea where it is now?'

'No.'

'And who had the one he thought Clarissa had?'

'She didn't say, but you can bet if Clarissa didn't have it, Edward did. He was always around, making deals, worming his way in. He looks harmless, but *don't be deceived!*'

'What about the painting in the cupboard in your bedroom? That should be in Majorca, shouldn't it?'

'Mayonnaise,' said Ross.

'*Mayonnaise?* What's that?' said Corey.

'That's what I used to say at school if someone was trying to bully me. It always worked.' He continued to stare out of the window.

Corey laughed scornfully. 'That's rich: *you bullied at school!*'

'It's a fucking copy, that's all,' said Ross in a sullen voice. He was silent for a while. Corey got the Uber driver back on track towards central London. When they reached Clapham High Street Ross said, 'I'm going to kill someone shortly.' The non-specific death threat indicated his spirit had started to revive. 'First I'm going to harm that duplicitous ponce Edward and his poncy wife. And then I'm going to get my paintings back off this Bastion. If he's flogging them round Mayfair, I'll find out where he's keeping them.'

'No,' decided Corey, feeling suddenly charitable, 'I'll let you know where they are; then you can try getting them back, if you want.'

He parted with Ross on the Fulham Road. As he climbed out of the car, Ross was insistent. 'You can bet it's Edward. Tell the Collariis.'

Forty minutes later, while exiting Green Park tube station, Corey's mobile rang. It was Max. He was not disposed to be long-winded.

'Any news?'

'No, no news.'

'There's another person you need to consult about nineteen eighty-two: Dermot O'Flynn. Ever heard of him?'

'Yes, of course.'

'Did you know he's publishing a book of his poems and Campbell Carter's written the introduction?'

'Yes, I did.' Not for the first time, Corey was unnerved by how well-informed Max was. He wondered how long it would be before Max learnt he'd already spoken to Ross.

'So much for Campbell Carter wanting to get on with the second volume of the Post biography! Going off on these kind of tangents is annoying! It seems strange to me... and to Peter! According to Peter, O'Flynn was a great friend of Gustave's when Gustave was in Berlin. I asked Angela to go through the gallery records and apparently my father paid O'Flynn three thousand pounds in nineteen eighty-two. It had something to do with Gustave's Venice exhibition.'

'Yes, he wrote a two-page introduction to the catalogue.'

'Really?' He thought about that a bit. 'Even today, three thousand pounds would be generous for a couple of pages of scribble, never mind then! Look into it, will you? I want to know why Campbell Carter's promoting O'Flynn.'

Corey wandered into Green Park. So, in nineteen eighty-two there was a substantial financial element to the relationship between Gustave and O'Flynn. He agreed with Max's estimate that three thousand pounds was an excessive amount of money for what he'd written. What other assistance had O'Flynn provided? Could it be, he wondered, that he had helped curate the exhibition in Venice? Or had his services been more those of a boon companion in a time of difficulties?

FORTY-ONE

It was four when Corey arrived back at the Collarii Building. He was told Waverley had been looking for him all day. It was said with an air of disapproval, as if he had behaved negligently towards her. He ignored the implication that not knowing where he was had troubled Waverley, and didn't call her. After ten minutes sitting alone in the archive room, he changed his mind. There was no reply, but no more than thirty seconds after he'd rung off she called him back.

'I'm in the basement,' he said curtly.

Waverley arrived. He had dreaded this moment of seeing her; he had convinced himself that everything would be different. It wasn't.

'I thought I'd lost you,' she said, slightly breathless.

He laughed, his thought exactly. 'What's up?'

She shook her head as though it was obvious what was up. 'Why didn't you come? What are we going to do? You haven't told me anything! Did you go to Devon? What did Ross say? *Where's the bloody Omega?*'

The latter question jolted him; he'd forgotten about the Omega. He reached into the inside pocket of his jacket and brought it out like a prize catch in an angling contest.

'Thank you; that's wonderful,' she said with relief.

'How's Fishman getting it back?'

'He's not. It's going to the same place as the others: Dover Street.'

She perched on a stool, blocking his way out. He wondered whether it was intentional. He eyed her but held his tongue as she pocketed the Omega. He didn't care to make conversation; that he left to her.

She held up a sheet of paper. 'Do you want to know about Dermot O'Flynn... *or not?*'

'Yes. What d'you have?'

'Poet, IRA sympathiser. Proselytised for them, actually. Nineteen seventies: highly successful tours reading his nationalist poems to Irish-American sympathisers. Suspected of raising money for weapons. Internationalist, with connections to various left-wing, revolutionary groups in Germany and elsewhere. Wrote a major poem about the Munich Olympics massacre that got him banned in Israel. Knew Dolours Price. Became disenchanted with the Good Friday Agreement, and particularly with Gerry Adams. Disappeared for a while; fallow period, eschewed politics. Wrote a poem entitled "Gerry Adams, From a Land of Monsters Came" when Adams's abusive family background became public knowledge. Last twenty-five years he reinvented himself as a poet of the Irish landscape –' she checked with the sheet of paper she was holding – '"as a determinant of its cultural soul".'

Corey was cutting. 'Conventional bloody arc from radical internationalist to rural conservative, then?'

Waverley winced as though his response was a slap in the face.

'Sorry,' he said. 'I've got things on my mind. They're going a bit crazy.'

'Tell me about Ross. What happened?'

He did his best to shake off his mood. He wasn't going to tell her he'd just come from seeing Ross, just as he hadn't told Max. Obstinately, he was determined to keep what he knew to himself while he mulled things over. Instead, he described Friday's meeting with Ross in the coffee shop, omitting the financial transaction Max had insisted upon. He knew if she saw Ross he would brag about having been paid to return the Omega. It was another dishonesty he was sliding into and he realised he'd have to tell her eventually, but now was not the time. He wanted to ask her why Max had rolled up in a big Audi and intervened between her and Fishman in the way he had, but he couldn't bring himself to do that either. Instead, he told her about finding *Composition with Movie Magazines IV, 1975*. She was suitably indignant. She urged him to make him return it.

Corey shrugged.

'Anyway,' she said stubbornly, 'he wants to see me. He's asked me to go to his studio, so I think I'll go.'

Corey knew she was trying to provoke him. He cradled his head in his open hand. 'I don't think you should go. I…' For a moment he was tempted to try dissuading her by telling her about Ross's equity-release scheme debacle.

'If he's stolen a painting from his father's studio in Majorca,' she reasoned, 'isn't it a good bet he's got hold of the Berlin Wall painting as well? Maybe the same way? He should be made to give them both back. Incidentally, did you give him my mobile number? I didn't, so somebody did.'

'Oh… I did.' Corey looked crestfallen and shifty. 'He asked me for it.'

'You did, huh? So maybe you think I'm a fallen woman and you're not going to protect me from him? Is that it? It's okay now if I get naked and pose for him, is it?'

'No, of course not. I made a mistake.'

She looked at him severely. 'I don't actually believe you, Corey. Giving him my number wasn't the act of a gentleman, certainly not a disinterested gentleman.'

Corey was in a bind. He could see that they were at cross-purposes, but he was afraid his protestations would make it clear to her how abjectly he was under her spell. He cast about for a way to change the direction of their conversation.

'Can I show you something?'

She waited while he found the volume of the Post *catalogue raisonné* for eighty-two.

'Ruthie put me on to this.' He leafed through the pages of illustrations until he came to the end of the paintings produced in Berlin. He turned the page and tapped his finger on the next picture.

She leant in to look, very close, tantalisingly close.

'I was doing some research in the daybooks last week and didn't realise… What's striking, once you think about it, is the difference between Berlin and the rest of the year. Look at the date of this painting. It's January, nineteen eighty-three. There's nothing from June to December! Ruthie told me Gustave was having trouble doing anything in the studio. Until she said it, the real significance of what happened hadn't registered. This gap isn't a record-keeping blip, he actually went six months without producing a single painting!' He leafed on through the volume. It was clear that in the New Year, Gustave had resumed work with his usual vigour. The first paintings were largely versions of compositional inventions from his time in Berlin. They conformed to something familiar in Gustave's work procedures, and which Campbell Carter had examined in some detail in volume one of his Post biography: one step back, two steps forwards. The illustrations showed nothing that resembled *Berlin Wall Lament No.1* until the second half of the year, when the landscapes that Ruthie had drawn his attention to began to appear.

'A break of six months! Don't you think it points to something major disrupting his peace of mind? He couldn't work!'

She nodded.

'And when he restarted, he spent several months trying to break the mould. *And* I found something else.' He went and fetched the third daybook for eighty-two and turned to the November entry about the studio furniture and materials sent to Majorca. There, appended to the end, were the words "Studies to be framed: 22?"

'The way it's written it's hard to know...' she observed, hesitantly.

'It is,' he agreed. 'It's difficult to tell whether the studies are part of what was sent to Majorca, or a separate instruction.'

She was unclear where his thoughts were taking him.

'According to the *catalogue raisonné*, Gustave had six months when he produced nothing, yet this entry seems to suggest that's not so.' He took out his copy of Dermot O'Flynn's *Barriers to Barricades* and showed her Gustave's epigraph in the front: "The Truth of my life lies always in my work." It had been on his mind. 'What manner of truth might those twenty-two studies reveal?'

Waverley looked at him, still puzzled. 'Meaning what? Where's all this leading you?'

There was only one answer to that. The stolen painting in Ross's possession, the twenty-two studies, both pointed to one destination: Majorca and Villa Besugo, future home of the Gustave Post Museum and Study Centre.

Corey paced the room. 'First the Berlin Wall paintings escaped my cataloguing, now these studies. There's a chance the studies are there. I want to see if they can be found; see if they reveal anything about Ingrid Steinmann.'

'So, what are you proposing?' she asked as though he were being purposefully obtuse.

'Don't go and see Ross. Keep away from him.' It was half advice, half plea. 'Let's go to Villa Besugo instead.'

Villa Besugo had been under lock and key since Gustave's death – four years in November – the settlement of his estate still inching towards resolution. In the meantime, the property waited, held in a kind of dowdy suspension, caught between past and future purposes.

FORTY-TWO

Dermot O'Flynn was smaller and frailer than he looked in his photograph; more withered than rugged. There was a good crowd. Corey was not surprised to see Campbell Carter in attendance. Campbell saw him and made a little grimace of salutation. Room had been cleared for the reading but there were not enough chairs, so people were sitting or standing wherever they could find space, making a spontaneous arena around the informal stage where the seated O'Flynn was due to read. As the starting time neared and a hush settled over the audience, Campbell lumbered forward and made a short speech of introduction, paraphrased some of the themes of his introduction to O'Flynn's book. *Radical… poetic innovation… lyrical… warp and weft… nationalist sympathies… pantheist*. A couple of employees from the publisher stood in the background, whispering and goosing one another.

O'Flynn's performance was less fun than the surrounding fuss. He read, in a reedy monotone, mellifluous phrases that spoke to the Irish diaspora of hearth, home and heath. When it was over, one or two young women sitting on the floor who had spent the entire reading hugging their knees, were delicately in tears. Less susceptible, Corey had occupied the time trying to see through O'Flynn to Gustave Post, imagining O'Flynn as a medium, a portal to the hereafter. However hard he tried, Gustave would not materialise, even when the poems were confabulations of remembered landscapes and the heroic struggle of the artist. As the reading finished, quite a crowd moved forward with their pre-bought books. There was some ineffectual herding by the two representatives of the publisher as they tried to form those who wanted O'Flynn's signature into a line, pointing at the desk where he was about to be seated. While the signing was proceeding, Corey went over to talk to Campbell.

'Evening, Corey.' Campbell was clearly in a better mood than when they had last spoken. 'I'm surprised this is your kind of thing.'

'I didn't realise poetry was your territory either, Campbell, but I have to admit you've done a good job.' Corey was determined to be complimentary. 'As I told you, I hadn't registered O'Flynn and Gustave were such kindred spirits until I read your essay. It does make a lot of sense, though.'

'I'm not Irish myself, but I admire the lyrical sensibility. I've had some amazing pastoral experiences on the Shannon…'

Culinary, more like, thought Corey uncharitably. 'I have some questions for Mr O'Flynn about Berlin and the Venice Biennale. Do you realise how much the gallery paid him that year? I was wondering what he did for it. Oh, and I want to ask him about *Berlin Wall Lament No.1*.'

Even that didn't dent Campbell's good humour. Thirty-five book signings later, when O'Flynn rose uncertainly to his feet, Corey was still engaging him in flattering small talk.

'Ah!' noted Campbell. 'The oracle needs his whiskey… before I tuck him up in bed. There's a pub out the back. Won't you join us?'

Corey was rather slow in making his way out through the Jermyn Street exit. When he reached the pub there was a summer evening's crush on the pavement but no sign of O'Flynn or Campbell. Wherever they'd gone, it certainly wasn't the Red Lion.

'Damn! Where the hell are they?'

He went back into Waterstone's and found the two employees of O'Flynn's publisher clearing chairs.

'Weren't you looking after Mr O'Flynn?' Corey asked them.

'Ooh, no, Mr Carter's been very solicitous of Mr O'Flynn's care,' said the more fey of the two. 'Wanted to do it personally.'

'Where's Mr O'Flynn staying? Do you know?'

'Mr Carter's taken him to Victoria for the Gatwick Express. He's staying at a hotel at the airport tonight. Early flight back in the morning.'

Corey was flabbergasted. 'What, back to Ireland?'

'Ooh no, not Ireland, *Majorca*.'

Corey was bewildered. He wondered what was going on. Had Campbell purposefully deceived him to keep him away from O'Flynn? The near certainty he'd been duped infuriated him. It was the usual suspicion rekindled: did Campbell have, in O'Flynn, a witness of what had happened in Berlin... to Ingrid and her paintings? And what part might O'Flynn have played in their disappearance to have been paid so much by Gustave's gallery? Here was another reason to go to Majorca!

FORTY-THREE

The Collarii brothers weren't about to talk to Marc Bastion; he was *persona non grata*. Having agreed to go instead, Corey was presented by Max with a Picasso Madoura jug of an owl.

'A token of our appreciation I know you'll like.'

Corey was getting a taste for intrigue. Marc Bastion was a smart guy with a two-day growth of beard that never grew any longer. He had a sharp suit and a narrow, striped tie from Asprey. Corey decided he wasn't very impressed. He thought Bastion looked like the kind of guy whose idea of fun was collecting second-hand Omegas. They talked. They were on different planets. Bastion didn't know a Post from a Piper or a Pistachio nut. He admitted as much: 'Art's not my thing. Post's blue chip, but you have to know when to sell, even with blue chip investments.'

Corey was even less impressed. 'Are you sure they're yours?'

'Of course. The contract stipulates a mutually agreed expert who says they're strictly comparable to the ones sold last week: same general size, same period.'

Corey shrugged. He wasn't going to argue about the relative value of Ross's collection of his father's paintings but he did ask by what process a mutually agreed expert had been appointed. '"Elected by members of the consortium"? That's a novel understanding of mutually agreed,' he decided. 'Ross Post might contest your expert's competence. In any case, you've missed the boat. The vested interests have been buying in. It's the only way you can protect yourself in the short-run.'

Bastion took fright at that. 'Turbulence?'

'Turbulence. Brexit. There's a group of museums in Germany and Switzerland unloading Posts. And the Collariis won't buy from you. You'd be better holding off until the pound turns. Where are they?'

'Under the stairs.'

Corey smiled indulgently at the witticism, then decided there might be an element of truth in what he'd said. 'Can I see them?'

'I sent photographs.'

'Not the same.'

'Maybe... another time.'

He decided that Bastion probably had *Falling Woman,* the pick of the bunch, somewhere in the building to show prospective buyers, but the rest were elsewhere.

'The foundation has a store: temperature, humidity, everything controlled. We'll look after them for you, if you like...'

Bastion rubbed his chin and smiled as though he knew he was being pushed about.

'...*And* verify they're genuine,' Corey continued smoothly. 'Provenance: it's like the lineage of a good racehorse.'

'Bullshit! D'you know what the loan-to-value is?'

'No, tell me.'

'Eighty per cent. That means we've a twenty per cent margin to play with before we lose a penny.'

'All I'm saying is that the private sale of big-ticket artists is a reputational business. Confidence is everything. The Collarii brothers won't even talk to you, but I can act for you... with them.'

'Ha, ha!' squirmed Bastion in his leather chair. 'I see: you have your principals, I have mine. I'm quite open to putting what you've said to mine. They're long-term investors but they might be interested. On the other hand, blah, blah, *blah*!'

They left it at that. Corey came out onto Curzon Street feeling like a tough guy for once. He was right about *Falling Woman* being in the building. Bastion had weakened and shown him it. What's more, he'd wheedled out of Bastion the location of the rest. Corey knew exactly what kind of place it was: a hi-tech, secure warehouse built with the aid of an EU rural business grant in the abandoned farmyard of a smallholding merged into the estate of a big shot private equity friend who liked to dabble in modern art and enjoyed having West End galleries as clients for his storage.

Yet again, he congratulated himself, he'd put in a shift for the Collarii brothers. He was pleased with the Picasso owl and, for once, felt sufficiently recompensed. He thought of Waverley as he skirted Berkeley Square. For a while it seemed it might be her ahead of him, but when he caught up with the young woman, she didn't even look vaguely like her.

A chance meeting would have been nice. He'd been shutting her out since the scene with Fishman and Max in Ross's studio. Was it that she had disappointed him in some way? How? After all, he had nothing beyond a suspicion to go on, and little enough evidence to suggest anything felt by Max had been reciprocated. But he had a feeling of betrayal and he knew he had been paying her back by keeping her at arm's length. It struck him now as churlishness prompted by thwarted ardour, the comical aspect being that no ardour had ever been expressed. He supposed he would come round, but maybe something magical in his feelings for her had been destroyed by the unwarranted intrusion of Max into their affairs. He couldn't forget the look on Max's face. He shook his head as if it were possible to shake the memory out of his ears.

As he entered Grosvenor Street, his thoughts returned to his interview with Bastion. Ever more delicate tasks seemed to be accumulating around the issue of who was trying to sell *Berlin Wall Lament No.1*. He readily acknowledged that, having volunteered to act as an emissary, the extent of his involvement was of his own making, but if Max was having Waverley, he wanted to be better paid all round, not just a separate consultancy for negotiating with Bastion. Immediately, he felt a prick of shame. He knew it was unworthy of him; in his mind he'd turned Waverley into a bartering chip. Still, when he reached the Collarii Building, he felt inclined, as a point of principle, to make his feelings on his financial recompense known to Max, but Angela wouldn't cooperate.

'His diary's full. I've already got you down to meet him tomorrow.'

'No, matter,' said Corey faintly. As he left, he looked back and saw Angela three quarters from the back and suddenly it struck him that it was her he had seen in the Audi, and she who had raised the anti-paparazzi blinds to conceal her presence. Face on, there was no similarity, but it was the curve of her neck and the way the second curve of her blond hair rested behind her ear that had done it. Why, he wondered, would she be there, unless... unless there was some unspoken dimension to her relationship with Max? Could it be...? No, his imagination was creating some kind of compulsive Lothario of Max, and surely Angela was far too upright and business-like to be caught having an affair with her boss? But it set a small alert; it was something to be wary of...

In a small act of rebellion, he sent Ross a text: "*Falling Woman* in Curzon Street. The rest in a storage facility in Norfolk. Can give you the addresses if interested."

FORTY-FOUR

Max took Corey's report of his meeting with Bastion without much comment. In truth, there wasn't much to comment on, apart from his confirmation that the paintings Bastion was selling were Ross's. What Corey had experienced as a bravura diplomatic performance now seemed unnecessarily aggressive in a way of which he knew Max would not approve. Max regarded his encounter with Ross as being of much greater significance. The moment was right for Corey to unburden himself. He spoke into a studied silence. Max was already on his feet, pacing.

'Ross has broken ranks. He's telling tales on Edward... now that Edward's landed him in a mess.'

'Oh?' Max's look was penetrating 'The equity release thing? Go on.'

'He denies having *Berlin Wall Lament No.1*. But he admits he overheard Clarissa and Gustave discussing both Berlin Wall paintings. This was when they got back together in the late nineties... when Ruthie left Gustave and went off to Devon.'

Max looked incredulous. 'They got back together? I didn't know that.'

'I don't think it was much of a thing, but they did, so Ross says... before Gustave hooked up with Neema. Apparently, they each had one of the paintings after Ingrid disappeared. Gustave wanted Clarissa's back. Ross pretty much said that she couldn't give it back because she'd already given it to Edward.'

'Edward!' Max nodded grimly, as though Corey's news was another assault on his equanimity. 'Good God, I'm shocked! I thought he was... If that's the case, I'm going to have to put it to him directly. What about the other painting, the one Gustave already had? Does it still exist?'

'I don't know. Maybe Gustave destroyed it. Maybe he destroyed it before he left Berlin and he wanted the other one back from Clarissa for the same reason.'

Max looked disappointed, 'Otherwise we'd have found it by now, I suppose.'

'Yes, it seems likely. There's something else: Dermot O'Flynn.'

'Dear Jesus, not more! Did you find out what the hell the money was for?'

'Haven't been able to speak to him. Did you know he has a house on Majorca?'

'*No!* What, near Gustave's place?'

'Seems so.'

Max looked troubled, but the more he thought about it the more his brow cleared. 'Well, I suppose lots do… Artists spending time on Majorca, I mean.'

'He was here doing a reading and I wanted to ask him what he knew about what went on in Berlin, but Campbell Carter kept him away from me. Very sly, it was. Shipped him off without giving me a chance. Straight back to Gatwick for the early plane to Majorca. I'm beginning to think Campbell knows about Ingrid Steinmann. What's more, he has some big dirty secret about Gustave that he wants to keep as a scoop for his next volume of the Post biography… and O'Flynn is his source! What if it's something really ugly? You wouldn't want that, would you?'

Max's pacing had taken on an agitated edge. 'No, not really…'

'What if it was something to do with Ingrid Steinmann, some scandal?'

'God knows! Could it damage Gustave's investment status? He's already seen as a man who didn't live by the rules, so tales of bad behaviour shouldn't make that much difference to us… unless it's really distasteful. Not to say we wouldn't want to be prepared. Nothing worse than being caught on the hop. If Campbell's got something I'd like to know.'

'So, I'm thinking I should go to Majorca. There are several things on my mind. I'm feeling a bit like an archaeologist tinkering about on the edge of something major. I want to chase down O'Flynn and ask him what he knows about Gustave's time in Berlin.

He was something of an agitator and an activist in those days; no saying what he might have been mixed up in. Then there's the money the gallery paid him. I'd like to ask him what that was for. I also think things at Villa Besugo might not be to your liking. Ross is denying it, but I'm pretty sure he's managed to wangle a painting out of there, maybe more. I don't know when, but I've a suspicion it's since Gustave's death.' Corey took out his mobile and found the photograph he had taken of the painting in Ross's cupboard.

Max looked at it and pulled a face, as if he wasn't sure he wanted to be convinced. 'I don't know; maybe it wasn't part of the deal with those hedge-fund boys.'

'No, I've checked, and the date's wrong. It's never belonged to him; it should be in Majorca, although Ross claims it's a copy.'

'Javier runs a tight ship; I've every confidence in him.'

'Do you want the details?'

Max gave Corey a look that said his mind was in danger of being cluttered up with too many explanations. He made a gesture of assent, but with extreme reluctance. 'Corey, I want this sorted! I'll warn Javier you're coming. I assume you'll go by yourself.'

Corey saw that Max had it in mind that Waverley should remain in London. Something in him baulked at the idea. It was too much. A sudden anger flushed through his brain, a cold, deliberate anger that he wasn't about to reveal. 'I don't need Waverley any more. I think that stage of what you asked me to do is over, don't you? Will you be putting her back to work in the gallery?'

This was not what Max was expecting. His sense of discomfort was palpable; a set of circumstances to his liking was in danger of being unsettled. He rubbed his forefinger back and forth across his lips, obscuring his mouth. To Corey it was a sure sign that he was deliberating.

Finally, he spoke. 'I was wondering what we're going to do with her when all this is over. Any ideas? She has been a help, hasn't she?'

Corey was already regretting his outburst. He felt uncomfortable and a little guilty; they were parlaying unscrupulously over a young woman's future. 'I don't know what the future holds for her. She's perfection now.' He said this mournfully, as though it was understood that time could only eat away at that perfection. 'She's proposed nearly every step forward in this investigation. I think you should give her a big pot of money and tell her to go away and use it.'

'Good grief! Doing what?'

'Dealing in art; she'd be extraordinary.'

Max laughed.

'Otherwise she'll get bored and fall back into her old ways with Fishman, or someone like him.'

Max, Corey could see, was determined to treat the subject of their conversation as a matter of barely any significance. He was good at containing his feelings, good at riding out the kind of emotional impulses by which less savvy operators gave themselves away. Did any part of the discomfort he had experienced when Corey first broached the subject of Waverley's future remain? Corey didn't think so. Equilibrium restored, Max was once more manoeuvring pieces in a game of personal gratification.

'After all, Corey, I think you should take Waverley with you.' He raised a finger as if to stress the irrevocable nature of his change of mind. 'While she's out there, I'll consult. Peter and Erik might have some ideas. Best if she's out of the way. As a human resources issue it deserves some serious consideration, don't you think?'

There was a pause; they were equally baffled by one another. Corey felt a faint erotic frisson, as if he were stealing Waverley's sexual favours from under Max's nose.

Later in the afternoon, Peter caught up with him on the back stairs. Since Peter considered the Post family to be Max's business, he was, as usual, the amused, quizzical bystander.

'I'm wondering whether there might be some studies by Gustave from the second half of nineteen eighty-two hidden somewhere at the villa,' Corey explained. 'There's a promising entry in the daybook. It's not entirely clear, but it does seem possible some went there. If they did, we certainly haven't found them yet. They might be in the back of a cupboard or mixed up with all that paper in his drawing studio. You never know.'

Peter might not deal directly with the Post inheritance, but he knew only too well that there was a wealth of half-finished and abandoned paintings and preliminary studies at Villa Besugo. They had not been considered worth itemising individually when the inventory of the villa's contents was being drawn up.

'Fair enough,' he decided, 'but just a tip, Corey. Bring things to a close. I don't like the Post atmospherics. Know what I mean?'

Peter made to continue on his way up to the second floor, but Corey detained him with a question.

'By the way, what is *Ginger and Pickles*?'

'Ah, *Ginger and Pickles*! Ginger is a tomcat, Pickles a terrier. They run a shop. They want to eat their customers – mice and rabbits – but they refrain for the sake of the business. Misguidedly, they also extend unlimited credit to everyone, so gradually they go bankrupt. Beatrix Potter: I read her to my girls at night. I suppose the moral is that Ginger and Pickles were useless with money. They should have eaten the customers, instead of giving them credit. The shop wouldn't have lasted long but at least that way it would have given them some gratification.'

Corey had one more idea, one more task to attend to before he left for Majorca. At the end of the day he packed a copy of Campbell Carter's biography in his briefcase and took the tube to Caledonian Road. Ten minutes later he was ringing the bell to Alice Shawcross's door. For a moment she didn't remember him, but then she was welcoming. 'That lovely young thing you came with. Such charm. Not quite French; something English that goes down well with balletomanes.' They both laughed at the idea.

Over a diminutive glass of amontillado, Corey took out the Gustave Post biography. He opened it so she could see the portrait photograph on the back flap of the dust cover. 'You remember the man who came to ask you about Ingrid Steinmann some years ago? Is this him, do you think?'

She took the book from him so she could examine the photograph more closely. 'Yes, I think it is. I remember that beard. Yes, I'm sure of it. Who is he?'

'His name's Campbell Carter. He's the author. Haven't you seen this book?'

'No, I can't say I have. Is it any good? I'm not a great reader, you know, but I would be interested in reading this.'

'Well,' decided Corey pleasantly, 'please, do keep it. I'm certain you'll enjoy it.'

As he departed, Corey had one more question for her. 'Do you remember someone called Dermot O'Flynn in Berlin?'

'Dermot…? Sounds familiar, but there were a lot of flies buzzing around Gustave.'

FORTY-FIVE

Wednesday. South terminal, Gatwick. The early flight to Majorca. Corey was waiting for Waverley. The giddy sense of intoxication she had inspired in the early days of their working partnership had turned to something more realistic: he was concerned she would arrive late and make them miss their flight.

But no, there was still plenty of time remaining when she arrived. He greeted her soberly. She ducked her head. They went up to the BA club lounge. She had a package under her arm. When he sat down with a bowl of cereal and saw it leaning against the back of the sofa opposite him, he felt a thrill of alarm. He knew things had been going too smoothly. Waverley was at the counter getting something to eat. He waited for her return, eyeing the parcel as one might a suspected bomb.

'Well? Tell me!' he said, indicating the parcel, oblivious to the fact that she was in hyperactive, confessional mode. Later, he was to wonder whether her response was a reaction to how distant he had become.

'He took me to Browns and we had S-E-X!' She said with lowered chin, knowing it was a bad thing, although she glowed as she spoke.

It struck him that by rights she should be anguished, and he was scandalised that she wasn't.

'Not at the Westbury Mayfair, then?' he said dryly.

'No, Browns,' she insisted. 'It was great, I'm not on the pill and he's had a vasectomy!' She said this with such enthusiasm it felt wrong not to feel pleased for her. Corey decided he'd better recalibrate. This wasn't the torment he was expecting, at least not when he was with her. He should put a brave face on it. After all, it had taken Max to release her from the pernicious hold of Fishman.

'It's crazy, I know,' she said, suddenly sobering. 'Don't ask me about the deception and betrayal, that's his share.'

'You're a beautiful object, Waverley; that's what beguiles him, but you're not a fabulous sculpture; he can't own you like a Rodin.'

'I can't help being what I am; I didn't ask for it.'

Corey gave a bitter laugh like a cough. 'But you've grown to relish what it does to men, haven't you?'

'I don't think about it. With Max, it was different. I felt...' She couldn't find the expressive means she needed and spread her hands in a gesture of supplication. 'I yielded, passively, permissively, perversely...' She said the words like a catechism. 'And then he released me. I'm sorry, it was marvellous, like a drug.' She put her hand up to her face, her fingers sliding into her hair, and closed her eyes.

He laughed. 'Surely you didn't *yield*!'

Slowly her head tilted back, as though she were surrendering to vertigo. All expression drained from her face; Corey had never seen it so stilled. She arced towards the horizontal, the line of her throat exposed, her expression beatific. It was like her swoon in Cannes, but self-imposed. Suddenly he was alarmed she might lose her balance and slip to the floor amidst a clatter of cutlery and crockery. He half rose from his seat to prevent her falling, but with a sudden jolt she pulled herself upright, her face disappearing beneath the cascade of her hair. He was shocked. Here was evidence of the enormity of what had happened; a kind of unconscious portrayal of her submission. As with all such insights, it was oblique, though with Waverley, propriety's mask was pierced. Had that not been a moment of... what? Abandonment? The doxy! Yet again her loveliness swept all thoughts of disapproval aside. What lay between them might well be a glancing blow, but there was no doubting its intensity. Had she taken possession of Max? If she had, what must be going through his mind? Corey wanted to know what Max was thinking; he saw him as the one who was in jeopardy, but Waverley seemed to have no psychological insights; or if she did, she wasn't saying.

'Why are you telling me this?' There was an edge of brusqueness to his demand.

'I needed to confess.'

'Christ!' he said, with a sudden sense of foreboding. 'Where will it end?'

She laughed defiantly.

'*Christ!*' was all Corey could say. Christ, Max's wife and four children! Christ, Max's brothers! The stability of the Collarii Foundation! Christ! Waverley's future, her friends! *Christ!*

She saw his despondency and it did not tally with her mood. 'Come on, Corey, I'm a bad lot; you've always known that. That's why you wanted me on your team.'

'What *is* that?' he demanded, jabbing a finger in the direction of the package.

She gave him a supercilious look. You know *very well* what it is.'

'Oh? *Do I?*'

'Well, it's obvious, isn't it? Do we even need to discuss it?'

'I take it you don't want to.'

'No, I don't.' She picked up a copy of *The Times* and hid behind it.

'Where was he at the time?'

'What time?'

'The time you removed it from his studio.'

'Yesterday? He was in Norfolk … According to Quentin, he went with a crowbar.'

'*With a crowbar!* There's a novelty. How come you're in touch with Quentin? And why a crowbar?'

'I don't know. If I did, I might be aiding and abetting, mightn't I?'

Corey wanted to tear his hair out. 'You are thoroughly annoying. You know that, don't you?'

Waverley crushed the newspaper in her lap and examined him with a reflective gaze. 'I sincerely try not to be. Strictly speaking, since he gave me a key, it's not stealing, I'm just relocating it.'

Corey had put his cereal aside, his appetite quite gone. 'Eat your sandwich. We're going to be late.'

He rose to his feet. She followed suit, leaving the sandwich.

'You keep making mistakes,' she said.

'I didn't…! Another? *What?*'

'You said I was a beautiful object.' She clutched his arm for a moment and gave him a smile that was positively impudent.

It was twelve minutes to their gate. Their flight was half-empty. When they entered the plane the steward who greeted them was dubious about Waverley's package, thinking it was too large for the overhead lockers. For a moment it seemed as if he was going to send it to the hold, but Waverley was persuasive. The steward, smiling obligingly, helped her as she tested out its size on an empty locker at the front of the plane. At a diagonal it fitted, just. Corey found the whole episode sickening. That was the sort of mood he was in, as far as Waverley was concerned.

FORTY-SIX

The repercussions came soon enough: first, a furious text from Ross, in speech terms, a tirade. They had scarcely reached the terminal building at Palma de Mallorca. By whatever means, he had deduced that Waverley had stolen *Composition with Movie Magazines IV, 1976* from his studio and Corey was implicated. No, not implicated, *responsible!* Secondly, soon after they had arrived at their hotel in Cala San Vicente, an icy email from Max to the effect that Ross had been to the Collarii Building and had caused a scene about a painting he was claiming had been stolen from him by Waverley. He had threatened all and sundry, firstly two of the girls on the desk, subsequently Peter, and had left with the declared aim of catching a plane to Majorca, to "sort them out!", i.e. Corey and Waverley, plus anyone else he could lay his hands on. Clearly, someone at the Collarii Building had told Ross they were on their way to Villa Besugo.

Corey felt he had every reason to be aggrieved that both these messages had been sent to him, not Waverley. As a matter of fact, to his disgust, her mobile had been utterly inert the entire journey. He couldn't work out whether Max's email was a warning, or one of his ploys to make him feel entirely responsible for what had occurred. Whichever it was, Corey judged it high in content but low in intent to advise. It had the mannerisms of an inter-office memo, and Corey suspected Angela had drafted it on Max's instructions, in his absence. "Rebuked by memo" was a new one on him and he sent Waverley a text: 'Castigated by email over Ross'. In five minutes she was knocking on his door. Corey's faculties were scattered. Events were making him feel somewhat hysterical.

'I need a drink.'

'Why not,' she agreed.

They went downstairs to the bar. Corey knew the hotel well. He had stayed there several times while working on the inventory of the paintings at Villa Besugo. In the beginning he had tried staying at the villa, but after dark he had found the atmosphere oppressive. The hotel was one of those built in the great seventies boom. It was modernistic, had an interior with plenty of veneers and was nicely situated with a picturesque outlook. It was busy, but spacious. The bar was at the back of the hotel and gave onto the swimming pool terrace. Beyond the grounds, the land dropped away to a rocky landscape studded with villas: patches of white and pastel amongst the rough and tumble. He checked the time. Amazingly, it was still only four o'clock. They opted for coffee. Corey looked Waverley up and down, as if making an inventory of her affects. Her hair was up in a ponytail and once again he found himself fascinated by the way even the smallest motion of her head made it swish with the animation of something finely bred and highly-strung.

'Did you consider the consequences of stealing that painting from Ross?'

'Meaning?'

'Like getting the sack.'

'He can't, can he?'

'Who? Max?' Corey reflected on that while he slipped a cube of sugar into his *cortado*. 'Ross is a Post, don't forget. That carries weight with the Collariis. But no, I suppose not. You know, don't you, Ross is threatening to come after us?'

Her eyes widened. Corey thought she actually looked a little scared.

'*To Majorca?* We could stay here and hide. I like this hotel; it's super swish.'

There was something charmingly teenagerish in the way she said, "super swish". It couldn't be said his heart melted, but his smile was a little less wintry.

'I've taken it in the neck because he thinks I put you up to it!'

She leant towards him with a mischievous smile. 'Ah! Poor you!'

'It's actually laughable. This is the second time you've done this to me in the space of a couple of weeks!'

'You'll survive,' she decided, brushing aside Corey's concern for his standing with the Collariis. 'I think you've become pretty much indispensable. Max is being so charming, *so very, very charming all the time;* he can't bear to be disagreeable to anyone.'

'Hah! You think that because you haven't seen the memo he sent me.'

'You're needed to meet the people he doesn't want to meet. In the end, Peter's going to put a stop to everything, but until then we're both safe.'

'Peter! That actually sounds rather alarming... although, yes, I know what you mean.'

'Max is a darling, but Peter's watching from the wings. He is the one, you know, with the real business head. He won't let Max have his own way much longer if this thing doesn't get sorted. He thinks the Posts are bad for business, and the more we stir them up the worse they become. Running artists' estates is meant to be super-discrete and super-confidential, not mad fuckers trying to kill members of staff.'

Corey thought that a touch disingenuous. 'Then why go out of your way to rile Ross? I mean, what if the painting is a copy after all, like he says, and the original is up there at Villa Besugo? What then?

'Can't you see?' she said with sudden vehemence, looking him directly in the eye. 'I have a commission from the *New Cognoscenti*. They want to publish part of my work on Man Ray. I need to finish it on time. *I'm precipitating the endgame!*'

It was wonderfully logical and he laughed.

FORTY-SEVEN

They drove up the coast to Villa Besugo in their hire car. It was still hot and torpid but the sun was declining in the far west. Lengthening shadows cut up the landscape into jagged fragments that zigzagged down to the sea not far away. Beyond, a bleached headland basked in unattenuated sunlight. Corey wondered where the beach was on which Gustave had propositioned Ruthie: "You should try me in the bath". *Ridiculous!*

The boundary wall was high and the gate closed. Corey got on his mobile and after a few minutes, Javier came to open the gate. He was dressed in black and looked like a notary: sallow, the stuff of ledger-readers. He greeted Corey warmly enough, in his *Opus Dei* manner, and shook Waverley's hand when she was introduced.

'*Encantado, encantado,*' he muttered in the very moment of turning away. He pushed the gates open wide enough for Corey to drive in.

As the gates closed behind them it was as though the outside world had dropped away beyond the horizon. The pine-shaded drive led straight towards the main house. It could be seen through the trees, its façade severe but golden brown. During Gustave's lifetime, the grounds had never been particularly well tended and, although things were better now, there was still an air of encroaching nature about the place. To their left, facing the long façade of the villa, there were glimpses of balustrades and urns on a terrace, and set below it there was another, larger terrace with a swimming pool and a tennis court. The slope between the two was a profusion of lanky weeds and overgrown shrubs. To the right, shadowed by more pines, was a range of buildings, once farm buildings, and the caretaker's house where Javier lived with his wife. There was a certain gloomy austerity about the approach that Corey thought unbecoming of a place that was destined to be Gustave Post's lasting memorial. He knew the sweeping views down to the sea from beyond the swimming pool terrace had much to recommend them and, not for the first time, he thought that once the outstanding legal issues surrounding Gustave's estate were finally resolved, and before the museum and study centre were opened to the public, a more fitting approach should be constructed in that direction.

Gustave's presence hung heavy in the air as Waverley and Corey entered the villa. Javier remained standing at the threshold, uncertain whether to follow or let them go about their business unaccompanied. It was Waverley's first visit, and she was quietly awed. The plain exterior had not prepared her for the grandeur of the ornate staircase; nor for the imminent feeling that the guiding spirit of the place had only just departed, a sensation given substance by the Edinburgh tapestries, based on some of Gustave's most celebrated paintings, that lined the walls of the stairwell.

She held out the wrapped painting she was carrying under her arm. 'Where does this belong?'

Corey laughed. 'Well... not here. The rooms on this floor were where Gustave worked.' He indicated double doors to his left. 'That was his studio. Upstairs was more for living. Let's go up,' he suggested, 'and see the paintings.'

Corey released Javier, telling him he would call by his house when they were ready to leave. They climbed the stairs and found themselves walking through a succession of rooms running the length of the front facade, not opening individually off a corridor but leading directly one from another. The lowered blinds let in a translucent glow. There was scant furniture, leaving Gustave's paintings to populate the rooms with their golden effects. Corey was thrilled afresh; it happened every time he visited. Framed and unframed, large and small, the walls were hung several deep with paintings from every period of Gustave's life. It was a bravura display. Waverley went from room to room with her mouth open. As they proceeded down the line of rooms, they passed through one with the vestiges of domestic use: a sink and cooking range as well as a table and chairs, and a broken-down sofa.

'It's incredible,' said Waverley more than once. 'So many paintings!'

Corey agreed; it *was* incredible. Forget that the long-term value of what they were seeing was almost inestimable; here Gustave Posts were two a penny.

'Isn't it risky them being here?'

'They can't be moved until everything's settled,' he replied. 'They're safe enough.'

Not least, they were safe because, beyond the immediate family and the staff of the Collarii Foundation, their existence was practically unknown. Even so, as Corey was well aware, there were yet more paintings – the ones Gustave had considered important – stored in a doubly-secure building alongside the caretaker's house.

'It's thrilling, *really*!'

When they had completed their tour, she chose a place to unwrap *Composition with Movie Magazines IV, 1976,* the painting she had taken from Ross's studio. She leant it against the wall under several other paintings of the same vintage and stood back to admire her placing.

Corey was touched. 'You've got a good eye,' he said approvingly. It wasn't a copy. There was even a space where it had once hung.

She looked at him doubtfully. 'Nobody would have missed it, really, would they? I mean, the family is the family, after all.'

He laughed. 'Is that an offer to surrender... when Ross gets here?'

She smiled ruefully.

Corey had other things than Ross on his mind. 'I want to show you Gustave's drawing studio.'

They returned to the far end of the succession of rooms. Turning right, there were more rooms in a wing that ran at a right angle to the main axis of the villa. The first one was what Corey wanted her to see.

'This is where there's still treasure to be found,' he said.

The drawing studio was cool, looking north, sheltered from the sun. Corey skirted the pair of long tables, placed some distance apart in the centre of the room, and opened the windows. A breeze came in and out, almost like waves breaking on a rocky foreshore. Waverley still stood in the entrance. To her immediate right, a mantelpiece, an ornate affair in marble, dominated the wall. Either side of the chimney breast there were deep built-in cupboards. Their doors were open and many different types of drawing paper, some still in their packs, filled the shelves. The other two, windowless walls were lined with plan chests, stacked several high. They were of all types and sizes, some plainly quite ancient.

'There's enough paper here to keep a whole team of artists going for years,' explained Corey. 'Most of the plan chests are full. I spent a little time in here last year and I found the odd thing – you know, one or two doodles – mixed up with the unused paper.'

Waverley pulled open a drawer at random. It was heavy; three quarters full of paper, dense, carefully stacked, creamy white. 'I see what you mean,' she said, pushing the drawer to with difficulty.

'The times I've been here since Gustave died, my focus has been on documenting his paintings for the *catalogue raisonné*. Nobody has bothered with all this. If the studies mentioned in the daybook came here, this is the most likely place to look for them.'

Waverley was surprised. '*What, start now?*'

Corey shrugged.

She scanned the tiers of plan chests, slightly daunted. 'There must be at least sixty, seventy drawers… plus the cupboards!'

He was determined they should make a start and so explained how they should conduct their search. 'One drawer at a time, we take out the contents, and place them on the table. We go through them sheet by sheet, unless it's obvious we're looking at a stack of paper that's never been separated. How about that?'

'To do them all will take all night!'

'Just a preliminary look.'

They set to work, refining their procedure as they went along. After some three quarters of an hour Corey called a halt. They reviewed their finds, which they had retrieved from vast amounts of unused paper – raw material for every conceivable purpose to which paper could be put, from handmade rag paper, through machine-made cartridge to newsprint and acid-free tissue. They had found a sheaf of posters for one of Gustave's exhibitions, a large number of illustrations ripped from magazines, a trial proof for an etching, and a sheet of paper squared up as though in preparation for something that never materialised. Between them, they had been through just seven drawers.

'It's getting late,' he said. 'I'm tired. How about you? We should go back to the hotel, eat and plan tomorrow.'

FORTY-EIGHT

A crowd of people were drinking on the terrace beside the swimming pool. Raucous teenagers, their bodies like sucked sweets, were still ducking and diving in the pool. Corey and Waverley sat at the bar with *cañas*. They had the place to themselves apart from the two barmen who were busy coming and going, taking supplies to those outside. Conversation was sparse while they set themselves up with food and wine. Some altercation outside attracted Waverley's curiosity, and Corey did not attempt to bring her attention back to him. At last, the mood settled into something comfortable.

'Quite a day!' he said warmly.

Waverley was looking into her glass as though it was an aperture to some other kind of space. He wasn't quite sure, but he thought she was reflecting on the wisdom of her confession about Max. Just as he was thinking this, she said, 'Every woman needs a Max.'

Corey smiled. 'Every Max needs a Waverley, I suppose.'

'Perhaps it's not a good idea if they succeed in finding one another. I can't fathom out how it happened. He offered me a lift…'

'In that Audi?'

'No, no, in a taxi. He went out of his way to drop me off. I don't know… one kind of kiss became another. You know, the farewell kind.'

He smiled ruefully. 'Ah, yes, the transmutation of the kiss!'

She laughed as though he had released the comic potential of what she had said. 'Yes, the transmutation of the kiss! Well, Mr Templeton, your cynicism is finely tuned.'

'I regard it as a sardonic investment in irony,' he replied, 'in the Pickwickian sense, of course.'

'No doubt.' She sighed and looked about her reflectively. 'I'm glad to be here, anyway.'

The moment seemed right to tell her Max had put up two thousand euros to persuade Ross to return the Omega. She pulled a face but made no comment.

'I have to confess,' he said, hesitantly, 'I've seen Ross more recently than that.'

He explained how Ross had been caught out by the equity release scheme. 'That's why he's in a dangerous mood. That's why we should be careful. You've taken the last painting by his father he had.'

She looked suitably discomforted at the thought of having baited an already enraged Ross.

Cory picked up the thread of his story, telling her how he'd gone to see Ross at the behest of the Collariis, and how, from what Ross had said, it seemed that Gustave might have had the second of the Berlin Wall paintings.

Now Waverley was listening as though bewitched, folding and unfolding the corner of a paper napkin lying on the table between them, so concentrated was she on what he was saying.

'According to Ross, Gustave believed Clarissa had the other one, and he tried to persuade her to give it back to him.

She looked him in the eye. 'Where, then, is the one Gustave did have?'

Corey gazed at his beer meditatively, running a finger through the condensation. 'I doubt it still exists. I think he wanted Clarissa to return hers so he could destroy it too. Maybe because of his guilty conscience about how they had been taken back from Ingrid. In the event, the only one he could destroy was the one he had.'

Adamantly, she shook her head.

Corey was too attached to the idea to be moved. 'The way Ross tells it, his father had his Berlin Wall painting all the time he was with Ruthie, but I showed her a picture of *Berlin Wall Lament No.1* and she never saw it all the time she was with him. Doesn't that suggest he'd already destroyed it?'

Waverley was still not convinced.

'What about the air of secrecy and shame around the disappearance of Ingrid?' he insisted. 'All along, Gustave must have had feelings for her. Something bad had been done to her. Something criminal?'

'Destroy it? I don't think so,' she said softly. It was as though she was thinking about Gustave living and working at Villa Besugo. Having been immersed in the atmosphere of the place, she had come to a new understanding of the way he thought. '*You know,*' she added suddenly, '*it has to be here!*'

'What do you mean?'

'I can feel it. It went from Berlin to London and then it came here. It's been here all along.'

Her air of certainty amused him. Among the paper he had with him in the bar were the photocopies of the entries from the nineteen eighty-two daybooks, folded in an A5 pocket file. He opened them out and turned round the top one so she could read it. 'Then what about this: the daybook entry for the paintings sent from Berlin when he gave up the studio? All of them were checked and logged when they arrived in London. There's no doubt about their identity; they're listed. No Berlin Wall painting; nothing that size came back from Berlin, even.'

'What if Gustave hid the paintings? What if he arranged for the one he had to come here?'

'It didn't happen!' He said it vehemently. 'No paintings came here; only materials and equipment for use in the studio.' He selected a second photocopy, the entry listing the items from the Berlin studio that had been sent on to Villa Besugo. This was the entry with the final cryptic line, "studies, to be framed: 22?" that had instigated their search of Gustave's drawing studio at the villa.

She brushed the air with her right hand as though to push his evidence aside. 'I mean, what if it was disguised? The entry says canvases, doesn't it?'

'Well, yes, it does.' His amusement had become mixed with a degree of thoughtfulness. 'You mean, it looked like a blank canvas?'

'That's *exactly* right! Somebody concealed both paintings with an extra layer of canvas. You're right, *Gustave was ashamed!* He never unwrapped his. He wanted to make sure the other one was never seen, but he failed to retrieve it. He couldn't bear to destroy the one he did have. He couldn't do that... *but it was as if he'd buried it!* He just left it as it came... *hidden!*' This she said with a conviction that was radiant.

218

He had to admit he was beguiled. Even though his habit of mind was to trust in the infallibility of the written record, he was inclined to indulge such passionate advocacy, especially when it chimed with his own feelings about Gustave's sense of guilt. 'One, and most likely both, had the title written on the back of the stretcher bar,' he observed. 'Somebody would have noticed.'

She had a ready answer to that. 'When the second layer of canvas was stretched over the first, it was taken right round, covering the back of the stretcher bars. It was fixed so close to the inner edge you couldn't see the bars at all! Does the daybook give the sizes of the unused canvases sent here?'

He glanced at the photocopy to be sure his memory served him right. 'No, it doesn't list them. It just says, "consignment of sundry canvases and drawing paper".'

'Then we see if there are any canvases at the villa the same size as *Berlin Wall Lament No.1*. If we find one, we strip back a corner of the canvas and see if there's more underneath.'

He was consulting his mobile. 'One eighty centimetres by one twenty.'

She laughed delightedly.

When they went upstairs there was a moment outside her room, as they parted, when they came within a finger's breadth of kissing. She smiled at him mockingly, daring him to see what would happen. Corey thought about the transmutation of the kiss. The anticipation was exalted *and* visceral, ineluctably linked. To precipitate it would have been too True Romance. The joke: they were turning bowdlerisation on its head!

FORTY-NINE

The next day, before the sun made it too hot to move, they returned to Villa Besugo. For the moment, their search for the twenty-two studies was put aside. Now there was a bigger game afoot. Still unburdened by doubt, in this matter at least, Corey was determined they should examine every blank or unfinished canvas. They began on the ground floor of the villa. The inward opening doors of Gustave's studio revealed an unfathomable darkness. Bright pinpoints of light shone through the hinging gaps between the leaves of the shutters. Once they were opened, the room was revealed to be the villa's principal salon.

'This hasn't been touched since Gustave died.'

The room was a frozen tableau of artistic endeavour. Its decorative grandeur was somewhat at odds with the way Gustave had used it. Evidence of his creative industry was everywhere. The wainscots were stacked with canvases, most with their faces to the wall. Scattered about the room were some small bedside tables, several drinks trolleys and a vast sideboard, ornate with ormolu, which might always have been there. Each surface was littered with half-squeezed tubes of paint and used palettes, some improvised out of plates, pieces of window glass and even the top of a shoebox. Hopelessly clogged brushes were abandoned everywhere. It was as if Gustave had left off painting only an hour before, but look more closely and one could see that the tubes of paint were dusty and had dried out over several summers, the palettes likewise. Corey watched as Waverley wandered the room, occasionally turning round one of the canvases to see how far Gustave had taken it towards a finished state.

'You see, they're all beginnings, fragments...' said Corey. 'Things abandoned. Barrel scrapings.'

Waverley crouched to examine a canvas with a glimpse of landscape in the top right-hand corner. 'I wouldn't mind this,' she said, looking up at Corey conspiratorially.

'I know, some are marvellous. The Collariis consider them inconsequential, but because they're by Gustave they'll be pored over by experts through the years. It's inevitable.'

'Did he come here alone?'

'Not often. There was always room here for whoever wanted to join him.'

'What, Ruthie, Ross and his brother?'

'Yes, and Clarissa before her.'

'And Neema?'

'Yes, they all came here.'

'A place of secrets, then.'

Corey laughed. 'I suppose you could say that.'

On the far side of the room there was another pair of double doors. Waverley pushed them open and they went into a second room. The shutters here were open. The room, smaller than the salon, was at the far corner of the villa, with almost continuous windows in the two outside walls. From here there was a panoramic view of the terraced grounds and, beyond, an expanse of hillside running down towards the sea. The water was pea-soup green. It stretched out to a heat haze that obscured the horizon. The view was magnificent. So magnificent, thought Waverley, it must have been here, on this very spot, that Gustave had stood when he resolved to buy the villa.

'I'd like to go down to the sea,' she said approvingly.

'Yes, there's a path down. Quite private too, the beach,' said Corey, who had walked that way on previous visits.

The room was empty but for the stacks of unused canvases in assorted sizes leaning against the walls. There was one canvas hanging in the centre of the longest wall that had very obviously been worked on. It was a kind of muddy turmoil, not at all like Gustave's beginnings in the previous room. Waverley stopped dead to examine it, uttering a small cry of recognition. She was horrified.

'I know what this is: *it's Ross*! He's been here painting!'

'Yes, I'd forgotten about that. He was here the summer before last.' When Corey saw the look on her face he added, hastily, 'it was a one-off.'

She said something under her breath about never being sure, where Ross was concerned.

'He had to be warned off,' Corey admitted, making a gesture of helplessness, as though regretting how things had been then. 'Security has tightened up since Javier arrived.'

Waverley was eyeing the stacked canvases that would now forever await Gustave's attention. 'Remind me again,' she said.

Corey had the measurements off by heart. 'One twenty centimetres by one eighty.' He walked over to where a number of metal rulers of different lengths were hanging on the wall. He came back to her with a metre measure. There was no need, the evidence of her eyes had already told her they were on the wrong track.

'There's none here that big.' She walked over to the window to take a second look at the view, almost as if she were consulting it. 'The thing is, Corey, he wouldn't keep it here, would he? He'd keep it in the store, with the other paintings he thought important, don't you think?'

The logic seemed right. They went across to the caretaker's house to fetch Javier. During the clement months of spring and autumn, Gustave had used the biggest of the buildings adjacent to Javier's house to work on large-scale paintings. Towards the end of his life it had been turned into a secure store.

Javier switched off the security system and unlocked the door. There were twenty or thirty paintings in racks, occupying the wall opposite the barred window. The single object that nobody had taken any notice of until now, because it was untouched by Gustave's wilful talent, was now the most apparent thing in the room: a blank canvas carefully wrapped in clear polythene, as if to keep it clean. Corey was abashed; he had moved it several times when cataloguing the paintings. He broke a fingernail ripping up a corner of the canvas, fixed with staples to the back of the stretcher bars. Once the canvas was lifted, it was immediately evident there was a second layer beneath. It was as Clyde Diggle had stretched it: secured on the edge of the stretcher with copper tacks. Waverley wouldn't let Corey stop until the painting was fully revealed. Then he sent a text to Max: "Found *Berlin Wall Lament No.2*. It's definitely a twin. Worth twenty trips here!"

He was right. It also added ten million dollars to the value of Gustave's estate, enough to get Max on the next available flight from London.

FIFTY

That wasn't the only discovery that morning. Waverley had left Corey with the painting and wandered over to the main house to resume the search of Gustave's drawing studio. It was nearly noon when she came upon a large manila envelope sandwiched between two unopened reams of drawing paper. There were the instructions, written in Gustave's hand: "Send to Majorca. DO NOT OPEN. 22 Studies. Not to be framed." The envelope was still sealed. Whoever had transcribed the instructions into the daybook had misrepresented them. When Corey arrived, he fetched a palette knife and slit open the envelope.

The drawings could be read like the recounting of biblical stories in medieval paintings, those in which several key moments of dramatic edification are illustrated within a single picture. There were many fine, linear images of men and women coupling in outrageous abandon, but there were also episodes with the hieratical stiffness of Egyptian friezes depicting dispute and despair. Corey recounted to Waverley the story Ruthie had told him about Gustave dreaming he was Macbeth, and having murdered Clarissa. He remembered Ruthie had laughed mercilessly as she described the dream: He lived in a black castle. There was a dark tunnel leading to a black forest... Everything in the dream was pitifully gloomy. Gustave had murdered Clarissa and dragged her down the tunnel to the forest where her body was consumed by savage beasts.

'This is it, isn't it?' he said. 'This isn't what happened to Clarissa; it's what happened to Ingrid.'

They left the villa and walked down to the swimming pool terrace. The pool was empty and beginning to fall into disrepair.

'I think,' said Corey, 'that Campbell Carter knows about this.

You remember Alice Shawcross said someone came to see her several years ago and asked her about Ingrid Steinmann? It was Campbell.'

'How do you know?'

Corey confessed he had been back to see Alice. 'She told Campbell pretty much what she told us about Ingrid.' He hurried his explanation, knowing Waverley was disappointed in him for having gone to see Alice without her. 'Maybe for Campbell, it's a cold case that came back to life when he discovered O'Flynn knew even more than Alice. That's why he kept O'Flynn away from me. For Campbell, it's the scoop of a lifetime. He's just waiting until *Berlin Wall Lament No.1* makes its public appearance in New York.'

She laughed a sort of "whatever next" laugh. 'Does Max know about this?'

'Some. The pieces haven't quite settled, have they?'

'No, I suppose not. Drawings aren't evidence, are they?'

'I'm pretty sure there isn't *any* evidence, not in a forensic sense.'

She shook her head. 'Why would O'Flynn tell Campbell Carter, after all this time?' Her gesture, a bodily tremor of exasperation, spoke more eloquently of her unease than her words. She found it all too elusive.

'I don't know. Campbell must have got close to O'Flynn to write about him. Something ridiculous happened. Maybe writing the introduction to his book was a *quid pro quo* for ancient reminiscences!' He rose to his feet. 'Let's go and ask him.'

She started at the suddenness of his movement. '*You know where he is?*'

'Not exactly, but I know he has a house here, in Cala San Vicente.'

FIFTY-ONE

They drove into the centre of Cala San Vicente. It was a typical touristic sort of place: plenty of bars and busy with holidaymakers. The sun blazed down, forcing them to walk in the shade.

'What are you looking for?' Waverley wanted to know.

'I'm looking for a bar with a Guinness sign.'

Soon enough he found one and an enquiry to the proprietor produced the information that Sr. O'Flynn sometimes came in for a drink. The proprietor didn't know exactly where he lived but he gave them directions to a bar further out where O'Flynn was thought to drink regularly. He reckoned he lived nearby. It was as he said: O'Flynn was well known at the little, flyblown bar with its plastic-topped tables and blaring TV. He had a villa further up the hill. It was sideways on to the road with a green pantile roof. Corey slowed the car to a crawl so they could see through the chain-link fence that divided the garden from the road. There was a terrace with steel chairs and a little table, and an old man pottering in the shade of a fig tree. Corey reckoned the bottle on the table was whiskey. He let himself in the gate and approached the shaded figure.

'Mr O'Flynn? Excuse me, sir, but we've come out from London with the hope of speaking to you.'

The old man looked at them suspiciously, his deep-set eyes examined them with an uneasy flicker. 'London is it? What can you be wanting with me, now?' he wondered in his querulous, reedy voice. 'I don't suppose you're journalists, are you?'

'No,' Corey shook his head. 'We're not from a newspaper, Mr O'Flynn.'

'Then what is it you're wanting?'

Corey produced his mobile and called up the photograph of *Berlin Wall Lament No.1*. 'I'm a historian, an art historian. I'm trying to trace the owner of this painting. I believe you saw it when it was being painted in Berlin; nineteen eighty-two.'

O'Flynn looked, pursed his lips and grimaced. 'Never seen it before. It looks like Gustave Post, though. Is there a tale pertaining to it?'

'You know there is!'

O'Flynn was unmoved. He took himself over to the table and poured a finger of the whiskey. 'Why in the name of God do you think I'd tell you, even if I did?' He chuckled into his glass. 'You art historians seem more interested in the dirt than art, if you don't mind me saying so. And who's she, the angelic one?' He indicated Waverley with his chin.

'She's... er... my associate.'

He looked Waverley up and down appreciatively. He had the wandering eye.

'What art historians?' said Corey. 'Campbell Carter, I suppose.'

'Now there's a gentleman with quite the manner to him,' said O'Flynn, taking a sip of his liquor and giving Corey a new, more extensive appraisal. 'As a matter of fact, I was wondering why he was the only one asking.'

There was a profound silence.

'What is it? Three and a half years?' wondered O'Flynn.

'Four in November...'

'Ah, *precision*!'

'We've been searching the Post archives at Villa Besugo.'

'Going through Gustave's rubbish bins, don't you mean? I hear there's not much happening up there. People wonder when the museum will come. It would be good for business around here. Work, you know, is scarce. And four years is a long time to wait.'

'Gustave left his affairs in a mess; it's been protracted, and lawyers... You were with Gustave in Berlin. You know what happened to Ingrid, don't you?'

O'Flynn bristled. 'What tout's peddling that nonsense?'

'We found another painting at the villa that once belonged to her: *Berlin Wall Lament No.2*.'

'Now there's a thing!' He laughed with a rueful shake of his head and poured himself another shot from the bottle. He held the bottle out to Corey. Corey accepted the offer on behalf of them both. He knew they would do a circuit of the poet's memories of Gustave in Berlin several times before they got where they needed to be. Then it would be easy, like the Boston College tapes.

'I suppose I've no objection to telling you what I told him.' He lowered himself onto a chair and indicated they too should take seats. There was a silence as, ponderously, he gathered his thoughts. 'Belfast in the seventies, Berlin in the eighties. Nationalism, internationalism.' He shook his head wearily, as though it had become all the same to him. 'Life's little ironies! Revolution and resistance need their poetry. Living in Berlin was seen as an act of solidarity with Berliners. You know? Standing up to Soviet tyranny! Give him credit: Gustave meant it… politically speaking, I mean. His studio was next to the Wall. He saw it as an affront. He was close to Berlin groups interested in crashing the Wall. He went out with graffiti artists who used the West's side for political purposes. The East Germans couldn't stop them. They tried, of course. It was considered dangerous because they were so unpredictable. Then it was the eighties. American abstraction had been in total dominion for years and suddenly figurative painting came back. Gustave was famous; the IRA turned to politics, I turned to the pastoral.'

So it was that they drank whiskey and went round the same route three times: stirring, companionable times in the shadow of the Wall. Finally, O'Flynn said, 'I'll tell you who killed Ingrid. It wasn't Gustave. He wouldn't do something like that. It was those boys; stupidity mostly. I should know; I cleaned up their mess. She was disappeared. Gustave was in touch with a group who had used the sewers to get people out of East Berlin. The VoPo had closed the operation down years ago; sealed the manholes in East Berlin with tamper-proof fittings. Nothing to stop things going in the other direction, provided you didn't want to get above ground.'

'What, she was dumped in the sewer?'

'Deposited under a bricked-up factory, beyond the Wall.'

'Who? Edward and Charlie?'

He nodded.

Corey was disturbed by how matter-of-fact it all was. 'How did it happen?'

'They were teenagers. She was trying to set fire to the building. She wanted Clarissa dead. It was inevitable, you know. High-spirited... Over-reaction. Gustave was in Venice, so I had to take responsibility. Otherwise those boys would have made a terrible mess of things.'

'So, that's *it*?'

'It looked worse than it was. Cut-up, he was, when he found out. Very cut-up.'

'Gustave?'

'I had to tell him; he was going to start a big search for her... Ingrid had a foul temper when she was crossed. Even Gustave was terrified of her. She had a gun.' He laughed at the memory. 'She was a danger to herself.'

'*A gun?*'

'An Armalite.' His eyes took on a sly twinkled. 'Made in Dagenham.'

Up to that moment, Corey had seen Ingrid as somehow a copy, a distant inflection of Waverley: high-spirited, utterly seductive, but somehow grounded. Now he remembered something Alice Shawcross had said – "She was a gifted terrorist" – and his image of Ingrid underwent a sudden transformation. "*She was a danger to herself*"!

'Is this why he had the gallery pay you all that money?'

'*Money?* It wasn't that much.'

'Back then it was.'

'I couldn't say.'

The conversation had run its course. It seemed likely, Corey concluded, that O'Flynn's greatest service to Gustave had been the thoroughly practical matter of contriving Ingrid's disappearance in a manner not unknown to the Troubles. Once more, whatever O'Flynn had actually done, whatever his real part in Ingrid's disappearance, he had confessed to sinning and was, for the moment, absolved and at peace. He dozed gently in the shade, and Corey and Waverley took their leave.

FIFTY-TWO

They ate companionably in a restaurant in Cala San Vicente. They couldn't bring themselves to discuss what had happened to Ingrid Steinmann. In truth, what they had discovered didn't seem real, but then their visit to Villa Besugo had had an air of unreality about it from the very start. It was as if they found themselves gravity free, located at a point from which earthly concerns were observable, but the accidental luxury of their condition meant that everything reality seemed to entail – and require – could be put aside for another day.

Later, they returned to Villa Besugo, disinclined to formulate anything more purposeful. By then it was late in the afternoon. Waverley wandered off to take another look at the studies she had found. Corey felt drained. He'd followed the whiskey drinking with wine over lunch. He went to the room where the remnants of domesticity meant there was somewhere to sit down. As soon as he fell onto the broken-down sofa he received a call on his mobile. It was Max.

'Ah, Corey! It's Max.'

'Hello, Max.' Corey waited, wondering why he was silent. When Max finally spoke the reason for his reticence became clear: it was serious.

'Corey, this fellow you spoke to about Ross's paintings.'

'Marc Bastion?'

'Yes, Bastion. Angela's had him on the phone. Apparently there was an attempted break-in and fire the night before last at the place where he's got Ross's paintings stored: some warehouse in Norfolk. The police have been called in. No actual harm done to the paintings but someone caused absolute uproar. He's swearing off about Ross. There's CCTV, but whoever did it was well covered up. You didn't speak to Ross, did you?' Max had become very measured. 'Because Bastion seems to think Ross was tipped off about them being there and had decided that if he didn't have them, nobody would.'

'I know nothing of this, Max.'

'Okay, that's good… but Corey, the police are involved and it's possible they'll try and access Ross's mobile.'

'I see. I thought Ross was in the gallery causing a stink yesterday. So, it can't have been him in Norfolk, can it?'

'The break-in was the previous evening. How many times have I said this: *Ross is capable of anything*.'

'Where are you, Max?'

'In Palma. I'll be there this evening.'

Corey had scarcely put down his mobile before he received another call, equally jarring. It was Edward Post.

'Templeton, I heard you were out here. It seems business is brisk when it comes to Papa's struggle with the oil paint! What gives? I gather that little minx of yours has upset Ross.'

Corey laughed. 'I think you're responsible for Ross being upset, Edward. He's threatening to off you. Where are you?'

'I'm on the island.'

'Good heavens, what a coincidence, Max is here too!'

'Where are you?'

'At the villa.'

'I see; as I thought. It seems there's a coming together going on. We need to talk. Meet me at the bar. And no funny stuff, I'm not in the mood for pranks.'

'Which bar?'

'Your hotel.'

The phone went dead. Corey wondered how he knew where they were staying. Somebody at the Collarii Building was definitely talking to the Posts.

He told Waverley about the imminent arrivals. Neither made any comment but a feeling of apprehension lay between them. The suspension of reality was about to end. It seemed inevitable that some sort of confrontation lay ahead. Was this the moment when the distrust between the Collariis and the Posts finally became open warfare? Was it now that Max's entanglement with Waverley would become the stuff of gossip, with all the consequences that that would bring in its wake? He gazed at her, full in the face. She looked back steadily, and he thought he saw that her desire, like his, was to be a bystander to whatever was about to unfold. Which of them was the greater shirker, he wondered? He seemed to remember her saying to him in Cannes, '*No, you're counted in. Too late, I'm afraid. You're in!*' If ever there was a time to say that to her, it was now, but once more, he kept his thoughts to himself.

FIFTY-THREE

As the day progressed the heat had grown sticky, oppressive. Come the evening, they made their way back to the hotel: lambs to the slaughter, dragging their heels. From reception they could see Edward in the bar, waiting for them. It was busy, but his Hawaiian shirt and Bermuda shorts were hi-vis.

Waverley excused herself and went straight upstairs to her room. Edward was sitting at the counter, facing a large scotch over ice. His vacation wear was excessive in the way of those who rely on the strictures of convention for guidance. He looked, thought Corey, like a glaucous booby dressed for the *mardi gras*. To one who tried to look like a well-heeled local when travelling, the effect was magnificently ludicrous. Here was a man who put on beachwear in the same way as he donned a dark suit and black Oxfords in proximity to money making. Corey was only too aware that he had been warned off in Cannes, now it seemed likely he was about to be on the receiving end of something less cordial, possibly foul-mouthed.

'I'm told you've come here chasing after O'Flynn,' Edward began at a rush, noticeably bad-tempered. 'After trying at Waterstone's book launch, or some such. I'm here to tell you to leave it alone. I really think this sleuthing of yours has gone on long enough, don't you?'

Corey indicated to the barman he'd have what Edward was drinking. 'I thought,' he said with deliberation, 'you wanted the truth "out there".'

'Look, maestro, you're treading on toes. I know Max won't call you off, but I do think taking this business to the very end is entirely unnecessary, and, frankly, going to be rather too messy for all concerned. That hoodlum Ross lost his paintings because he's a bloody fool. I never expected him to borrow so much against them. He's been living high on the hog for years on the back of that deal. It was never meant to be like that. *Never!* I don't want him on my case, blabbing to all and sundry.' Nervously he took a sip of his drink. 'I'm going to tell you what I know, and perhaps you'll understand why you should leave off; loyalty to the cause, and all that. How about it?'

Corey considered his offer for a moment and nodded just enough to indicate his agreement, while not giving much away. Edward was more on the back foot than he had been expecting.

'This is between you and me, *right*?' Edward emphasised the urgency of this requirement with a chopping motion with his hand on the edge of the counter. 'I need your absolute discretion because this can't come out. You've a lot invested in the Post legacy, so it's self-interest.'

Corey settled onto his stool, making a conscious effort to be as neutral, as non-existent as possible.

'O'Flynn knows where the body is.'

'Really? Ingrid Steinmann's?'

Edward was loathed to repeat what he had just said.

Corey smiled to himself. 'I got there ahead of you. I found O'Flynn's place this morning and talked to him. I don't know how much credence to give to what he says, but certainly he claims to know what happened to Ingrid Steinmann. I was thinking it might explain why you ended up with *Berlin Wall Lament No.1*. We've just found its pair up at the villa.'

'That's rather good news, I take it,' he said caustically.

'Which part?'

'Oh, finding the painting.' Something caught his eye over Corey's shoulder and he straightened up. 'Ah, here's Max!'

Corey swung round to see. Max was standing at the entrance to the bar, talking to someone from reception. Corey thought he was probably reorganising the housekeeping to suit his wants.

Edward leant forward and lowered his voice. 'Before he gets here, let me say I don't have any such painting *and* it was O'Flynn who killed Steinmann. He's hardly in a condition to remember straight, is he?' He looked up and, for Max's benefit, an incongruous smile creased his face. 'Whatever he claims, it'll sully the family name. Max can't want that, can he?'

Max had been about to make his way towards them, but before he could, Waverley appeared at his side. Corey couldn't tell whether they had come down together or just met. He was gripped by apprehension at what might happen next. He watched over the rim of his glass, an act of unconscious and fruitless concealment. She was standing, half turned towards them, as if about to enter the bar. Max spoke to her. Corey noted he avoided eye contact, like a dog with a Pavlovian aversion. He wasn't the only one watching with keen interest. Edward too was focused on them, making soft, guttural noises in his throat.

Corey felt a furious compulsion to annihilate his smug disapproval. 'O'Flynn says you and Charlie killed her.'

Apparently unperturbed, Edward averted his eyes to gaze at the shelf of exotic liqueurs behind the bar. 'She's trouble,' he said, signalling in Max's direction with a cock of his head. 'I could tell she'd be trouble when I met her in Cannes.'

Max was still talking, now looking in their direction. He turned to her and held up his fingers, indicating he needed five minutes before she joined them. She met his gaze, her head slightly thrown back, emphasising the exposed curve of her throat. Corey couldn't take his eyes off her. Edward gave a disgusted click of his tongue. She always looked, Corey thought, so untouched. There was something defiant, more than a little provocative in the way she was dressed, as if she didn't give a fig for whatever business had brought the three men together. She turned and drifted off towards the swimming pool terrace. Max came in their direction, his brow, usually innocent of any such thing, was furrowed with lines of concern.

'Well, well, another foregathering in the name of Gustave Post!' he declared, embracing them with a taut smile. 'Evening, Edward. Corey, I congratulate you on your discovery. It truly is a red-letter day when we can say we have the twin to that New York painting.' He breathed in deeply. 'I love coming to the island... Better than the south of France, I think.'

His expected measure of genial preamble having been delivered, although less smoothly than was usual, he turned to examine, rather pointedly, the way Edward was dressed. Apparently, he too was affronted by its garishness. 'I wasn't expecting to see you, Edward. I assume you're not here to lie on the beach, even if appearances suggest otherwise. Shall we huddle in the corner and be frank with one another?'

Obediently, they followed Max to an empty corner table. There were several armchairs too many and pushing them out of the way smacked of a badly organised business meeting. A waiter came across and Max saw to the ordering of fresh drinks. It was obvious to Corey, if not to Edward, that Max had finally decided that expectations of decency and fair play from the Post heirs were not good enough. The interests of the Collarii Foundation required something altogether firmer. Corey had the distinct feeling that Max was a man distracted by pain and the road ahead was scattered with body parts.

'You know, Eddie,' Max began in the stern tones of a magistrate being disrespected from the public seats. 'I have only one interest in this business. It's discipline. I can't have the family selling your father's work behind the Collarii Foundation's back. If you'd been straight with us about this painting, none of this –' he gestured towards Corey – 'would have been necessary.'

Max's gesture made it clear that, for the purposes of their present encounter, Corey was nothing more than an instrument of his will. That being the case, Corey hoped Max was admonishing Edward for good reason. If so, it could only be that something had happened in London to turn Ross's assertion, which he had conveyed to Max when last they met, into a certainty. More likely, he feared, there had been no such occurrence and Max, plainly discomposed, was venting without bothering to consult him on the state of his investigation. And the chief reason for that discomposure was, even now, taking an enforced stroll around the terrace.

'I can see you're thinking my presence on the island implies guilt,' said Edward smoothly. 'You reason: why else is he here if it isn't to cover his tracks?'

He was right, but Max wrongly assumed that Edward was there to prevent himself from being revealed as the owner of *Berlin*

Wall Lament No.1. Corey feared that, in his befuddlement, Max had concluded that he – Corey – was in possession of the proof.

Edward had straightened, his face suffused with annoyance. 'You're making the same mistake as Corey – probably he's put the idea in your head – *I don't have any Berlin Wall painting*!'

Sure enough, Corey felt Max's eyes turn on him, expecting him to contradict Edward's denial. All he could do was shrug.

For Max it amounted to a coherency break. '*Fuck!*' he cried, his confrontation with Edward – as he saw it – sabotaged. He threw up his hands in frustration. 'Who the hell has it, then?' he said, giving Corey the look of one betrayed.

There was a morose silence while the drinks were delivered. Corey was uncomfortably aware that he was sitting on the real reason for Edward's rush to Majorca. Explaining Edward's wish to prevent him meeting Dermot O'Flynn inevitably led to the matter of Ingrid Steinmann's disappearance; an occurrence that had, for him, taken on the character of an obscenity. Once it was out, he knew there would be repercussions. For the present, given its total lack of immediacy, her disappearance was a cause for little more than raised eyebrows, but he was not so sure the world at large would see it that way. What is more, he suspected he knew who had prompted Edward's rush to the island: Angela, Max's PA. Edward had identified her by acknowledging he knew of Corey's attempt to buttonhole O'Flynn at Waterstone's. Apart from Max, Angela was the only person at the Collarii Foundation who knew he had gone to the reading. He didn't suspect Max, yet he had no idea why Angela would leak to Post family members, unless it was a consequence of some murky aspect of the long-standing links between Gustave's heirs and the foundation. The fact was, all three of them were inadequately informed. Their little meeting was rank with half-baked accusations; a noxious whiff of neurotic asymmetry was in the air.

Corey took a first sip of his second scotch. 'I thought the reason you flew down was to see the *other* Berlin Wall painting,' he reminded Max.

Max sat up, the prospect of a diversion momentarily lightening the gloom, but before he could respond further, Corey's mobile rang. It was Javier.

'Excuse me while I take this,' said Corey, rising to his feet and moving away from the table. In a moment he was back. 'That was Javier,' he announced. 'There's an intruder at Villa Besugo.'

There was a moment's puzzled silence.

'*Ross!*' said Max, suddenly vivacious. 'Let's go!'

'What, *mob-handed?*'

'Yes, yes, all of us, *now!*' Max took a parting quaff of his drink, feverish to quit the scene of an embarrassment.

As they rose to follow in Max's wake, Waverley appeared from the direction of the terrace. Max's five minutes was up. Corey was amused to think she had taken it literally, almost to the second, he reckoned.

Damn!' Max was saying. 'I've let my driver go for the day. Who has a car?'

For a moment Corey's thoughts wandered; he caught a glimpse of the situation from Waverley's point of view, heading towards them. A sense of the odd inequality struck him. Did they, to her, look predatory? Had she and Max talked upstairs, he wondered. By the time Waverley reached them they had abandoned the table and their barely-touched drinks. She was, for a moment, whirled about by the insincere warmth of Edward's greeting. Corey had his eyes fixed on her, trying to make out the expression on her face, even as she turned away from him. Neither Max nor Edward seemed to notice she was wet. Droplets of water hung from her earlobes like small diamond earrings. Her limbs were slick with water and the floor was already pooled where she stood. Momentarily bewildered, Corey wondered if she so conformed to what Max and Edward expected in a bar such as this – a bar giving onto a terrace alongside a swimming pool on a hot Mediterranean evening – that they saw nothing amiss. To him it couldn't have been more incongruous had she just showered in soda water, fully clothed. The atmosphere was all *non sequiturs* and superlative stupidity. In the derangement of the moment, he decided, they wouldn't have noticed were she a mermaid.

In his haste to be gone, Max was hustling them towards the entrance. The performance struck Corey as garish: such quick-fire mood changes were not the stuff of Max. Waverley was slow to understand.

Corey held out his hand to her. 'We have to go.'

There was a moment of cross-purposes as they reached reception. Edward was a picture of reluctance. Max's hunch that the intruder at Villa Besugo was Ross did not go down well with him.

'I'll handle Ross,' Max promised, not entirely convincingly. 'It's not a problem.'

While the persuasion continued, Corey hung back, quietly explaining to Waverley that there had been an inconclusive confrontation over *Berlin Wall Lament No.1*. 'He claims he doesn't have it,' he said of Edward's denial, 'and probably Max feels the need to apologise. He wants to get him in his car by himself so he can.'

'Yes, Edward probably doesn't have it,' she decided abstractedly. 'The next person to turn up will be the one who does, I wouldn't be surprised.'

Corey laughed. 'There's an intruder at Villa Besugo. Max thinks it's Ross.'

'*Ross?*' She gave him a saucer-eyes look. 'Is that where we're going?'

'Yes.' He leaned into her, his arm coming away wet. 'Hang onto your hats!'

Somehow, Max had settled Edward's funk, and he turned back to make it clear to Corey that he should come separately with Waverley.

'It wasn't wise to take his painting,' he reproved Waverley, giving her barely a glance. 'I know Ross. He's been to that place in Norfolk causing havoc, now he's here. And Corey, if you told Ross where Bastion had his paintings stored, that's tantamount to aiding and abetting.'

'I think that *is* aiding and abetting,' suggested Waverley.

Max stared at her blankly. 'Don't you need a cardigan, or something?'

Before she could respond he had turned back to Edward and was urging him towards the car park.

'You'd better change,' said Corey. He didn't look at her; he couldn't.

It was ten minutes before she reappeared. Edward and Max were long gone. As they met, a middle-aged woman came up to them, with a look of concern on her face. 'Are you all right, dear?' she said. She turned to Corey. 'She wasn't looking where she was going and walked off the edge of the swimming pool; nearly struck her head. She needs to be more careful.'

Corey thanked the woman for her concern and they made for the entrance.

'What's going on?' he said, as they reached the car.

It was barely dark, one of those soft twilights that cloak the Mediterranean littoral in summer. He turned the radio down to a low burble.

'Nothing,' she said dismissively, without the slightest pause for thought.

'You frightened her.'

'The pool, that's all.'

'*You weren't looking where you were going?*'

She didn't answer.

'Is that why the others didn't seem to notice: you wanted to drown?'

'Corey, that's *ridiculous!*'

'Did you talk to Max upstairs? Something's going on.'

'What, when you were in the bar?'

'*Yes,* when I was in the bar! *There's an atmosphere!*'

'"I can't go on; I've made a mistake." That sort of thing?'

'Something like that, *yes!*'

'No.'

'Really?'

'*You're driving on the wrong side of the road!*'

Brainless introspection seemed about right.

FIFTY-FOUR

Even a little further from the sea, the night was darker, the heat clammier. The gates were open and there was no sign of Javier, or the others. Corey parked short of the main house, instinct telling him they should make their final approach on foot, the better to attune themselves to the surroundings, which, insensibly, had taken on a menacing character. When he shut off the ignition, they could hear something wild calling. They sat for a while, each a silent comfort to the other.

'This is crazy.'

'Fucked up,' she agreed.

They both climbed out. The last door to close dowsed the car's interior lights, leaving them in a landscape of blacks: black earth, black vegetation, black buildings. Above their heads, the pine trees were a canopy of black blots against the indigo of the night sky. The front door of Javier's house was ajar, a single source of illumination.

'I suppose Ross wants his painting back,' she said.

'It isn't his,' Corey reminded her.

'He thinks it is, *obviously*.'

He wanted to quibble, but restrained himself. They came upon Edward's hire car, a red Honda, empty. They couldn't hear anything. There was no sign of life at the villa.

'They must be round the back.'

'What's behind, anyway?' wondered Waverley.

'Nothing much. There's a quarry. It's a big drop and not very far.'

'What kind of quarry.'

'I don't know what kind… Stone.'

There was a sudden thrashing noise from the direction of the swimming pool.

'There's lots of things people can fall into, rushing about in the dark,' said Corey fatalistically.

'That was somebody forcing their way through undergrowth,' decided Waverley. 'I think we should go and see.'

A breathless voice called out of the darkness. 'Has he been here?' It was Max.

'Who? No,' answered Corey. 'We've just arrived. What's going on?'

Max materialised out of the darkness, peering in the direction they had come. 'There was somebody hallooing a minute ago. I've lost Edward. He thought he saw Ross. I think he went that way.' He hardly paused, so intent was he on proceeding, and in a moment he had gone past and become a spectral shadow. 'Corey, turn the villa lights on,' he called as he went.

Corey peered at Waverley, as if to say, "what a palaver". On they went towards the villa. Either side of the door there were tall, narrow windows that let onto the vestibule. The glass in the nearest had been knocked out. Fabric – it could once have been a blind – trailed over the sill.

Waverley stood in front of the window, hands on hips. 'This sure looks like Ross!'

Corey tried the door. It was locked. 'I'll climb in and open it from inside.' He stepped over the low windowsill and, gingerly, slid through sideways.

'I thought this place was protected!' she hissed. 'Why isn't an alarm going off?'

He shrugged and disappeared to switch on a light. A moment later he was back. Several muffled grating noises and he had the door open. Nearby, he pointed out to her, leaning against the wall, were three or four paintings of a size easily packed in a suitcase. Just then Max came panting out of the darkness.

'They're scrapping on the tennis court. *Corey, quick!*'

His urging was peremptory. All three of them made haste along the terrace to the front of the villa. Max was already ahead, his instinct to foster brotherly accord spurring him on. Corey and Waverley cautiously took the steps that led to the lower terrace. The tennis court was at the further end of the terrace, beyond the swimming pool. From that direction they could hear grunts and scuffling noises. Max was already there, trying to make sense of what was happening. He couldn't find a way through the wire fencing. The gate wouldn't open. By the time the others joined him he had already shouldered it repeatedly without success. He turned his attention to the catch. He and Corey nearly clashed heads, crouching to examine it. Simultaneously they came to the realisation that a padlock was dangling from the catch's sliding bar.

'*Corey, they're locked in!*' declared Max, breathing hard.

At that moment the larger of the shadowy figures struggling in the centre of the tennis court knocked flat his stout, but much smaller opponent. There was a moment when nobody, including the combatants, stirred. Then Ross materialised out of the shades, the very image of the mad prankster. He addressed Max.

'You'd better hurry, Fishman's turning the villa into a bargaining chip. He's an expert arsonist is Fishman.'

Max needed to hear no more. He turned and stumbled off into the darkness.

'Don't switch on any lights upstairs!' shouted Ross after him. 'Booby trapped light fittings are a Fishy speciality!' He laughed fiercely and turned his attention to the others. 'Hello, Waves!'

'*You brought Fishman?*' exclaimed Waverley accusingly. 'Ross, why? You're just getting him into trouble. *Jesus!* Was he in Norfolk with you when that warehouse caught fire?'

'Look, Waves, Max isn't going to let any of this come out, is he? Can't afford to have the boat rocked. And there's got to be a bit of a rebalancing, hasn't there? Rebalancing in favour of the Posts, I mean!' He gestured towards the villa from where the faint sound of voices raised in anger drifted. 'Look at that place, stuffed with my dad's work. *Fucking liberate it, Max, liberate it!*'

Just then the dark shape on the asphalt sat up and groaned. Ross turned to look at it pityingly.

'Templeton, I've an idea,' he said. 'Let's get Eddie to tell us who owns that Berlin Wall painting you've been wittering on about these past weeks. He knows!'

Ross went over to Edward and hauled him upright. In a moment he had the collar of his shirt twisted in a grip and was propelling him towards the gate, forcing him forward until his face was pressed against the wire.

'They're never going to get it out of you, are they?' said Ross. 'But you'll tell me, won't you? Otherwise we're going to chase one another round this tennis court until your little legs drop off.'

He pushed him away and let go. Edward staggered off, but there was no escape. He did a circuit round the sagging net and stopped. When Ross saw he wasn't running, he chased after him. Edward gave a yelp, realising he was in for more of Ross's treatment and set off in a futile attempt to stay out of his clutches. Ross soon caught up with him, despite circling very wide as if to give him more of a sporting chance. Finally, he engulfed him in a bear hug and bundled him back to where Waverley and Corey were standing.

'This is what we call "direct action"!' he explained with pedantic clarity.

Neither could muster a response. There was something intractable and merciless about Ross's demeanour.

'So, Edward, who does own Berlin Wall number one, or whatever it's called?' He jerked him about by his collar like a rag doll.

'Templeton, where's the key?' pleaded Edward as he teetered to and fro. 'Tell him I don't have the painting!'

'*I* don't have any key!' protested Corey. He put his weight to the gate. 'Ross, where *is* the bloody thing?'

Ross stopped. He came right up to the wire so they could make out his features. His manner was all mild reasonableness, as though imparting something of value to everyone's wellbeing. 'I don't have the key; the hired help'll do the honours when he's finished up at the villa.'

At that moment there was a loud bang from that direction.

'Was that Max or Javier?' wondered Ross, with a kind of quizzical glee. 'I came here quite a bit in the old days, you know. Used it as a base before it was set in aspic.'

A car started up. They all turned to see headlights picking up speed along the front of the villa.

'Ah,' continued Ross with some satisfaction, 'Fishy must have fixed up the villa because here he comes, making mayhem. I think it's your car, Eddie. He's going to drive it into the swimming pool, I expect.'

Hardly had he time to finish speaking before there was a crunch of metal and plastic, and the car's progress came to a sudden halt.

'I do believe he's hit one of those urns,' laughed Ross. 'Oh, dear, something else for Max to fix!'

Corey felt beset by incongruities. Just behind him there was a bench. He backed up and sat down with a sigh, drained of all inclination to participate. There was no doubt about it; despite Ross's raving, the situation had its ludicrous aspect.

On the upper terrace, Fishman's mayhem was playing out. The urn, or whatever it was that he had collided with, had snagged the car. He was revving the engine until it screamed, then letting in the clutch. When the car refused to move, there was a succession of ghastly noises as he crashed the gears.

'Well, this is quite a circus!' said Corey, not even bothering to look what was happening. 'Apart from airing your grievances, Ross, what's the point?'

Disturbed by the air of violence, Waverley made a half-hearted attempt to appease Ross. 'I'll fetch your painting, if you like,' she offered.

'Thanks, Waves. That's big of you! Shouldn't you be ministering to Fishy?' All this time Ross had hold of Edward by the scruff of his neck. Again he released him. 'Reparation, Templeton! And this little rat is going to squeal, or I'll know the reason why!'

Edward backed away. Ross was playing with him, just failing to seize hold of the front of his shirt. Then came a repeat performance of the chase, two dark, running shapes circling the tennis court. Ross was in no hurry to catch his prey, following his own orbit round the net. He made a pantomime of attempting to grab Edward as their paths crossed, uttering a blood-curdling yell as he failed to do so.

For Corey the performance brought to mind something Peter Collarii had said; something about Ginger and Pickles. He couldn't remember the details, but the names had stuck. Here they were: Ginger and Pickles, one chasing the other like two cartoon characters in a smackdown. Was Pickles chasing Ginger, or was it the other way round? He couldn't decide. Whichever way it was, he was beginning to think his presence was inciting Ross. He stood up. 'You can sort it out between you,' he announced. 'I'm going up to the villa to find Max. Fishman is capable of any amount of superlative stupidity.'

It was true, the atmosphere was febrile, and anything might happen, mostly by chance. Corey was thinking of Ingrid Steinmann ending up dead, and how something equally foolish could happen here, in this fetid darkness. He looked round and saw he was alone. Waverley had slipped away. He decided not to follow her. He was perfectly sensible to the fact that something had gone wrong between her and Max, and knew it would be best if he avoided finding them together. Instead, he decided, he would look for Javier and stop him calling the police, if it wasn't already too late.

'Wait!' shouted Ross. He had caught Edward and was dragging him back to the wire. Edward was clutching at his Bermuda shorts, which he was in danger of losing.

'Now then, *Edward* –' Ross spat his name in his face – 'who has that bloody painting?'

'For Christ's sake, Ross, let him go!' said Corey disgustedly.

Ross was delighted by Corey's disapproval. 'Don't you want to know? You've been labouring away at this puzzle, and here's the easy way to find out. It's called "enhanced interrogation". *Let the oracle speak!*'

Corey wasn't having it. He set off towards the villa. He could see Edward's Peugeot close to the steps that led down from the upper terrace. Ross had been right in saying it had collided with one of the urns spaced at regular intervals along the length of the villa's facade. The urn had toppled, and the base was half under the car. A struggle was going on, illuminated by the vehicle's interior lights. Someone had the driver's door open and was trying to haul Fishman out of his seat. It was Javier.

'Wait!' wailed a voice behind him, 'don't leave me here with fucking Ross! I'll tell you who has the painting. *Just stay!*' There was real fear in Edward's voice. It struck Corey that, after all, he shouldn't leave him alone with Ross. There was no saying what might happen if he did.

Edward's face was again crushed against the wire. 'It's Campbell Carter's,' he said between gritted teeth. '*Campbell Carter!*'

'*Campbell Carter?*' That struck Corey as immensely droll. He gave an awkward gulp of laughter. 'How come?' He approached the wire cage, incredulous. Campbell Carter wasn't his idea of a man who owned a painting worth ten million pounds.

'He got to Dermot O'Flynn; O'Flynn told him about Ingrid Steinmann. This was years ago, when he was researching Papa's biography.'

'Yeah, but why would O'Flynn tell him everything?'

'He knew I had the painting and he wanted it.'

'Who did? O'Flynn or Carter, for Christ's sake? I don't get what you're saying!'

'O'Flynn did, but Campbell Carter sidelined him, bought him out.'

'*Bought him out?*'

'O'Flynn was afraid... implicated. Carter had the whole story, O'Flynn didn't. Then *he* had the hold over us. In the end we bought him out.'

'So, *now* you bought *him* out – Carter?'

'The painting in exchange for no volume two of Papa's biography. No Ingrid Steinmann, no scandal, no enquiry. Carter knew a good deal when he saw one. No book to write, stuff that wouldn't earn him a hundredth of the value of the painting.'

'Wait! *That means...!* You mean Campbell Carter's never had any intention of ever finishing...? *Jesus!* That explains...!'

With sudden clarity Corey saw who had warned Edward he was on the trail of O'Flynn. It was Campbell, not Angela. Now he understood all Campbell's hedging and dodging, the paucity of his notes, the lack of generosity, the mealy-mouthed dribs and drabs of information about Gustave's time in Berlin. *No volume two!* He was stunned; past putting thoughts into words, but the way he clutched his head in his hands said it all.

'I told you! *Did I not tell you?*' demanded Ross, utterly delighted with himself. 'I just got the bloke wrong. Poor little Edward gave it to some scrivener to preserve the family name! *What d'you know!*' He threaded his fingers through the wire mesh of the gate and pushed. Corey was already too dumbfounded to be surprised as it opened outwards with a squeal. Standing in the lea of the bench where he had been sitting was a bottle of *supermarché* wine. Ross picked it up and took a swig. 'I'd better go and save Fishman before he gets hurt.'

Corey examined the gate in a daze. They had shoved and pushed in their attempt to intervene between Ross and Edward, but never pulled. A single wrench would have been sufficient. And although their fumblings had demonstrably shown the padlock's shank was locked shut, it was threaded through the gate's sliding bolt to secure it immovably in the disengaged position.

He felt for Edward, and he waited solicitously while he adjusted his Bermuda shorts. He sensed the dignity of a man who had sacrificed for the family, and who, even in his present miserable state, was determined there would be a reckoning. What it would be he didn't care to guess, and didn't want to know.

FIFTY-FIVE

They chatted amiably on the plane. A new beginning had been declared. Max had poured balm; The Powers That Be had made an accommodation, even with Ross... although perhaps not with Waverley. As ever, there was no doubting the diplomatic skills of the eldest of the Collarii brothers. As Corey began to assemble the night's happenings and its aftermath into some coherence, he saw that a complete *volte face* had occurred. When he had been recruited by Max to find out which of the Posts had broken their agreement with the Collarii Foundation, they had been as one, on the side of the angels, the Posts the opposition. Now it was he and Waverley who were on the outside. The turn-about did not puzzle him for long. He could see the interdependency of the Posts and the Collariis stretching out into the future. "A fifty-year horizon on the disposal of works belonging to the family trust", Max had said. Now, in close-up, he was seeing that idea in action. It was Max the fixer, the go-between. The magic of Gustave Post lived on, not just as postcards, monographs and museum fare; it was blood, inheritance, genealogy become entitlement. *A small biographical incident* some forty years before had been erased by Edward's sacrifice of one Gustave Post painting. But, collectively, the family had gained its pair! No doubt, in time, some recompense would be arranged. As for Campbell Carter, he could sell *Berlin Wall Lament No.1* without let or hindrance. No Collarii or Post would object to his anonymity. His loss: an incomplete biography – an outcome satisfactory to all, it seemed. Even Campbell Carter's publishers would be recompensed in due course by the appearance of *Golden Eye, Evil Eye: Gustave Post, Man and Myth*, a personal memoir by Clarissa Post. Meanwhile, a painting by Gustave Post would turn up occasionally, a chaotic life ensured that, but no member of the

Post family had broken the terms of the trust that ensured their wellbeing. So be it; Corey Templeton would be there, custodian of the *catalogue raisonné*, ready to bring order to a chaotic life, to sort the genuine from the fakes. Meanwhile, he could turn his mind to other things.

What would happen when they got to Heathrow, Corey had no idea. He made sure they came out of arrivals together. There was a dismal drizzle.

'I'm going on the tube. What about you?' he said.

Waverley rested her flight case and threw back her hair from her face. She fixed him in the eye. 'Max is giving me a lift.' She looked about her and laughed lightly. 'He thinks we're going to be business partners. I'm to be the apprentice. He wants to discuss it in the car.'

'Ah! What are you going to tell him?'

'I'm going to say *no*.'

Then Waverley did something full of symbolic intent. She undid the clasp of the silver chain around her neck from which the little silver whistle hung. She pooled the chain and whistle in the palm of her hand and made a fist. Corey held out his hand, sensing this was to be a moment of exchange. She reached out and funnelled the necklace into his open palm.

'If you want anything, just whistle,' she said with a slow, secret, tender smile. 'You put that thing to your lips and… *You know!*'

OTHER TITLES BY GJ BABB

LARA BLISS LOVES
ROSE MADDER GENUINE

The Emsbury locals call them "grockles", summertime visitors that flock to the beautiful estuary of the river Em. The most famous grockle is Meade Daguerre, controversial artist with an international reputation to uphold. Lara Bliss, local artist and president of the Emsbury League of Artists, sees Daguerre as one of her own and takes him under her wing when she hears that journalist Jack Palanga, *the Celebrities' Confidant*, is in town after a story.

Palanga is playing his cards close to his chest, but gradually it transpires that he suspects the crew of Daguerre's racing yacht, which is berthed in Emsbury marina, are using it to smuggle something – possibly illegal immigrants – ashore.

Daguerre, with a deadline to meet, is beset by another distraction: nighthawks searching for a horde of gold with metal detectors have plundered an archeological site on his estate. The archaeologists guarding the site are attacked at night in an apparent attempt to drive them off. Matters become even more serious when Daguerre discovers a bloody chaos in the cabin of his racing yacht. It appears a murder has been committed, and the five members of the crew have disappeared.

With the holiday season in full swing, the police, journalists and amateur sleuths – led by Lara Bliss – seek to solve the two mysteries. As Bliss gets on the trail of the culprits she begins to see that the clash of two communities – and two cultures – means that things are never quite what they seem!

LARA BLISS
LOVES
ROSE MADDER
GENUINE

A NOVEL

GJ BABB

NUDE, NOT NAKED

University London Central, a middling university, finds itself in a scandalous mess. The new vice-chancellor, Professor Clifford Conquest, is a seasoned public sector enforcer, a dedicated organisation man facing multiple challenges. As he sets about putting the university to rights he finds himself exposed to a terrible temptation. His conflicting desires – to succumb to temptation *and* to manage his university judiciously – put him in danger of becoming the target of the very machinery of academic disciplining he has set in motion. Schemes designed to rectify the ills of the university begin to crumble: inept academics defy his attempts to discredit them, an insurrection by Chinese students turns ugly and a symbolic dismemberment threats all.

At the centre of this whirlwind is Professor Archie Pomfret, the unworldly head of the Department of Art. Is his department harbouring the vice-chancellor's nemesis? Can Conquest continue his rise to greater things? Or will the forces of disaffection biding their time in the darker corners of the senior common room bring him down? Surely, even a man driven by ambition, and a belief in his inevitable rise to the very top, cannot live by the righteous sword of administrative rectitude alone? There must be more, however great the risk!

THE PERFECT CAMBUS NOVEL FOR #METOO TIMES

NUDE,

A LOVE STORY...

NOT

SORT OF

NAKED

GJ BABB

AUTHOR OF LARA BLISS LOVES ROSE MADDER GENUINE

 **Matador**

For exclusive discounts on Matador titles,
sign up to our occasional newsletter at
troubador.co.uk/bookshop